Empress Octavia

A Romance of the Reign on Nero

Wilhelm Walloth

Empress Octavia: A Romance of the Reign on Nero

Copyright © 2018 Indo-European Publishing

The present edition is a reproduction of previous publication of this work. Minor typographical errors may have been corrected without note, however, for an authentic reading experience the spelling, punctuation, and capitalization have been retained from the original text.

ISBN: 978-1-60444-873-3

CHAPTER I

THE gray stone seats of the Circus Maximus were already beginning to fill; the gates were opened, throngs of people were crowding through the corridors, pouring from the doors of the boxes into the narrow passages, which divided the seats, rushing like a cataract down the steps, or rising like the waves of a stream which threatens to fill a valley. Soon not a vestige of the marble in the building was visible, the vast interior was packed with heads up to where the last pillars of the outermost enclosure touched the blue sky.

Heads, nothing but heads, buzzing, roaring heads, a sea, a mountain of heads, in whose vast circle the white sand of the arena burned in the sunlight. How peacefully lay that white sand, soon to be dyed scarlet, how intently those thousands of eyes gazed at it. Now the dazzling sunbeams still glittered on its grains, but the Roman populace longed to see It smoke with blood. Death was to stalk over it like a Phoenician dyer, when he crushes purple snails upon a white woollen cloak till the dark juices trickle down investing the snowy vesture with a crimson splendor. Banners wave, bronze statues shine in the morning light, the seats of the Senators await them, and before the Emperor's golden chair a superb hanging swells out like a sail into the arena. Now the scene darkens; high above the heads of the spectators a cloud is rolling, depriving the sun of the right to annoy the citizens of Rome by its fervid heat; a gigantic screen, woven of variegated material, stretches from one summit of the human mountain to the other, waving, swelling, and concealing the sky; the multitude greet with enthusiastic cheering the cool shade that is slowly extending over them.

The attentive ear often catches a dull roar, or a hoarse, long-drawn growl, which dominates with its bestial sound the buzzing voices of the throng. Expectant hearts thrill, and one man nudges another, saying: "Do you hear the lions raging behind the grating?" His neighbor, rubbing his hands gleefully, replies: "How hungry the animals must be!"

The last belated arrivals enter, and the slaves arrange cushions for them on the reserved seats. A youth, scarcely beyond boyhood, who has been here since before sunrise, takes his breakfast—consisting of a few peaches and some bread—out of his pocket, and a poor weaver tries to eat the sausage he has brought, while people crowding past him almost knock the mouthfuls from his lips. Men from the cookshops offer their steaming pasties for sale, and the patrician dames in the front row of seats below flutter their fans, laugh, and nod to one another. Lovers seated close to each other sometimes receive a jesting admonition to move a little nearer, which calls forth a universal peal of laughter; an unmannerly boy throws fruit stones at girls sitting below him, and is roughly called to order by the soldier on guard with the handle of his lance. Now the Senators' chairs gradually fill; the crowd is growing more and more impatient. A moment's silence follows; helmeted warriors, on whose weapons the sun flashes, appear in the imperial box; soon he must enter, the Lord of the World, the

1

Emperor of Rome, Nero. How intently the throng is watching; now the heavy hangings stir, black hands draw them aside; there is Spiculus beckoning to a stately man in a flowing toga to take his place in the front row of chairs, and that is Petronius, the manager of the festivals, who is officiously arranging the golden chair. And now, hailed by the thundering cheers of the populace, the man for whose pleasure Jupiter created the world stands surveying the assembly. A gracious smile hovers for a moment around his beautiful but pallid lips, a feigned expression of affability flits over his flabby, effeminate, almost womanly face, and Seneca, to whom the Caesar has just whispered one of his acute remarks, bends forward and instantly repeats it to his companions, who of course receive it with the most animated applause, especially as Seneca himself pronounces it uncommonly witty.

Now the Emperor approaches the front of the box. The Senators rise, but he motions to them to resume their seats. Still leaning on the railing, the monarch scans the vast amphitheatre, and some of the spectators awaken great amusement, which he expresses with mingled mirth and cynicism.

"Who is the big man up yonder in the third gallery?" he asks with a careless laugh; "it really is hardly seemly to exhibit such a paunch in the Circus. I should like to see the fellow run away from a couple of leopards. And the one over there with the long nose which he is constantly sticking into people's ears, must be a barber. Tell him not to forget to wear a mask during the day time in future. How can one insult the air with such a nose! But I would like to see him in a fight with the nets. And that lean fellow. Tell him to pour lead into the soles of his sandals, that the wind may not blow him away. Aha! And there sit my Senators, who, spite of their purple-bordered pomp, are only the puppets of the Caesar's will. What is to prevent my showing them some day naked to the people in the arena? Look yonder at Piso, he grows older and gloomier every day. And there is the chaste Aemilia; I should like to have her, too, in the arena, or hide a young buffoon in her chamber at night. But how the beautiful Justina has adorned herself today; I should like to know where her husband gets his money—"

So Nero talks on, without waiting for a reply, drums with his fingers on the edge of the box, gazes through a polished emerald at the spectators, and at last lapses into a bored silence. The Consul Piso whispers to his neighbor: "He looks ill, Justinus." In fact, the Caesar, as he takes his seat, whispers to his freedman: "The sea-fish, my dear Aperinus, lies very heavy on my stomach; tell the cook not to serve it to me again, or I'll have him put into his own pots."

The sovereign's angry expression changes to one of assumed good-nature, as Spiculus arranges the folds of the toga artistically, but it seems to the attendant courtiers as though Nero was struggling with sleep, for sometimes his broad neck droops, sometimes his eyes close, then he suddenly opens them again. Now he even represses a yawn and asks why the games do not begin. Petronius apologizes for the delay. There is a very beautiful Christian maiden to be given to the wild beasts: would the Caesar prefer to have her death reserved until the last, or should she enter the arena first? The Emperor drowsily replies with a word that Petronius does not understand, and to which, in order not to ask a second time, he replies: "Yes, my Lord!" Burrus, stern Burrus, whispers to his neighbor, "The Caesar is drunk again." But the other pretends not to hear the blasphemy. Petronius waves a white kerchief and the tuba sounds, giving the signal for the commencement of the games. The combats between the wrestlers which now take place, bore the populace; it wants stronger fare, and while the men struggle, gasping and panting, the occupants of the galleries talk on without even looking at the bloodless battle.

"Agrippina, Agrippina," now runs in a whisper from seat to seat. "See how proudly she moves."

Nero's mother enters her box. Tigellinus ventures to approach the dozing ruler and inform him of her arrival. The Emperor's face darkens, it is true, but swiftly controlling himself, he shakes off the last remnant of drowsiness, salutes the Empress, nay, even sends a slave to invite her to witness the games at his side, and Agrippina then appears in her son's box, where he embraces her before the whole populace. Otho, with his beautiful wife, Poppaea Sabina, now appears in a row of seats at the right of the Emperor's chair. Vatinius, the Caesar's jester, succeeds in giving his master a secret sign which the latter had evidently arranged with the dwarf; for, as soon as he receives it, Nero turns his head toward Otho's box, a faint flush mounts into his face, and he speaks with twofold graciousness to his mother. Sabina, too, blushes and whispers to her husband. It does not escape the notice of the courtiers that, while conversing with his mother, the monarch often glances, as if by accident, at Sabina, and that the beautiful woman returns the look. The couple seem to be noticed by the audience also; many inferences are drawn from the eloquent language of Sabina's eyes, many bold assertions are made.

"How is my illustrious son pleased with his young wife?" Agrippina asks in the course of the conversation, while the gladiators below are vainly striving to attract attention. All Rome knew that the relation between the imperial pair was by no means the most tender; Agrippina, who has also noticed her son's restlessness since Sabina's entrance, has intentionally put the question. Nero bites his lips. As he turns away, his eye meets his mother's and it betrays that she is again in a fault-finding mood. Agrippina does not cease to praise Octavia's virtue. Nero makes no reply, but gazes down into the arena as if he did not hear the paeans in honor of his wife's fidelity. Finally, when his mother unmistakably blames his indifference to the daughter of Claudius, the sovereign's face wears an expression of impatience; he interrupts Agrippina's words with the exclamation: "She is too virtuous for me," and beckoning to his favorite Spiculus, whispers an order into his ear.

Spiculus vanishes, but soon reappears in the Caesar's box and secretly thrusts a long strip of papyrus into the folds of his toga. The son scans his mother's features suspiciously to discover whether her penetration has detected the secret correspondence, and lets the strip of papyrus slip lightly through his hands—but not a word of writing is legible; the receiver of the letter must wait until he returns home and scatters charcoal upon the characters written with milk.* Not until then will they become visible in black outlines.

*Ovid: Ars Amandi.

"Sly Sabina," murmurs the delighted Caesar.

Meanwhile the crowd is murmuring, and the complaisant director of festivals, to whom its will is law, orders the gladiators to retire. The iron grating at the extreme end of the building rolls back, a huge form creeps from the dark cage, a short growl is followed by a deep roar that shakes the very air, and, directly after, the lion's tail lashes the sand of the arena. He, the terror of the caravans, was dragged in huge carts through the provinces of the Empire and now must extort the admiration of the populace by his fury. The people receive in silence the king of the wilderness, the monarch of the desolate ravines of the Atlas Mountains, who so short a time ago watched for his prey on the rocky plateau and sprang boldly through the air to the neck of the giraffe, and now, with drooping head, slinks along close to the wall, snarling discontentedly. Then he lies down, raises his head with its floating mane, yawns, and licks his bristling lips with his red tongue; the yawning chasm of his jaws close, his eyes blink sleepily, he crosses his fore-paws and looks like a statue.

The walled ring gradually fills with animals from the desert, the forests, the mountains, the marshes; the gratings rattle constantly, the whips of the overseers crack; the people greet the savage guests with acclamations. The lithe Indian tiger steals spitefully around the auroch of Germany, the Northern bear scans with his little red eyes the sullen boar, the wolf licks his jaws hungrily with his hanging tongue, the serpent rolls itself into a coil, the Egyptian hyena, with its sinister green eyes, steals from one hiding-place to another. Timid gazelles tremble, ostriches fly, claws, hoofs, manes, tails, move in a strange medley, and, like an orchestra tuning its instruments before the concert begins, the beasts gathered from all the quarters of the globe into the arena growl, roar, howl, and grunt together.

The spectators fume, cheer them on, utter angry curses; the animals, finding themselves surrounded by a mountain of heads, grow timid. Scarlet cloths are flung among the beasts to irritate them, red-hot iron poles are thrust through the gratings to stir the sluggish ones. Suddenly the first applause breaks out at the southern end of the circus. A bull whose sharp horns came too near a lion, had received a blow from his paw that laid its right hip open to the bone. The first blood is greeted with cheers, and as if by magic, a universal struggle, all fighting against all, begins. The sand whirls up in tall, white columns; the bear rises on its hind legs, tearing the air with its terrible paws; the lion crouches to spring; snapping teeth strike in necks dripping with blood; horrible sounds of rage, sharp death rattles, hoarse bellowing delight the ears of the multitude, which constantly grows more frenzied. Heads bend forward, people point to the confused medley of combatants, the gaping wounds.

But the sovereign people is not yet satisfied with the spectacle. These scenes still lack their highest charm; the horrors of death as yet encompass only unreasoning brutes,—how it must please the eye of man, endowed with intellect, to see beings also possessing intelligence shrink in terror from these gaping jaws, these uplifted paws! Are there no more criminals? Why don't they seize some of that Jewish sect, the Christians? What sight is fairer than to see the bosom of a girl of sixteen bleeding under the claws of a lion? Pity, horror, and the charms of the senses blend so bewitchingly in the breast of the spectator, when she raises her beautiful arms imploring aid. What a study for the sculptor is the innocent youth, when his slender limbs struggle against the hug of the bear! How every muscle stands forth, how touching is the haggard gaze with which he looks his last at life! And the old man, how his quiet submission teaches the philosopher to despise death! What a pathetic sight is the infant with its thumb in its mouth, laughing at the animals, ignorant of the coming doom, and how its mother clasps it to her heart, hiding it as the wolf's muzzle reaches her! Such a spectacle makes the blood flow faster through the veins, and, for the first time, one realizes what it is to be safe.

The shout: "Men, men!" rises everywhere; the spectators wish to see human beings struggle with the beasts. The directors of the games are ready to gratify this desire too.

At the extreme end of the circus is an outbuilding where the persons destined for the combats await their turn. It is a vaulted structure, through whose grated windows daylight scarcely ventures to penetrate. The damp stones are overgrown with green mould, against which the wan faces of the condemned men stand forth in strong relief; around them, armed with lances, are soldiers on guard, gazing pitilessly at the scenes of misery before them. But it is not seemly for Christians to wail aloud. They sit quietly side by side on the stone benches, or clasp one another's hands. Mothers exhort their children, old men their sons; they speak tender words of comfort, words uttered by the Saviour as He hung upon the cross, and many an eye sparkles with a radiant light. The iron- bound door opens; the roaring of the beasts, the frantic shouts of the multitude grow louder, like distant thunder or the howling of the storm. The captain of the guard chooses the first couple who must enter the arena,—two youths, leaning shoulder against shoulder as they sit together. The younger, scarcely beyond boyhood, gazes with pallid face at the floor; the older, of stronger build, embraces his timid companion with his bare arm. The boy, shuddering, leans his head upon the other's breast, clasps his hand convulsively, and raises his large, mournful eyes to his. A submissive smile, a sorrowful quiver of the under lip, are the sole response of the older youth. What can he say? • What comfort can he offer his young comrade? The captain shouts: "Why do you delay?" and they approach the door. There the boy's strength fails, he hides his beautiful face, and the older, overpowered by grief, supports the tottering form. A soldier attempts to force the sinking lad to stand.

"What am I to think of you, my Drusus," murmurs the older youth, thrusting back the soldier, whose rough hand violently shakes the almost senseless form. Now the boy, trembling, clasps his friend's neck, and the latter bears him out, his face, distorted with suffering, and eyes dimmed by tears, turned toward the distant arena.

The iron-bound door closes, and the roaring of the conflict reaches the hapless beings within less distinctly through its heavy boards. In the darkest corner of the room stand two old men convicted of being Christians. They had been friends from boyhood and at nineteen shared the expedition to Germany. In those days their motto was to live, to enjoy, and they did enjoy until the strange tidings of the Man on the Cross reached them; they loved and drank, and now they were talking about the immortality of the soul, and their eyes sparkled more joyfully than when they dashed together into battle with the Germans. Slaves, too, are crouching on the ground. Whom could the example of the gentle Conqueror of the World inspire more, what bondman's heart did not throb faster when he heard the message of the brotherhood of man and the liberty which death bestows? The eyes of the slaves yearn for this freedom, the blow of the lion's paw is welcome to them.

But the most touching group among those condemned is one standing locked in a close embrace near the door. Even the sullen browed soldier, the Jew Rufus, leaning against it with the spear in his sinewy hand, would fain turn from this scene; yet his deep-set eyes cannot wander from the girl kneeling on the damp stones to take leave of three little brothers who are too young to understand the meaning of what is passing around them. His gaze is constantly attracted by the slender white figure, whose movements are so swift, so bewildered, and whose mortal terror is visible only in the large eyes, whose dilated pupils seem lost in vague, unknown distances. She turns from one brother to another; she cannot give enough proofs of love, encouragement, admonitions, farewell kisses, but her caresses are not returned; a paralyzing stupor rests upon the aged parents, the man with the long white beard, the woman with the wrinkled face.

"Father, tell sister she must stay with us," sobs the youngest child, pressing his wooden horse to his eyes. "Let us go home, I'm so hungry."

The father and mother look down at the children silently; they must lose their darling Lucretia who, without their knowledge, has professed Christianity. Secretly the thin, hollow-eyed youth beside her, who is pressing the crucifix to his brow, initiated their daughter into the mysteries of the new superstition. Yesterday the soldiers captured both as they were kneeling in the catacombs before the crucifix, and to-day they must atone for their boldness in having scorned Jupiter and clung to a fanatic.

"And you, my Regulus," Lucretia whispers with rigid, motionless features, clasping her youngest brother's hand, "you will be good, won't you? You will obey our parents when I am no longer here, as you have obeyed me, and love them as you have loved me. And don't break the toy I

6

gave you, and think of me very often, though I can no longer pray with you in the evening, nor put you to bed. Do you hear? Remember that I shall be very happy, and that you must be good, so that some day you can come where I shall live forever."

But the boy hides his face in his mother's dress, his sister's eyes look so strange to-day as she talks in such hasty, excited tones.

"My Brutus," Lucretia turns to the other boy, pushing the black curls from his brow with her hand, "you will understand me; your heart beats strongly and bravely, though you are so young; and I know you will do great deeds some day. God has given you much, my child; honor Him in using your talents."

"Where are you going, Lucretia?" he asks. "I will go with you. They shall not let you face the wild beasts alone."

But the sister has already turned to the third brother, who, almost as soon as she speaks to him, bursts into tears without knowing why.

"He must leave me; he will rob my soul of all its strength with his tears," she says to herself, then, looking reproachfully at him, rises. Does she feel compassion as she sees her grief-stricken parents wringing their hands? Her gaze expresses bewilderment. The door has opened again; the command rings out; a number of victims leave the room at the same time to enter the arena; Lucretia notices it and averts her face from the departing figures. Has she fought the last battle? Has her heart, has her mind, been so torn by conflicting emotions that claws and teeth can no longer harm the flesh? Does Faith really possess the power to destroy human nature in human beings? As the despairing shrieks of the lacerated victims penetrate the cell, she lays her beautiful hand on her father's arm; does she need comfort? She would fain console him, but a deadly pallor overspreads her features. The groans of anguish send a shudder through her frame, and she murmurs: "Everything, everything, great God, only let me not hear."

She covers her ears with her hands. Her mother, with a hollow groan, sinks upon the stone bench; no one can go to aid the fainting woman. The door opens once more; again the shout of command and the clank of weapons are heard; more victims are wanted. The thin, fanatical youth, with scarlet spots on his hollow cheeks, approaches the maiden and silently holds before her bowed head the crucifix, sure of its sustaining power. What is his amazement as she stares fixedly at the Crucified One and shakes her head!

"Where is your faith, Lucretia?" he says hoarsely, frowning. "Will you do your teacher so little honor, has your zeal to fathom the divine life proved so small, and where has your trust in the help of Christ fled?"

Lucretia is about to clasp the cross, but now frightful sounds, such as no human ear has ever heard, echo from the arena, blended with bestial yelping and howling laughter; it seems as if mortal agony was striving to find tones to touch the heart of savage curiosity. Of what scenes these sounds speak, what blood-stained visions they hold before the eyes! How

7

they describe the fearful torture of mangled bodies dragged by gnashing jaws over the smoking sand!

Lucretia draws her hand away from the Redeemer's image; the Man on the Cross has forsaken her; even His example no longer raises her courage. What would she give if, instead of the untenable consolations the fanatical believer is whispering in her ear, instead of the invisible presence of Christ, a visible saving hand would rescue her from this prison! Her gaze wanders helplessly from her mother to her father, and from him to her own body, now beautiful in its symmetry, whose charms must serve as food for the wild beasts of the wilderness. Then her glance falls on the Jew, Rufus, who still leans against the door, his head bowed, his lips compressed, staring at the young girl. Her livid mouth is distorted, the reddened lids of her eyes open widely, and her expressionless gaze is almost like that of an animal, but she does not utter a word. Yet she is still beautiful in her anguish. The Jew sees how she struggles to control herself, how she strives to hold the fear of death at bay, and, to numb it, clasps her brother to her bosom.

"Help me, my Brutus; comfort me, my child!" she murmurs. "Oh, to what can my soul cling in this hour of need! My parents, have you no consolation for your child? Father, you who gave me life, kill me with your strong hand—to be torn by snarling beasts before this throng of people— Hark I hark! How they groan! If only dying does not hurt much! but, oh, father, I fear it does."

And cowering on the floor, not knowing what she is doing, she drags herself to the Jew's feet, clasps his bare knees, and falters wildly: "If you are a man, thrust your spear into my breast."

Rufus turns pale, sighs, and lowers the spear as if he intended to fulfil her entreaty. Then he shrugs his shoulders and gazes with fierce indifference in another direction, as if he did not feel a tremor as the hapless girl's head rested against his knees. Lucretia, with throbbing temples, remains in this attitude for a time, as if half unconscious; but Lucius, the fanatical convert, approaches, and lifts her from the floor. He is trembling as he embraces and kisses her.

"Lucretia, the hour of death looses my tongue," he whispers as if enraptured. "Listen to me: I have kept silence until now; but I have loved you, Lucretia, since I first saw you, since I taught you to pray to the Christian's God. The arena shall be our nuptial chamber; what do I care for death, since it gives you to me?"

He clasps her to his breast; she does not heed it; she has scarcely understood his words; he continues to stammer mingled prayers and vows of love, which she hears with an indifferent, meaningless nod of assent. At last she seems to realize the significance of his ardent kisses, and pushes her curls over her cheek.

"I do not love you, Lucius—may the Lord be merciful to me—I do not love you—but give me your hand—there—let me clasp it firmly—you must forgive me for saying this to you, but I am so weak I scarcely know what I am doing—my parents abandon me—at least be my friend, Lucius."

8

The tuba interrupts this strange love-talk; the door opens; the shout of command rings out; the captain chooses a group of victims, among whom are Lucius and Lucretia. Rufus's lips part as if to utter some exclamation; he grasps his spear more closely, then shrugs his shoulders as if he were saying to himself: "What is the girl to me? I can't help her."

The old father sinks down on the stone bench, weeping and muttering to himself in childish grief; the mother rises, rushes noiselessly to her daughter, and clutches her dress convulsively, while her chin moves as if she were talking in her sleep. But now that the die is cast and death opens his iron arms before Lucretia, courage returns, at least the nervous feminine courage, the reckless defiance of death, the feverish hardihood of despair. She beholds the world steeped in crimson light; she could laugh aloud, her heart throbs so high with joyous terror; the whole world whirls around her, shining strangely; she moves toward the entrance as if borne onward by burning clouds. A soldier has attempted to remove the old woman's hand from her daughter's dress, but he finds it impossible, and is obliged to hack the garment away with his sword.

The roar of the surging sea of the populace already deadens every other sound, and now heart-rending shrieks pierce the air. Again Lucretia turns back; she sees her mother prevented by force from following her, sees the poor woman struggle, then clasping Lucius's hand closely, whispers: "When I fall, Lucius, arrange my stola, I beg you, that I may not lie with garments disarranged before the throng."

She adjusts her dress, hiding her bosom with her long hair, in half-unconscious modesty. They approach nearer and nearer to the place whence the deafening noise proceeds. Lucius, raising the crucifix toward heaven, begins to sing a hymn which dies away in the uproar. Clasping the girl with his right arm, his eyes, almost starting from their sockets, survey the vast arena as if defying the wild beasts; mortal terror, enthusiasm, contempt of the world, are all depicted upon his haggard features. The grating before the entrance rises; some resisting victims are thrust forward with red-hot iron poles.

Now the young pair stand in the arena; the grating closes creaking behind them. The girl rests her beautiful arm against the stone blocks of the encircling wall; the dense clouds of dust, through which are seen, as if in a mist, the mountain of heads, the hairy bodies of the wild beasts, the mangled human limbs, all appear to Lucretia like a shapeless vision of the imagination at which she gazes in wonder.

The thundering roar seems to lull her senses, the cries of fury, the sharp, shrill, hungry howls of the animals appear like flashes of lightning; the blood-soaked sand, into which she sinks to the ankles, seems painted; flames dart around her; everything shimmers, quivers. So she stands waiting, with her beautiful arm braced against the thick pitiless wall; often the face of a girl friend rises before her, an affectionate word, a beautiful scene from the days of her childhood,—all swift, fleeting, vanishing. Then she feels as if consciousness were receding farther and farther, shrivelling more and more; she sees dimly, as if through a light, swaying crimson veil, a monstrous brown form with huge paws tower in gigantic outlines before her, beholds Lucius throw himself upon it and his head vanish in yawning jaws. Then, drenched with some warm fluid, she sinks beside the wall; something quivering convulsively rests upon her body.

CHAPTER II

MEANWHILE Rufus, who had been on guard before sunrise, was relieved. Instead of watching the spectacle, he left the Circus and, absorbed in thought, walked around the building, passing the booths of the shopkeepers under the arcades of the amphitheatre without noticing their wares; even the smile of the Assyrian dancing-girl, whose alluring gestures invited the attention of strolling idlers, could not efface from his imagination the image of the Christian maiden led forth to death. He felt a dull, vague compassion when he thought of Lucretia's head as the trembling girl pressed it against his knees,—a compassion which angered him, because he knew that whoever wished to attain a good position in Rome must contemptuously thrust pity aside as weakness, and to attain a good position had been the ambitious Jew's aspiration from his early youth. Hitherto he had not made much progress,—he was a private soldier in the fifth maniple of the Praetorians; but who, at twenty-four, loses the hope of being at least a centurion in the imperial guard when he reaches the age of fifty?

Rufus now tried to interest himself in the dancing of a Phoenician, whose nude limbs were relieved in artistic beauty against the dark archway, but the fair one's smile only called before his imagination, in still more vivid colors, the death-agony of the Christian maiden whose limbs were now perhaps quivering on the sand of the arena; and he could no longer watch the dancer's movements, which reminded him hideously of the last convulsions of a dying form.

As a Jew, his nature was more sensitive; and being averse to the brutal deeds of these Pagans, his sole consolation was that the girl's sufferings were over. To him a human life was of more value than to these Romans, and, though recklessly ambitious, he felt a certain respect for every human being that Jehovah had created. Yet, after all, what was this girl to him?

Shrugging his shoulders, as was his habit, he muttered to himself: "What do you mean, Rufus? She is dead! Have you the power to call her back to life? Nonsense! I forbid you to think any more about her."

Then he really felt relieved; military discipline had so pervaded his nature, he was so thoroughly convinced of its necessity, that he treated himself with the strictness with which his superior officer, whom he always implicitly obeyed, would have treated him.

As, clinching his black beard between his lips, he hurriedly turned around a pillar, he ran against one of the street astrologers, who usually enjoyed excellent patronage in this place. The man, an Assyrian, was crouching on the ground, completely enveloped in a long robe, which was intended to lend the necessary dignity to his lofty calling. His knees almost touched his chin; he clasped his pointed beard thoughtfully in his hand; his brow, with its bushy eyebrows, was bent over a tablet covered with all sorts of strange characters; while several bystanders were listening patiently to hear what the august man would read from the stars concerning their future. After some time he raised his head and beckoned to a muffled woman, into whose ear, as she bent near him, he whispered the result of his investigations She gave him money and hurried off with a light step; the news she had received of the future of her lover in Egypt had doubtless been pleasant. Another person

to whom the result of the calculation was communicated left the astrologer with less satisfaction. The heritage expected by the smooth faced young dandy would never come to him—if the learned man's opinion was correct.

Now the astrologer sat alone in the shade of the pillar. The burning noontide sun was blazing outside; the smooth leaves of the distant laurel-trees glittered as if set with tiny mirrors or gems, whenever a sunbeam touched their green enamel; high above, towered the stone I blocks of the Circus wall, partly covered with clinging ivy. Opposite to the Circus rose the Aventine, whose white temples gleamed in dazzling radiance against the deep blue sky. Not a human being was visible at the moment. Rufus pondered whether he should try his fortune too. True, his religion forbade him to meddle with magic, and he valued it no more than a dream, yet he could scarcely resist the impulse of his gnawing ambition. For what was he destined? He would but ask jestingly; Jehovah could not be wrathful with him for playing a prank with the Pagans. Yet his heart throbbed violently as, glancing timidly around him, he approached the crouching figure. The Assyrian started up, trying to assume a majestic air, as the excited soldier's footsteps cast gravel on his tablets.

"So you can unveil the future," exclaimed the Jew, while an incredulous smile hovered around his bearded lips.

The Magian, with a majestic gesture, answered: "Thou hast said."

"And how do you do it?" asked Rufus.

"How do I do it?" The Magian did not exactly trust the stranger, and scanned him from head to foot, while reflecting whether he was dealing with a scorner or a respecter of his art. The examination finally convinced him that he need not conceal his wisdom in the presence of a comparatively untutored soldier.

"Yes. How do you do it?" Rufus repeated, leaning his spear against the pillar, raising his helmet, and passing his hand over,. his hair, dank with perspiration.

"Do you suppose that this secret can be explained to you in a few seconds?" replied the other, almost insulted. "Young man, go with me to Egypt, visit the temples, become initiated into the mysteries of the priests of Isis, hold intercourse, as I have done, with Thrassylus, the astrologer of

11

Tiber, and Barbyllus, the astrologer of Nero, study medicine, mechanics, mathematics, astronomy, and live to be seventy years old; then perhaps you may have a vague idea of the wisdom I call mine."

The Assyrian again became absorbed in his figures, as if he did not desire to be accosted or questioned, muttered all sorts of Egyptian words, and drew strange circles with his stones, while Rufus began to feel some degree of respect for the knowledge of this observer of the stars.

"Have you studied all these things?" he asked in astonishment.

The learned man smiled contemptuously.

"And much more," he said, passing his hand across his brow with a bombastic gesture, which intimated that nothing was concealed from him.

"And your art," stammered Rufus,—" does it always tell the truth?"

"Truth?" replied the Magian, in a melancholy tone, and then suddenly added, stretching out his arm as if in ecstasy: "What is truth?"

After hurling this phrase, he remained several moments in his attitude of profound thought, but meanwhile secretly watching with a side glance what effect his acting was producing upon the young man. Rufus took his spear, leaned on it, and gazed intently at the ground.

"Yes," he murmured, looking watchfully about him, "it is strange! God must know what awaits us; why should not a sharp-sighted intellect endeavor to fathom His thoughts? If we could search into the councils of the gods—of God, I meant to say—"

We can," interrupted the sage, impetuously.

Yes, if one were God Himself, or, as that other called himself, the Son of God," added Rufus.

"That is wholly unnecessary," said the Magian, eagerly. "We need not be God; the gods are like little children in school,—that is, bad accountants. Yes, my son, everything in the world had its destiny fixed from the beginning, before the gods existed. Whoever can calculate how the elements were arranged when love brooded over them, can estimate how they are arranged now, can predict the fall of every grain of sand, the approach of every comet. The gods are but the servants of Fate, its torch-bearers: the gods know nothing, for they have no mathematics; but Prometheus is the great inventor of the science of numbers. Mathematics, young man, is the key of mysteries. Like a good hunting-dog, figures track the revolutions and courses of the stars, pierce the elements, and divide them into other elements, build temples, arrange the hewn stones like a sturdy Cyclops, and it is figures also which disclose the future of human beings, as a child's hand opens the closed bud."

Rufus was surprised; these words awed him. He felt a dread of calculations, and asked humbly if the sage would not reveal his future.

"Willingly," said the latter, clearing his throat, "but—it is again figures, according to which we value small as well as large coins."

Rufus understood. Horror of the mysterious figures disappeared, or rather it increased when the sage now named the sum after whose payment he was ready to announce the decree of fate.

"Five denarii?" asked the Jew,—" my pay for a fortnight! That 's too much. How am I to live?"

The sage pretended not to hear this ejaculation, which evidently proceeded from the depths of the heart, but played with his stones, and smoothed his Assyrian beard.

"How am I to live?" the soldier muttered again.

"And how am I to live?" answered the sage, coldly. "What is life? Unless you can be content with a sip of water from the hollow of your hand and a bit of mouldy bread, you are not worthy of the sun. Five denarii, young man, that is the will of Isis, the universal mother."

True, Rufus did not understand what the universal mother had to do with his five denarii, yet, sighing heavily, he resolved to pay them, and the Magian began his calculations.

"Will you not give me a short account of your family circumstances?" asked the mathematician after a brief silence. "I can investigate the course of your life better if I know its beginning."

"My father was a physician," said Rufus, frowning, and evidently dissatisfied.

"What is your mother's name?" asked the other.

"Esther. My father died, leaving us in poverty."

"Where do you live?"

"In one of the streets in the Tiber district, near the Covered Way."

"Have you any brothers or sisters?"

"No."

"How old are you?"

"Twenty-four."

"What is your favorite occupation?"

"Ask me no more questions," answered Rufus, sullenly; "it is enough for you to know that I—" he paused in the midst of a remark concerning his ambitious aspirations, and added, "that I don't like to be catechised."

"Very well," murmured the mathematician, and continued his calculations. The warrior intently watched the stones as they formed figures, shaking his head as he gazed at the curves which the soothsayer, with an air of the deepest thought, drew upon the tablet. Several passersby lingered, to the Jew's great annoyance. One, a young stranger, asked what was going on here. Rufus made no reply; he sincerely regretted having asked counsel of the soothsayer, whose whole manner was gradually awakening his distrust. Yet he awaited the answer with some little curiosity, and then asked the stranger what he wanted. The latter walked on laughing, saying that the sights in Rome were wonderful; except the rude soldiers, everything was quite different from the provinces. At last the work was finished. The old man raised his head, but Rufus motioned to him to be silent until the idlers had moved on. Then he made him a sign.

"Beware of woman!" said the sage, solemnly, "thus speaks the voice of Fate."

"Explain that," replied Rufus.

"Explain? What is there to explain?" said the Assyrian.

"I don't understand," answered the soldier.

13

"Can you expect me to understand the decrees of the gods?" said the sage. "Please give me my fee."

"But you just called the gods bad accountants," Rufus was beginning to expostulate, when the august astrologer interrupted with the exclamation: "Beware of woman!" and in the same breath added: "Will you pay me?"

The soldier drew out his purse and threw a denarius on the table, patting the sage on the back as he said: "You know how to calculate, my friend, and will be able to make yourself believe that this is five denarii as easily as you led me to think you could unveil the future."

The scholar, however, understood no jesting, and was by no means so estranged from all worldly things that he was willing to relinquish four denarii. Grasping the soldier's cloak, he vehemently demanded the remainder of his fee. But a sinister glance from the Jew's eyes rested upon him.

"You predicted," said the latter under his breath, "that misfortune would come to me through woman, my friend; with your leave, I believe the prophecy is false. I will now make a far more reliable one in the words: Let me go, or there will be a shower of blows."

The Magian did not seem to feel any special liking for this novice in the art of prophecy; he dropped his cloak and, muttering angrily, thrust the denarius into his pocket.

The Jew left the soothsayer, and, greatly dissatisfied with himself, strode off, passing the shops near the Circus without taking the slightest notice of the various invitations shouted by tavern-keepers, cooks, and pretty dancing-girls. "A base generation," he thought, scanning the various scenes, " a base generation, dreaming life away over these boiling sausages and steaming dishes of lentils." Rufus had imposed upon himself, as his supreme law of life, contempt for sensual pleasures; only by ruling his passions could he expect to reach his lofty goals. True, it was sometimes very difficult for him to refrain from responding to an ardent glance, but even when he yielded he always ruled passion with a cold curb of reason, which enabled him to cast pleasure aside as soon as he perceived that it might become an obstacle in the path of his ambition. He had secretly drained many a goblet of wine, but always remained sober; he had cradled many a Syrian beauty on his knees, and laughed at her the next day when she protested that she could not live without him. Meanwhile he secretly enjoyed seeing his comrades swimming in the pool of pleasure till they were stupefied and robbed of their senses; nay, like some destructive power of nature, he even led more than one youth into drinking, gaming, and libertinism, by which, in a certain degree, he made them subject to him.

Rufus had reached the extreme end of the Circus and was admiring a magnificent litter which had just been carried past him, ardently wishing at the same time that he might some day be surrounded with the same splendor, when he saw a bald-headed, corpulent old man stagger out of one of the Circus taverns, leading by the hand a boy who was evidently trying to support the reeling figure. Dragged to and fro by the unsteady hand of the gray-haired servant of Bacchus, the poor child was sometimes thrown into very strange positions, nay, was often literally dragged along.

"Why, father, what ails you to-day?" asked the innocent little fellow. "Take care! People are looking at us."

But the old man, with a foolish smile on his red face, framed by a white beard well suited to inspire reverence, vainly tried to force his legs into their usual gait. He stumbled and skipped, sometimes smacking his tongue as if he still tasted the Falernian. Sometimes he rubbed his hairy thigh, and at last even leaned against the wall for a purpose which it is not well to describe more closely,—in doing which he dropped both cloak and sandals,—and rubbed his shoulder persistently against a projecting stone.

Rufus laughed; but a bystander called out that he must not ridicule him, it was a very serious matter. When the old Silenus moved slowly on, Rufus, to his surprise, recognized the father of the Christian girl who had just lost her life. As he staggered past the soldier, he was talking volubly; and though the words were greatly mangled as they fell from his flabby lips, they afforded a glimpse of the overwhelming sorrow of the father's heart.

"My friend," he stammered, with his glassy eyes turned heavenward, "the gods are great, my friend, and man is little. Whoever denies it, by Zeus, is a drunkard! Have you thought of this? We must submit, my friend, submit. Fate is calm, very calm, and sometimes even cruel,—Oedipus learned that; but I would rather lead my own wife astray and marry my father than to deal with the Sphinx. But man has a comfort for his sorrows, my friend; behold it in me, for my heart is merry, very merry—" Then he began to sing a little Egyptian song, but never got beyond the first verse, which he repeated constantly, then with drooping head relapsed into silence, which he suddenly interrupted with the angry question whether anybody supposed that he was drunk? Then, when Rufus advised him to go home, he began to weep until the teardrops trickled down upon his beard. " Don't say that; don't say that," he sobbed. "It's no use for me to go home: I shall not find my child. Do you see the big house yonder? They shut my child up there, and she was such a good daughter; she always said: 'Father, take care not to drink more Falernian than is good for you,' and I obeyed her. You must know that I have a little weakness for Falernian; and now, since she can no longer give me this warning, I shall go downhill. It 's a pity; I know that very well. I should have made a good mime; it's a pity, a great pity."

He went off sighing; Rufus still heard him muttering: "A Stoic must not weep; a Stoic conquers pain." Then he saw the boy, who was dragged along, turn around a pillar, and walked on toward his home greeting every one who was standing near with studied humility. On reaching the neighborhood of the

Forum, he was stopped by a litter with closed curtains, surrounded by numerous richly clad bearers. It was obliged to wait for a moment opposite to the Temple of Vesta, because one of the slaves had sprained his

15

foot. The curtains were instantly pushed back; a woman's face, pallid but very beautiful, appeared, and the captain of the bearers gave the information requested. Rufus recognized the Empress Octavia. Her features wore an expression of sympathy as she heard of the accident to the bearer, who sat on the pavement, clasping his ankle. The royal lady wished to get out and walk, but the captain entreated her not to do so.

"Send the slave home," she said in a gentle tone, "and see that he receives the best possible care."

As she was about to leave the litter, a citizen, apparently a dyer, forced his way through the slaves.

"Permit me, august sovereign, to be your bondman to-day!" he exclaimed. " Come, my men, I'll take the lame bearer's place."

The Empress smiled.

"I cannot accept your offer, my good man," she said pleasantly; but when the dyer persisted, she murmured, with an expression of the most winning kindness in her large eyes: "Be it so, then."

The bystanders applauded, and the litter moved on amid the joyous cheers of the populace.

"Now I understand why the people love this woman," Rufus said to himself; and a baker at his side told his neighbor that Octavia had visited the funeral pyre of her father Claudius, which Nero had scattered, to weep there for the basely murdered Emperor, and perhaps to pour libations of wine upon the last remnants of the pile. Another citizen, laughing loudly, was relating Nero's last nocturnal prank. The Emperor, with his own hands, had flung into the cloaca a teacher who was returning home. Not a night passes," said the narrator, in which the Caesar does not play some mischievous trick. A few days ago he even robbed a cook-shop."

CHAPTER III

NIGHT had long since closed in upon Rome, the capital of the world; the noise of day had ceased; the squares and streets were illumined by the glimmer of the waning moon. It was the hour when the peasant drove his cart along the Appian Way to the city, in order to offer his milk and eggs early enough to the still slumbering masters of the houses. It was the hour when the Ethiopian maid rose, yawning, to prepare the rouges and salves, or to cleanse the combs, while her mistress, with hair in curl-papers, and a layer of dough on her face, was still resting; it was the hour when the slave, on his bed of straw, dreamed of the overseer's lash, to which he must again submit; the bakers were already stumbling half asleep to their ovens, and the trumpets would soon call the soldiers to their drill. Darkness still brooded over the seven hills; the first glimmer of dawn was quivering in a narrow gray streak over the Esquiline, overspreading the colonnades of the Temple of Venus with a leaden hue, and tingeing the gilded ornaments of Nero's palace, opposite to the temple, with a faint crimson tint which glided slowly over the imposing pediment of the building.

Just at this time a young man was walking along the Via Sacra, gazing dreamily at the cold splendor of the imperial palace, still sleeping in the twilight. So this was the abode of the Ruler of the World; from these walls the officials bore his commands. Here he celebrated his orgies.

Metellus had no other thoughts as he looked at this imperial residence. He moved wearily on; his handsome eyes were dull, and the lacerna was flung carelessly about him. Metellus, coming from Bilbilis, had landed in Ostia four days before, in order, as the phrase goes, to seek his fortune in Rome, or at least earn a living by his Art,—he was a sculptor.

Thus far the youth had not succeeded in obtaining employment; ever since the day of his arrival he had wandered penniless through the streets, thinking of his distant home and repenting that he had listened to the assurances of his friends, who promised him mountains of gold in Rome. Under such circumstances the beauty of the city made little impression upon his mind; he scarcely saw or heard what was passing around him. "If I only had a good muraena, fattened on human flesh," he said to himself, smiling bitterly, "I should probably be able to value Rome's architectural splendor better. The Temple of Jupiter, viewed with a satisfied stomach, may raise very* imposing pillars heavenward; in their present condition, I cannot blame my bowels if they forbid my brain to think, and silence all enthusiasm with grumbling impatience."

In truth, hunger and homesickness had put the youth into a strange mood: he thought of a little song, a gay little song, which he had heard the laborers in the harbor sing the day before, and began to whistle it; but his lips quivered painfully as he did so, his eyes glittered with unshed tears, and the ditty ended in a most unmusical whistle. His poor parents at home! He could not be angry with his father now, though he had had good reason; their separation lay like a reconciling hand on his resentful heart. The old man's image rose before his memory. He tried to drive away his sad thoughts by counting the stones in the pavement and mentally raging over the rude statue in a doorway; but he could not banish his mother's sorrowful face, which gazed at him from the dark street corners.

His father, a quick-tempered, somewhat severe man, who had moved in his early youth from Rome to Hispania, wished to make the lad an honest ironmonger; but Metellus resisted all the more vehemently because he had found an opportunity to visit a sculptor's studio whenever he chose. There he had nourished his imagination with the forms of heroes and gods; nay, he had secretly studied under the master's instruction. Here, too, he made the acquaintance of Martial, a youth of nineteen, who most zealously encouraged him to continue in his chosen profession. Our hero, in his present situation, could not help thinking of this friend, too; of the pleasant hours which they had spent walking arm in arm on the bank of the Salo, dreaming, planning, sometimes even improvising Alcaean verses or translating passages from Homer into their native language. Then came sorrowful days for the young sculptor. With the utmost difficulty consent to devote himself to Art was at last obtained; but as Art brought no income, the son suffered from his father's ill temper. To the old man an art was a trade, and whoever earned nothing by his art was an idler. The hardest thing for the boy to bear was the contempt with which his father sometimes spoke of his work.

"I shall yet live to see you go to Rome and die there as a wretched gladiator before the eyes of the mob," was the old man's usual remark; to which the son replied with an almost equally heartless answer. At great expenditure of time and money, the young artist finally succeeded in finishing his first work: a Sisyphus rolling the rock. The statue, which showed traces of the immaturity of youthful genius, found no purchaser; and the jeers the father heaped upon it severed the last bond that united him to the ambitious son.

In his despair, Metellus found his sole comforter in his friend Martial, who understood how to cheer him; but his courage had sunk so low that Martial had great difficulty in withholding him from committing suicide. The present had always exerted a predominating influence over the artist's mind; he was driven to despair as quickly as he was comforted, and could laugh and weep in the same moment like a girl. His careless nature, averse to reflection, was prompt to reach a decision, which was just as promptly executed. No one is more ready to cast life away than he who regards it as a light burden.

The mother took her son's part; and one day, when her husband told her that he could do nothing more for the son's training because it would lessen the daughter's dowry, she advanced the money, and Metellus did what he had already planned,—he hastened on board of a trireme bound for Ostia. Martial, when they bade each other farewell, promised to follow, which had no little share in filling the traveller's mind with joyous anticipations. Oh, enthusiasm of youth! When the boatman shouted, the two friends had kissed each other again, and promised not to break their vow. And what vow had they made to the eternal gods? Nothing less than to avoid women, that contemptible sex, and let friendship fill the place of so-called love. The works of the poets swarmed with instances of the miseries that women brought upon men; they two would live for each other, as Plato directs. One mild moonlight night they had embraced, and sworn to have nothing to do with women, but after the labor of the day to seek recreation in the serious conversation of men, not in idle love-dalliance. The ardor of their friendship resembled that of love, and they did not hear the waves of the Salo laugh mischievously as they took the solemn oath.

All these experiences, with their bright and dark sides, flitted before the mind of the nocturnal pedestrian; but as he had always believed that reflection over the past or the future was the most foolish act a human being could perform, he quickened his steps and laughed aloud when, after a prolonged search, he found two sestertii still in his purse. "I must seek a wealthy patron," he thought, "that I may receive sour wine and kicks daily as his client. But then, dear Metellus," he went on in his jesting soliloquy,

"I will have nothing more to do with you! I'll have no intercourse with a fellow who is regarded with contempt even by the slaves, and spends his life in paying visits and inventing flatteries; no, my good Metellus, I would far rather see your skin tanned in the gladiators' barracks. The possibility of dying an honorable death in the arena will at once relieve you from the obligation of being the slave of your tyrannical stomach."

The artist summoned up all the humor he possessed, and felt, as he thought, quite well, especially when he succeeded in dispelling his sorrowful thoughts by noticing what was passing around him. Sometimes his steps were checked by soldiers, whose ranks stretched almost entirely across the street Rude,brawny fellows, carrying spears, surrounded emaciated figures who held one another clasped in silent embrace. The latter, as the youth correctly surmised, were Christians destined at daybreak to serve as food for the wild beasts. Often, when an old man tottered along too slowly, he received a thrust from the handle of a spear.

Just as the troop reached the niche of the wall into which Metellus was pressing himself, a young, bold-looking soldier dragged an old man forward so roughly by his white beard that the boy on whom he was leaning for support laid his hand on the cruel fellow's arm as if beseeching pity. In return he received a violent kick, which hurled him out of the ranks, almost on the knees of our pedestrian.

"Forgive me," panted the lad; and Metellus, touched by the large tearful eyes fixed upon him from the child's face, raised the little figure.

"Hide behind me," he whispered, thrusting him into the darkest corner of the niche. Meanwhile the band had marched on; the soldier was occupied for the moment with the fainting old man, and when he hurried back to seize the boy whom he had thrust from the ranks, one of the leaders shouted an order which permitted no time for a thorough search.

So he went back, swearing furiously, to the prisoners. When Metellus looked for the lad, he was nowhere to be seen.

The veil of dusk still concealed everything in the streets leading to the Capitol; the sun hesitated to wake the " Queen of the Universe," the temples were not yet gray, and the sculptor, yawning, wished that daylight would appear. The pavement of the more distant quarters of the city often rumbled; then he saw heavy, rudely made wooden carts roll along, drawn by ten to fifteen oxen harnessed one before the other. Sullen roars echoed from these shapeless vehicles; a hairy muzzle, a tail, a paw armed with claws, often protruded between the clumsy wooden bars; so Metellus was not long in doubt as to what cruel strangers were here making their entry into Rome, and for what purpose they were transported during the night into the imperial gardens. At the corner of the street leading to the Carina, a beggar, over whose thin legs Metellus almost fell, lay sound asleep.

"Ho, ho!" cried the young sculptor, hastily supporting himself against the wall. The sleeper slowly rose, but instead of complaining, sighed, stammering drowsily, "Well hit, my lord, well hit."

"By the dog!" said Metellus, "is he thanking me for the kick I gave him?"

19

The other, meanwhile, waking more fully, rubbed his eyes, and seeing the disturber of his rest, said laughing,—

"Pardon me, my young friend; you have rendered me a pleasant service: you waked me from a disagreeable dream."

"How is that?" asked the sculptor.

"Just think," replied the old man, "I dreamed that I was sitting at the table of my patron, the Aedile, and he again played one of his rude jokes on me to make his guests laugh. I entertained him, as usual, with passages from the philosophers; in return he flung a ham-bone at my head, which jest I humbly applauded with the cry: 'Well hit!'"

"And do you submit to such humiliations without a murmur?" asked Metellus.

"O ye Muses! What will not a man do for the sake of a hot dinner?" replied the philosopher, yawning. "Besides, who humiliates himself the most,—the mocker or the mocked? And what are jeers when we look at them closely? Where is the person, who does not deserve to be derided, to be found in this world? Mockery is a merry reproof, and no one should be too proud to be reproved, young man."

With these words, the Cynic threw his tattered cloak around his lean body, spit vigorously into the gutter, and, scorning the dirt around him, leaned comfortably against the wall.

"Judging by your speech, you seem to be a Greek?" asked Metellus, curiously.

"I congratulate myself upon having been born under the blue sky of glorious Athens," replied the philosopher.

"And do you always spend the night in the gutter?" the sculptor continued.

"The highest virtue is contentment," said the Greek, taking from his pocket a bit of mouldy bread, which he began to gnaw.

"Up to this time I have not carried it so far as you," said Metellus; "I prefer a bed, no matter how hard, to the stones of the street."

The Athenian moved nearer to the unsuspicious artist.

"I know well," he began, scratching his left hip,—"I know well what value men usually set on gold. For my part, I utterly despise it."

Metellus, sitting down on a projection in the wall by the speaker's side, declared that he fully shared this contempt. The sage, laying his hand familiarly on his young listener's knee, went on: "Education, my friend, that is the capital with which to speculate,—a capital which bears interest, and which can never be stolen from you. But are you safe from thieves so long as a single sestertius remains in your purse?"

"Certainly not," said our friend, thoughtfully.

"A man who has education," the other continued, "possesses everything he needs, even virtue. But virtue is the highest good. By virtue I especially mean honesty. With it we can go far in the world, for how much easier it renders life if we need neither cheat nor steal; and really he does not possess the highest good who is obliged to live in perpetual anxiety lest he should be caught in some knavery. True, it is said that there is a certain pleasure in having overreached a blockhead; but it seems to me that the person outwitted must have more satisfaction in having been the man who was cheated, than the cheat, for many pockets are certainly very narrow."

In the course of this explanation the philosopher had edged nearer and nearer to his attentive pupil, and appeared to feel a keen interest in his cloak, which he felt cautiously; and when Metellus noticed it, the Stoic said reproachfully:

"What fine cloth you wear on your body! Feel my cloak; it is as rough as my beard. You seem to be an Epicurean."

Before the youth could answer, the strange fellow rose.

"I am in the habit of bathing in the Tiber at this hour of the night," he said; "it hardens the body. Farewell, my friend, and take to heart the lessons I have given you."

The Stoic moved off far more rapidly than would have been expected from a man of his fragile appearance, and Metellus admired the simplicity of his habits and the honesty of his principles. That is the life we ought to lead, he thought, ever ready to express our thoughts with the same dignity, whether we are at the Emperor's table or in the mire of the gutter; sacrificing all pleasures, scorning the world, meditating upon virtue, submitting to every insult without taking vengeance,—yes, that is indeed a noble existence.

With the enthusiasm of youth, the artist's childlike nature painted the advantages of a Stoic's career, though he was certainly the last person who would have found pleasure in such a life. But his raptures were soon to be thoroughly cooled. When, by accident, he thrust his hand into his purse, he found it empty; his two sestertii had been cautiously transferred to the pocket of the philosopher, whose beautiful maxims of honesty probably exerted a great power of attraction upon coins.

Metellus laughed aloud. He was not enraged with the old man who had taken advantage of his inexperience, but merely marvelled at the cunning and dexterity with which he had managed to cheat him. "Now," he thought, "I am really the original man; so long as I had money, there was a touch of artificiality in me. It's lucky that it costs nothing to breathe Roman air or to drink from the water-pipes. I could not even pay the ferryman of the nether world, if he should summon me to his boat now." He again burst into a peal of laughter which rang with childlike mirth through the quiet streets of the Subura, whose taverns were still closed. But it was suddenly echoed by approaching voices. Whistles, mingled with the noise of confused shouts, and reeling steps were heard.

Could these be watchmen, Metellus wondered as, turning the next corner, he saw several figures advancing toward him with the bearing of aristocratic debauchees, sometimes pounding insolently on the doors of the houses, sometimes, after the usual fashion of drunkards, affectionately embracing one another. All were muffled in strange, motley garments, while hideous masks concealed their features. The whole train was apparently trying to represent the gods, but there was something indescribably childish in the parade; nay, the gestures and insignia of the majority were unseemly in the highest degree.

Metellus remembered having heard that it was one of the amusements of Roman profligates to toss in blankets peaceful citizens who met them on their way home from their nocturnal orgies. So, though he did not lack courage, he resolved, as a stranger, to avoid a brawl, and was just evading the band when the torch held aloft by the foremost threw a broad glare of light upon the pavement. He was seen and instantly surrounded by faces whose motionless, dimly lighted grin inspired a sense of fear.

"Why are you laughing?" asked one of the disguised figures in a stern, feigned voice, and then whispered through the huge mouth of his mask into the ear of one of his companions. The latter, who was costumed in the insignia of Apollo, nodded; and the other, planting himself with legs wide apart before the sculptor, again asked with malicious emphasis,—

"Why are you laughing? The gods, who to-day condescend to honor the streets of Rome, ask the question."

I am laughing," replied Metellus, quickly, because you are vexed that you cannot laugh, too; for there is no dainty more delicious, my lord, than laughter: the gods envy us its enjoyment. But really I don't know myself why I am laughing, for I have no reason to be gay."

"Do you suppose you can trifle with Jupiter, miserable mortal?" growled another.

"Tell us at once why you are laughing," cried a third, raising his staff, "or your mirth will be instantly transformed to weeping."

"Fie!" replied the artist, apparently entering into the jest, "is laughing forbidden by the police regulations of Rome? But you shall never know, just because you wish to learn; and if the Emperor himself should stand before me, he would get no other answer."

"Apollo, do you hear, he disdains the Emperor," said the questioner, turning to his companions.

"Do you know the Emperor?" asked the Apollo, whose feminine outlines and reddish hair were recognizable in spite of his disguise.

"No, my lord," replied Metellus, peevishly; "I have been in Rome only a few days, and my friendly intercourse with coins is extremely fleeting, so I never had an opportunity to gaze at the Emperor's likeness more than two minutes."

The former speaker now turned to the group surrounding him, and with a gesture of mock solemnity said,—

"Cudgel him for not having yet seen the Emperor, and then put a red-hot denarius on his cheek to imprint the Caesar's image upon it."

"That is contrary to law," Metullus expostulated; "and if there are any watchmen in Rome, one will see whether your absurd masquerade is permitted to attack peaceful citizens; "but he had scarcely finished the words when blows from several thyrsus staves rained on his shoulders. Metellus, whose composure was wholly destroyed, chose the youth addressed as Apollo for the object of his wrath, since, as leader of the party, he believed him to be the instigator of the sorry jest. He quietly allowed the others to splinter their staves on his back, watched his opportunity, made a skilful side spring, snatched the lyre of the god of song, and dealt the Olympian's head so violent a blow with it that his mask was shattered into fragments, disclosing a very astonished face. His companions instantly fell upon the insulter of the divinity.

"Save Apollo! Throw him into the cloaca," was shouted as if by a single mouth; and, in spite of the most desperate resistance, Metellus was soon held firmly. Apollo watched the struggle with an angry laugh, but hastily borrowed another mask from one of his train.

"Is this the Roman method of fighting," groaned the ill-treated youth, when, after a long conflict, he at last escaped from the arms of his tormentors, "ten against one? If you are not drunken rakes or dishonorable highwaymen, choose one of your band, confront me with him, and I'll show you what Hispanian arms can do. I have hewn marble; do you suppose flesh fattened on pasties, bathed or anointed, is harder to deal with than a block of Parian marble?"

As no answer came, only a confused murmur running from one to another, the speaker went on,—

"True, the Roman of to-day tries his strength only in pressing the cushions of couches at the banquet, and is brave only against woman's virtue. So let me go my way."

He threw his cloak over his shoulders, cast a scornful glance at the party, and prepared to move on. His powerful though not tall figure seemed to intimidate the profligates. The haughty manner in which his muscular arm held the lacerna across his breast, his rough goat-skin garment from which his round knee protruded in the vigor of youth, his firm step, the clear gaze of his frank eyes, flashing with the influence of excitement, did not fail to produce a certain impression; and he had taken only a few steps when a voice shouted in a tone by no means unfriendly: "Stop." He turned carelessly and saw a figure attired as Neptune whispering eagerly to the Apollo.

"Wait a moment, young man," called Neptune, and again turned with eager gesticulations to Apollo. Metellus felt that the two were talking about him. Sometimes they scanned him intently, pointed at him, and appeared to be discussing the pros and cons of a plan. Although he had intended to go on, curiosity now bound the sculptor to the

spot. "What, by Zeus, can they be whispering about?" he murmured as he saw Apollo, laughing, shake his head and wave his hand in denial.

"Your plan seems too bold," he heard him say.

"By no means, my lord," the other answered. Then followed several unintelligible sentences, until at last Apollo was silent, while the other, taking advantage of the opportunity, appeared to crowd all his former arguments into a single long sentence.

"Then make the attempt," whispered Apollo, at its conclusion; and Neptune, bowing most graciously, at once approached Metellus, who had vainly racked his brains to guess the purport of this singular dialogue.

"Pardon our attack upon your precious person," said Neptune, courteously; " we were mistaken in you.. I am sorry that you chanced to be the one to fall into our hands."

"It would certainly have been better if another back than mine had chanced to have the honor of serving as anvil for your hands," replied Metellus, in his talkative fashion. "No one can take my blows from me; but I am glad that I have marked the divine brow of your leader, that rake, that Apollo, with a blue spot which will last several days."

"Then we will consider the incident as forgotten," said Neptune, adroitly. "My young friend, I address you in the name of my master, who, if you consent, is able to make your fortune."

"And who is your master?" asked Metellus.

"You will learn that to-morrow," replied the other, evasively.

"And in what way do you expect to make my fortune?"

"Call at the Emperor's palace to-morrow, four hours after sunrise. There you will receive an explanation of what is now concealed from you."

"The Emperor's palace?" asked Metellus, laughing. "I suppose you feel at liberty to make sport of me. Call at my palace, four stories high in the Jew quarter. There I, too, might explain many things unknown to you."

The mysterious mask's only reply was to ask the name of the youth, write it on a tablet, add a few words, and hand it to him. Metellus read the inscription by the flickering light of a torch; it was an order to the palace guard to admit the bearer of this tablet and conduct him to the Emperor's ante-room. The sculptor shook his head.

"If you are speaking the truth," he said, "I shall be still less inclined to accept your proposal."

"And why?"

"At least I should wish to know more definitely for what purpose I am summoned to Nero's ante-chamber."

"You will learn later."

"This is a serious matter to me," said Metellus, gravely; "for what do you take me? Do I look like a scoundrel who can be used for unlawful purposes? Am I a wily Greek? A poison-brewing woman? I have no fancy for the Emperor's palace. All sorts of tales are heard of what is done there—"

These words, spoken in a somewhat louder tone, were probably caught by the group waiting near; at least, they were greeted with immoderate laughter.

"What are those fellows laughing at?" murmured the young man.

"Do you fear us?" replied the disguised figure, joining in the laugh.

"Call it what you please, but I forbid your laughing at me; there is no cause for it."

"Your artlessness is delicious," said the other, patting him on the shoulder. "I like you, my boy, and I swear that you shall experience nothing unpleasant in the imperial palace. Clasp hands! Promise to be there."

"I'll think of it, but don't call me a boy, I beg; it is not very complimentary to my eighteen years."

"You are hungry, my friend, I see," replied the disguised speaker, " while at the same time you are too honest to steal, so you will not let this opportunity of earning a large, a very large sum, pass by. Your trade ?" he added haughtily.

"I am a sculptor."

"So much the better," was the reply. "A sculptor, a handsome person, and waving red locks, you possess everything necessary to make your fortune in Rome."

The masked stranger hurried back to his group of friends, leaving the bewildered artist to his amazement. Red hair was fashionable in Rome at that time. Metellus understood the hint; and since he had a little vanity and intended to make his fortune, his flatterer at once appeared in a pleasanter light.

The party of disguised revellers now went off with loud shouts, waving their torches till the houses were illumined to their roofs by the crimson glare. Our fair-haired artist looked after the retreating figures, shook his head, and decided that he was either a favorite of the gods, or a creature doomed to destruction.

"What can they want of me?" he asked himself again, but perceiving that it was as impossible to solve this enigma as to pierce the clouds and enter Olympus, he dismissed the whole matter from his mind,—which to one of his temperament, averse to reflection on any subject, was comparatively easy. Perhaps it might be some mysterious task, an imperial caprice; perhaps one of the Emperor's loves, whose existence no one was permitted to know, was to be modelled, thought Metellus, rubbing his hands gleefully; and though he had just been suspicious of the whole adventure, he suddenly resolved to go to the palace at the fourth hour. Then his thoughts wandered to an entirely different subject, till he suddenly realized that he was thirsty, and he stopped beside a fountain.

Bending down to the mouth of the marble lion's head to catch in his hand the silver jet which it was furiously spouting, Metellus washed his face vigorously with both hands; and while thus engaged in making his toilet, he saw a helmeted head reflected in the green crystal of the basin of the fountain. Turning, he perceived a soldier, whom he remembered having seen the day before. Yes! it was at the Circus Maximus, in front of an astrologer's booth, that he had encountered this Jew with the pinched, gloomy face, who had harshly rebuffed him. Rufus was standing behind the artist, cooling his brow by dipping his hand into the fountain and pressing it upon his temples. Metellus dried his face and turned familiarly to the soldier.

"Aurora is gradually beginning to raise her fingers above the capital of the world," he said; "at least I see her son, the morning star,, twinkling faintly above the Temple of Isis. A dim gray hue already illumines the pediments of the loftiest palaces; we must wash and comb ourselves to be in readiness for the awakening of Rome."

Rufus, who was not pleasantly affected by the unexpected meeting, had turned to go without answering the kindly address; but Metellus, in his artless heedlessness, did not notice that the Jew would have preferred to pursue his way alone so, joining the soldier, he walked silently beside the silent man.

One could scarcely imagine a greater contrast than that presented by these two figures, passing side by side through the empty streets in the deceptive glimmering light of dawn. The warrior, erect and sinewy, showed, beneath the iron clasps of his armor, muscles hardened by training. His step was firm; and when he raised his helmeted head, his shaggy beard bared a thin neck with swollen veins. The youth's rounded outlines were set off by a skin almost girlish in its fairness. Manly strength and feminine grace blended in him in the manner which is especially bewitching to older women. He was shorter than the soldier; waving locks fell over his forehead almost to his beautifully arched eyebrows; the curve of his cheek ended in a delicate chin. The fire of his glance and the virility of his slender figure lent his face dignity and nobility. But the loquacious artist could not endure this silent walk long. He criticised the badly painted signs of the vegetable or meat dealers, the unnecessary number of pillars in many of the houses, but Rufus's sole reply was a brief clearing of the throat or a distrustful glance. This, however, by no means disturbed him in his remarks; he even had courage to question the gloomy soldier about his silence.

"Do you know," he at last asked gayly, "how one can get a piece of bread without paying for it? I am hungrier than Tantalus."

Rufus smiled contemptuously, and silently offered the youth a small coin. Metellus pushed his hand back.

"I will accept no gift bestowed in that way," he said proudly.

Rufus pocketed his money again, shrugged his shoulders, and flushed to his helmet as he now spoke for the first time to his companion.

"What is your calling?" he asked half unintelligibly, as if it dishonored him to seem communicative.

"I am a sculptor," replied Metellus, irately, running his fingers through his shaggy goatskin garment.

"A stone-cutter!" muttered the Jew, scornfully.

"You do not seem to love the arts," answered Metellus, without taking offence.

"No, I do not!" retorted the other. "I honor the laws, and believe that a great orator, a great general, resembles your gods far more than Virgil, Homer, and Ovid put together; but least of all can I understand why people want to carve men from stones."

"That is a matter of taste," said Metellus, smiling sarcastically. "Nero loves the arts."

"He loves them, as I would love them, to shine by their means."

"There you are mistaken," said the artist, sharply. "Nero writes verses, models, plays the zither. Whoever pursues an art is ennobled by it: the Caesar cannot be as bad as people in the provinces try to represent him; his love for art proves that. Has he not had a colossal statue of himself made for his Golden House?"

"Yes, and behind the yew hedges in his gardens lurk many white forms: that is the fashion; everybody follows it. If I were as rich as a Tigellinus or a Piso, I, too, would place these pallid marble ghosts in the shadow of the elms, but I would laugh to scorn both statues and sculptors."

"Would you like to be rich?" asked the artist, to turn the conversation.

"A foolish question!" replied the other. "Why do we live? If I knew that I should never get any further in the world than to be a file-leader, would it not be senseless for me to live on?"

Metellus had a different opinion, but he kept it to himself, for the soldier's positive, bold nature disheartened him. The Jew began to prove the uselessness of the arts, represented reason as the supreme power of man's soul, and spoke contemptuously of that which was called imagination. The youth had few opposing arguments. He felt that Rufus was wrong, but at the moment he could not find the fitting reasoning. "Necessity is everything," said the gloomy man; "the rest is mere trifling. Life is too serious to fritter it away in amusement and beautiful marble faces; when stern, savage reality confronts you, you must not lose yourself in a realm of fancy." The two had changed characters: the artist was now silent and depressed, while the soldier grew talkative.

"A miserable world," he said spitefully, "in which it is only worth while to live when one has five million sestertii, or is a fool. The fools have the best of it; they secure honors and offices, like a Vatinius. I wish I had been born, like him, in a cobbler's shop, a hunch backed, long-eared monster; then I would soon hold this whole marble Rome in my hairy fist. A zither-player is well off, too, if he knows enough to let Nero win the victory. What do you think of getting ourselves places in the band of the Caesar's applauders? They have a yearly salary, wear fine clothes, and have nothing to do except clap their hands occasionally."

Amid such conversation the couple, leaving the Temple of Lares at the left, had reached the Val Murcia. The artist did not notice that Rufus was intentionally going toward the Circus. Metellus had proposed taking another direction; and Rufus, turning toward the Capitol, apparently assented to the suggestion, but in the course of their talk, he had managed to take the way leading past the wrestling-school on the Coelian Hill. While chatting continuously, he had often cast searching glances at his companion, who strolled unsuspectingly beside him, and was greatly surprised to find himself suddenly at the entrance of the Circus.

Here they beheld a scene whose terrible details gained a certain melancholy charm by the veil of the dim light of dawn. While in the distance the first travellers, singing and laughing, were already entering the city through the Capenian Gate, here sad-faced men were hurrying out of the door of the building; others followed weeping, bearing forms muffled in blood-stained linen; others again seemed to be watching at the street corners to give warning of the approach of danger.

The blood-stained burdens were dragged out of the entrance hastily and fearfully; often the end of a sheet escaped from the bearer's trembling hand, revealing, in the faint light of dawn, a mangled neck, a horribly disfigured face.

Metellus guessed that the Christians were carrying the bodies of their murdered brethren out of the arena to bury them in the Catacombs.

The body of a young man was just being taken with great exertion down the marble steps. The bearers—two sisters and an aged mother—forced back their tears; their sobs became panting breathing as they struggled to lift the corpse from step to step. A trail of blood, trickling from the linen, marked the way along the marble. The face of the body was covered; the nose formed a strange elevation in the gray covering on which the increasing light cast faint, dull rays. The morning breeze blew chill, bearing the odor of blood to the two spectators; the chariot of victory above the entrance gleamed redly; the goddess of victory hovered in a cold purple haze. High aloft in the grayish blue sky, majestic, unsympathizing, she curbed the rearing steeds, while the steps and pillars of the building were dyed with blood.

An old man, bowed with grief, walked in front of the corpse; his eyelids drooped as if he were on the verge of fainting as he tottered past the two spectators whom, in his bewilderment, he seemed to take for Christians. "My sole support," he wailed, extending his hand as if for a gift.

Metellus was not well disposed toward the Christians. As an artist, he execrated a religion which rejected all representations of the deity in sculpture and painting; the superstition seemed rude and bald, fit only for beggars and simpletons. Yet now, touched by compassion, he opened his purse, and, with a sorrowful shrug of the shoulders, showed that it was empty. The old man, smiling sadly, put his hand into his pocket and was about to throw a coin into the wallet. Metellus, utterly bewildered, pushed back the proffered alms. The old man went on; and as the body was carried past them, the sculptor could not refrain from lifting a corner of the cloth which covered it.

The mother noticed it, and, pausing, said in a passionate outburst of the grief she had been repressing: "Yes, young man, look at him; see how handsome he is; an angel has kissed the horrors of death from his brow." She raised the winding-sheet. Before Metellus lay the most beautiful youth whom he had ever beheld: a noble anger slept upon the ivory-white brow; defiance of death rested gloomily on the blue-black eyebrows; the exquisite lips were slightly parted as if about to utter a contemptuous word. The matron, who was still stately, even beautiful, in her anguish, clasped the hands of the departed one over his breast.

"I wish that he had been my friend," whispered Metellus, deeply moved, to the mother. The latter nodded, gazing dully into vacancy, while tears sprang to her reddened eyelids. Then she slowly covered the dead man's motionless face and helped to bear on the corpse. As Rufus, with sudden resolution, hastened up the steps to the entrance, the youth slowly followed. His heart throbbed heavily as he entered the cell of the condemned man, whose door now stood wide open, affording a view of the arena, strewn with corpses. The long rows of seats were empty; only a few bright spots, interrupting the monotonous gray hue of the stone stairs, showed that one or another of the spectators, instead of going home, had preferred to spend the night on his cushions in the Circus.

The pale light of dawn glimmered above the highest row of arches down into the arena. The moon looked wan in the white radiance of the early morning, as her indifferent, pallid face hovered above the heaps of corpses of men and animals, whose limbs sometimes still quivered, that lay scattered over the sand as if Death had given a festival. How many shades were doubtless already surrounding the gloomy ferryman! How silently the skiff was doubtless now gliding through the sluggish waves, past the distant rocky shores which men behold but once! How did they dwell in the eternal twilight, amid the croaking of the horrible birds! Hence, sorrowful visions! Clear up, frowning brow!

The morning breeze bore the warm, sweet odor of blood toward the sculptor, who would have shuddered at the spectacle of this battlefield had not the characteristic attitude, the noble outlines of the limbs of many a corpse awakened his artistic interest. The cool colors of the morning light softened the inhuman aspect of the scene and gave it a wild grandeur, an unprecedented beauty. He suppressed a yawn, wrapped his mantle closer about his shivering limbs, and prepared to enter the next cell. Far away torches, moving to and fro, twinkled like stars in the blue morning mist. Slaves were removing the bodies, shovelling away the blood-stained sand, driving off the ravens which hovered croaking over the piles of corpses. In the next cell a keeper of the beasts was snoring on the floor among his water-pails and brooms, digesting the leeks and onions which his wife had served up to him the evening before. Through the closed grating of the cage a lion was visible, pressing its head against the bars; while the blood, flowing from a wound in the hip, covered the floor. Metellus sympathizingly watched the royal brute, as it let its hurt bleed without a sound of pain, turning its angry eyes contemptuously away from the world. In this cell a sturdy keeper also lay asleep, still holding in his hand a bit of meat. Metellus again gazed at the dying lion, which remained motionless, then seized a butcher-knife and scrawled upon the table used to cut the meat the outlines of the dying brute. "There," he said, when he had finished the picture, "now I shall not forget you."

He went toward the arena in a more thoughtful mood than he had ever been before. He could not have explained the cause of his reflections; they rested upon his consciousness like a burden which could not be shaken off; a melancholy that he had never felt, a mournfulness which astonished him, occupied his mind. Striving to escape it, he paused before the body of a mother who was clasping her dead child to her breast, then before the corpse of an old man who grasped a strangled leopard. He scanned the lifeless features, sought to fathom the last thoughts of these pitiable martyrs, and gazed into their dull eyes.

Meanwhile the image of the handsome youth whom he had just seen borne away haunted him; and as the pale, reproachful face rose before his mental vision, the atmosphere suddenly grew so close and oppressive that

29

he gasped for breath and hurried on. He felt as if he ought to admire the beautiful dead, nay, envy his lot. What would he not have given to be able to live in the companionship of such a man, how he suddenly longed for friendship, and how lonely and desolate it seemed among these wan sleepers in great, unsympathizing Rome! For the first time in years he, .who found life so gay, felt as if he must weep, and that, with the tears, his happy childhood would flee, never to return. His heart seethed with resentment against Rome, which had so swiftly wrought a transformation in his feelings and opinions; he envied the slaves laughing yonder with heartless indifference and cracking jokes as they dragged the corpses through the sand; only base souls like theirs could be at ease in this city. Either the unwonted spectacle, or the hunger which had tormented him for hours, affected him with paralyzing weakness; but conquering it he went up to Rufus, whom he saw kneeling beside the dead body of a girl.

The Praetorian had found what he was seeking: Lucretia, whose face had haunted him more than he desired, lay before him. Around her were the clumsy bodies of dead bears; a leopard with a stab in his breast stretched its jaws wide open; another still clenched a woman's head with its teeth.

Lucretia was unhurt: she had been concealed by the dead bodies of men and animals; protected by the lifeless, she had been saved. As she lay rigid before the bearded man, who strove to banish every trace of compassion from his features, it was a strangely peaceful picture in the midst of these horrors, illumined by the dazzling rays of the morning sun.

The soldier brought a pail from the cell occupied by the keeper, and sprinkled the girl's face with water. The only sign of life was the rising and falling of her breast; the rest of her form lay motionless. Her black hair, moist with mire, blood, and water, was plastered upon her brow and cheeks, forming a frame in which the nobly formed, wan features, absolutely expressionless, had a spectral appearance. Her helplessness was well suited to awake compassion; the broad closed lids arched so mysteriously over the eyes, a faint smile rested on the livid lips, she did not look like a girl; there was nothing human about her.

Rufus harshly shouted to Metellus an order which the latter, in the drowsiness caused by his exhaustion, did not hear. He turned as if to fulfil it, toward the entrance, staggered down the steps into the open air, and before he was aware of it again stood in the street.

CHAPTER IV

ROME had now awaked; her marble roofs and lofty pillars were gleaming in the radiant sunlight. Crowds were already surging to and fro among the booths, past the tall houses with their tiny windows, around the statues at the street corners, and through the colonnades. The sumptuous buildings looked down in silent majesty upon the throng. The green foliage of trees broke the lines of the arcades with its refreshing hue and offered shade to the yawning idlers. Venders called attention to their wares; butchers offended the nostrils of the passers-by with their quarters, of beef thickly covered with flies; bakers Dressed their fingers into their cakes to show hungry customers their crispness; cooks praised their pease-puddings. Shepherds from the surrounding country came in with their milkpails and chattered at the doors of the houses with the mistresses. Metellus, while watching the scene, was tempted on account of the gnawing in his stomach to pay court to a young woman who was just taking the milk-pail from a burly son of the mountains. In his exhausted condition, he scarcely knew what he was doing when he addressed her, in the hope of obtaining a cup of milk as a reward for his flattery. Unaccustomed to woo, he asked for a kiss awkwardly enough.

What do you want?" cried the wench. You are so beautiful," stammered the starving man, pulling at his cloak.

"Am I?" she cried. "Well, my friend, you are as ugly as Achilles in woman's clothes. By Orcus! he smells of the distaff, and what dainty little fingers he has. Go; you are far too delicate for me, you stupid Ganymede." And she now began to berate him so vigorously about his goatskin garment and his smooth, beardless face that the sculptor retreated in great embarrassment, without answering. The grinning shepherd, who fairly reeked of the stable, remained in full possession of his rights, and instantly bestowed a resounding smack upon the girl's mouth with his thick lips.

Metellus's sufferings soon grew unbearable; his stomach urgently demanded food; the noise of the crowd sounded farther and farther away; and a gray veil already dimmed his eyes. But no one troubled himself about the pallid, tottering stranger; everybody was occupied with his own concerns. One pondered over his interesting law case; another thought of the rich old aunt who must soon go down into the nether world. This man was planning a clever bit of cheating; that one was considering how he could best overthrow Julia's virtue. Many were perhaps in the clutches of the usurers, while one was estimating the cost of his new villa in Tibur; school-children were declining words under the direction of the lean tutor; every person behaved as if he were the only human being in the world and his cause were the most important, his neighbor was heeded only just so far as he stood in his way. Metellus stopped in front of a pillar and heard, without paying attention, a portly citizen reading aloud to a laughing group a pointed epigram about Nero's "singing voice," which had been scrawled upon the wall; he heard a snub-nosed crier promising a hundred denarii to any one who brought back Senator M.'s runaway slave. He saw a ragged sailor, with a piece of the ship in which he had been wrecked in his hand, begging for alms, and a cripple on the pavement stretching out his withered arm or beating his sole companion, that was starving with him,— his dog. All these things were heard and seen as if in a dream; the whole motley throng began to whirl shrieking before his eyes; the houses no longer stood firmly; the nymphs and the marble lions spouting water into the basins of the fountains began to dance; the fruit-seller's donkey and the

31

knight striding proudly along, the grave Egyptian and the agile Greek, all the various costumes and figures blended into a thick mass, which was constantly stirred by invisible hands.

The corpses which the poor fellow had just beheld haunted his imagination; unbearable pain tortured his body; he could scarcely think, and dragged himself onward, his breast filled with an emotion of self-pity.

"If I should fall now, what would become of me?" With tears in his eyes, he went up to a fruit-dealer whose baskets were overflowing with figs and bluish-green melons, but in spite of his great need, he had not the courage to ask the man for a gift.

A rich magistrate, reclining in a litter, was borne along the street. The slaves walking in front shouted: "Make way; make way;" but Metellus was so dazed that he stood still, and received in consequence a severe thrust in the ribs from the sable Ethiopian. He no longer possessed sufficient strength of will to return the blow; he scarcely knew that he had been hit, and gazed after the satiated glutton, who lolled comfortably on his crimson cushions, holding a bunch of grapes to his lips and spitting the skins into the faces of the passers-by.

"O gracious Jupiter, what am I to do?" murmured the starving youth. "I expected something very different."

When a client, hurrying along in a shabby toga, stepped heavily on his toe and hastened on without an apology, he partially recovered his consciousness; the old spirit of defiance awoke, and without pausing to reflect, he entered the nearest tavern. The courteous host instantly appeared with his usual smile and his fat bowed neck. "What can I set before you?" he asked, and Metellus called for wine and common cheese.

"At once," said the host. It was a tavern of the lowest sort. Rough wooden tables, and a floor strewn with fragments of dishes, sausage-skins, fruit-peels, and seeds. The little stove at the entrance, used to prepare warm dishes, filled the dark room, open to the street, with thick black smoke, against which the white robes of the guests glimmered like the shades in the darkness of the nether world. In front stood the counter, on whose dirty marble top fruit, cheese, bread, fish, wine-bottles, and plucked fowls lay in confusion. The whole array produced the impression of being composed of remnants which kindly Ceres (she was painted on the sign) had dropped from her horn of plenty. Moreover, besides the noisy guests, there was no lack of little stinging fellow occupants, which instantly chose the sculptor's goatskin for their wrestling ground. The poor youth rested his head on his hand and summoned all the strength of his will in order not to betray his weakness; to divert his thoughts he counted the number of guests and scanned the rude sign displayed above the counter. Perhaps his pallor, his yearning gaze bestowed upon his beauty a greater power of attraction than the hue of health; at least the Syrian slave girl who was now filling his goblet from the wine-skin smiled at him most seductively.

"Refresh yourself, stranger," she said, pressing the neck of the wrinkled skin with her white fingers. Metellus, without hearing her, seized the cup and half emptied it.

"May Bacchus bless the drink to you!" she said, and Metellus, whose consciousness was fully restored by the strong vintage, ruefully reflected in his troubled mind that Bacchus would hardly help him pay for the wine. Soon the ever-smiling landlord appeared and placed on the table a little rush basket filled with cheeses, which he handled as though it contained the most delicious dainties.

"Appease your hunger," he said pleasantly, and when Metellus, sighing, seized one of the yellow cheeses, the portly host patted his shoulders, adding: "Don't sigh! What says Horace of youth?" Then he interrupted himself: "Whence? Whither? If I may venture to ask?"

"I am from the provinces," said the youth.

"Aha! Do you want to make your fortune in Rome? That is well! Always come to Rome. Money grows from the paving stoned."

Metellus sighed again, but the fat landlord went on,—

"Only don't neglect the women; always stick to the women. Courage, young man, when I was your age—" Again he did not finish the usual phrase, two soldiers called him to another table. With cringing affability he leaned his portly paunch over the others, whispering into their ears all sorts of jests about the rustic youth from the provinces, who had certainly come to Rome to be led by the nose by some old Senator's widow. "The landlord is a good-natured man," thought the artist, sipping the Falernian and chewing, the greasy, loathsome cheese, which, but For his excessive hunger, he would scarcely have touched. "The host seems to mean kindly by me. "After he had thus regained his mental composure, the boldness of his undertaking weighed like a twofold burden on his heart. Horrified at what he had dared, he flung down his goblet without hearing the words of the slave-woman who refilled it, for his mind was occupied solely with imagining the consequences of his cheating. They will call the lictors, I shall be in prison to-night, he thought, gazing at the jovial face of the landlord, who as yet had no suspicion that—or had he an idea of the baseness of his guest, did he not sometimes glance suspiciously at him? Metellus, you are on the point of becoming a vagabond: to eat, drink, and not pay!

The honest fellow suffered inexpressibly from these ideas; it was the first act of fraud which he had ever committed, committed in desperation, and in desperation he drank more and more Falernian, which instantly worked upon his empty stomach and used the opportunity to fire his heated brain. His cheeks flushed, his gloomy visions gradually receded; brighter ones entered his mind, and, all at once, he could not understand why the world was suffused with so roseate a light. The burden that had weighed so heavily on his shoulders half an hour before suddenly became as light as a feather, the landlord was a fool, money the most superfluous thing in the world, inability to pay a jest.

Several guests sat down near him, and, glad to relieve his heart, he entered into conversation with them. With the spirit of contradiction that so often takes possession of the gentlest nature when it feels in its veins the power of Bacchus, he had some criticism upon every remark uttered by the drinkers. One of the men who were present, a thin linen weaver, was relating what he had heard from his neighbor, the squint-eyed baker Naevius, concerning Nero's relations with his wife Octavia.

On the whole, people were satisfied with the government,—only the great had suffEred from tyranny; the rest received bread and games, and sometimes did not grudge the aristocrats the humiliations and fears the sovereign inflicted upon them. Of course the linen-weaver did not know where the baker obtained his news, but it was certain that yesterday the Caesar had beaten his beautiful young wife with his own august hands. All Rome pitied the gentle Empress, who was only nineteen years old; Nero did not dare to divorce her, because he feared the voice of the people; others raised objections, protesting that Octavia had deserved this treatment from the Emperor.

"Not so loud," interrupted the landlord; "you know that we are never safe from spies."

"Still worse tales are told in my quarter of the city," whispered a tanner; "they say the Caesar treats Octavia like a prisoner—starves her."

"And what reasons should he have?" began Metellus, loudly; then as "hush!" was uttered on all sides, he finished the sentence in a low tone— "for such conduct?"

No one could give a reason, and the artist, excited by wine, eagerly upheld Nero, while the rest, smiling, listened in silence.

"Do you know Octavia personally? Have you permission to enter the Caesar's apartments? Gossip, city gossip!" he cried, "you hatch it in your cobbler-shops. I don't believe a word of it!"

The enthusiast was allowed to talk on, and the others passed to different subjects. The circus stallion "Helios" was subjected to a rigid criticism, and they discussed the question whether he had reached the goal two or three feet in advance of "Cleopatra" as if the existence of the empire was at stake; Lucan's last pantomime, "Paris and Helen," was praised, certain airs from this work, certainly not the most seemly, were sung. It was said that rain had fallen in Egypt, and the news that the gladiator Claudius had died of his wounds was told with expressions of regret. Metellus asked whether Lucan's last epic was published; the poet was very much praised, he was even said to have aroused Nero's jealousy.

"A splendid fellow," interrupted a dwarfish sandal-maker; "what a giant! Such endurance, such changes, such buoyancy when he warms up, such a fig—"

"He is said to command a very graceful style of verse," interrupted the sculptor, overjoyed at this appreciation of art.

"What! Style of verse! I 'm talking about the gladiator," said the sandal- dealer, glancing contemptuously at the artist, "with his epic."

"I did not have the pleasure of knowing the gladiator," retorted Metellus, dryly.

"You ought to have seen him bleed," said a peaceful-looking joiner's apprentice; "it was magnificent when he received the thrust in his breast without the quiver of an eyelash."

34

"And how the other slowly drew the reddened steel from the gaping wound," observed a fat fruit-dealer; "oh, I shall never forget it. The white, muscular body dripped with the red life-fluid like a crushed mulberry."

"And how gracefully . he sank!" cried a third, enthusiastically.

"Ah! But we Romans were gentle," replied the fruit-dealer, "we pardoned him."

Metellus inquired about Seneca's last work. No one could tell him anything of it, they knew only his name; but they could inform him just how many Christians had been torn by the lion " Hercules " the day before. The sculptor asked a question about Amulius's last picture, but no one had heard of the man, though they told him, as a piece of very important news, that the cook Thrasycles had invented a new kind of fruit pasty. Some of the fat fruit- dealer's cleverest equivocal sayings made the young artist blush so painfully, inwardly and outwardly, that he determined to give the conversation a different turn.

"Haven't you anything more sensible to say?" he cried. "Circus stallions, pasties, what do I care about them? Now listen, I'll tell you a nocturnal adventure which perhaps will suit your taste. This is a beautiful Rome, your Rome by night." Then, with vivacious prolixity, the artist described his adventure with the disguised company of gods, which has already been related. The imaginative fellow was so deeply absorbed in his dramatic reproduction of the fighting scene, that he did not notice the fruit-dealer, who was scratching his head in astonishment, the tanner, who forgot to drink, or the cabinet- maker, who was moving restlessly in his chair. The landlord came gliding up, and the whole company gradually showed a singular, very unusual interest.

"Yes," said Metellus, ending his story with a laugh, "I spoiled Apollo's sport thoroughly. I dealt him such a blow with his lyre on his divine nose, that he'll carry an Olympian blue mark on it at least a week."

"What!" exclaimed the horrified tanner, "you struck him—in the face—"

"Certainly!" replied our friend, laughing, "I struck him. Didn't he deserve it! Is one to submit good-naturedly to such midnight assaults?"

The tavern-keeper tried to speak, but in a fright which made his face livid, could only gasp: "Is it possible, sir! Struck him!"

"And how did you say that this Apollo looked?" asked the sandal-maker, timidly. "Was he tall—?"

"Tall!"

"Slightly inclined to corpulence?"

"To be sure."

"Were his limbs somewhat like a woman's?"

"Yes. There was something mushy in his face—but I don't understand your excitement—tell me—"

"A broad neck, reddish hair?"

"Exactly."

"And he was the leader of the band?"

"The leader," replied Metellus.

"It was no other, by Pluto!" panted the little cobbler, nodding to his companions in terror.

"It is he, it was he. That is his favorite disguise," said the cabinet-maker, rising noiselessly from his chair. "I remember that I must go home, Milo the centurion is waiting for his broken table."

Every one suddenly remembered that urgent business awaited him at home. All who were present had turned toward the speaker at the commencement of his tale; now most of them hastily emptied their wine-cups, paid their score, and made off with frightened faces. The tanner also rose, the rest of the group at the table followed his example; some repressed a smile of superiority, the cabinetmaker uttered an audible, "Ass!" the sandal-maker muttered something about stupid provincials who endangered the lives of peaceful citizens. The whole tavern was suddenly emptied of guests. Metellus did not know what to think of this flight; he sat as if in a dream, staring after the guests and wondering whether he or they had suddenly lost their reason.

"Begone, you dogs," shouted the landlord to his slaves, "why are you standing about here!"

The slaves had been staring at the speaker with dilated eyes, and did not stir until their master had favored them with several kicks. Then, with eyes sparkling with rage, he turned to Metellus.

"Well? And you?" he shouted " you who drive away my customers, must I put you out of the door by force, or will you use your legs?"

"But, in the name of Zeus the omnipotent," began the sculptor, "tell me at least—"

"Begone!" shouted the landlord, scarcely able to control himself, "begone—"

Metellus rose timidly, fingering, as was his habit when excited, the shaggy hair of his goatskin garment.

"I am sorry I cannot pay you," he stammered blushing, "write down my score, I will work, I will—"

"Begone!" raved the other without listening, grasping him by the shoulder, "do you suppose I want to have my custom spoiled?"

He pushed the poor youth who, in his bewilderment, submitted to everything, into the street. On reaching it, he thanked the gods that the landlord, in his excitement, had forgotten to press for payment of his account. This happy certainty at first drove all other painful emotions out of his heart.

"What can I have done that they all ran away from me as if I were a leper," he pondered; "these Romans are really just like children."

He was already beginning, according to his habit, to regard what he had experienced in a merry light when, in the midst of the crowd, a voice whispered in his ear: "Fly, you are lost!" He turned and thought he saw the end of the little sandal-maker's robe just vanishing behind a portly matron. "I sha'n't fare quite so badly; Zeus won't permit an honest sculptor to be ruined," thought Metellus, strolling toward his lodgings, which were between the triumphal arch of Tiberius and the island of Tiber.

There were so many new things to be seen * in the streets that he had no time to listen to the voice of the monitor. The colors of the Babylonian carpets, the gems, the metal vessels from Greece, the Asiatic slaves, who stood ready to be sold, occupied his whole mind. Now that his physical needs were supplied, he began to appreciate the architectural magnificence of Rome. The colonnades elicited exclamations of admiration as he saw them in quiet majesty lifting the superb roofs heavenward; the marble forms that looked down so nobly from their pedestals upon the throngs below filled his soul with a rapture of beauty; he could scarcely tear himself away from the statue of a dying warrior: the submissive expression, the dignified bearing of the wounded man attracted him again and again. And above all this wealthy Rome was throned, like an image of Olympus, the temple-crowned Capitol, shaming the skies with the glitter of its marble. It rose like an ever present thought of divinity whenever the eyes were raised from the dark streets; its gigantic staircase seemed like the ascent from the heavy atmosphere of earth to shining heights.

The artist, with the glad surprise of a child illumining his handsome face, walked past the magnificent shops of the Septa Julia, the halls and temples. As he approached the Forum his way led by the temple of Jupiter Stator, and he stood still as if enraptured before the majestic beauty of the faҫade. A richly adorned litter, which seemed to be waiting for some very aristocratic nobleman, was at the foot of the marble stairs. The numerous slaves had seated themselves comfortably on the steps, where they were playing dice. The contrast could scarcely be greater: noble pillars which raised the gabled roof filled with images of the gods nearer to the sky, and below upon this staircase inspiring, by its sublimity, thoughts of devotion, vulgar every- day life, drinking, gossiping, dice-playing slaves. The gate was opened; within the cool interior of the temple Jupiter concealed himself; half hidden by the dusk, his white limbs seemed slumbering beneath a blue veil.

Metellus's piety awoke; he entered the sanctuary, and as, instead of the brilliant sunlight, the subdued magnificence, the consecrated dusk of the temple surrounded him, he could scarcely restrain his tears. No one was visible, silence reigned. A light bluish mist rose from the altar, hovering in graceful curves around the brow of Jove. The noise from the street sounded like the distant surging of the sea; a few sparks glimmered on the altar, at last the fire died out entirely. The sculptor wished to kneel in prayer, but could not find the right words; again and again,, instead of holy emotions, the image of the dead youth for whom, without suspecting it, his soul was mourning, rose before him, and he resolved to leave the temple.

Rising from the floor he saw behind him a woman, who was gazing with an expression of anguish up to the countenance of the god. Metellus involuntarily stood still. The lips parted as if to utter a cry of pain, the reddened, tear- stained eyes, the trembling fingers convulsively clasping each other,—all afforded him a keen artistic pleasure that stirred his tender heart.

Before the door the slaves were quarrelling; their harsh voices awakened reverberating echoes as if the sanctuary, incensed, wished to bid the wranglers keep silence. Outside the world was surging and seething, here solitary grief knelt before Zeus, moving its lips in mute petitions. Metellus fairly held his breath, fearing to be noticed by the sorrowing woman. He felt as if some secret emotion constrained him to reflect, as it were, her expression of suffering in his own features; he, too, opened his lips, just as she was doing, and gazed with childlike curiosity into the beautiful, pallid face. At last she rose; Metellus shrank back, but she had already met his eyes, overflowing with compassion. At first a cloud of anger darkened her brow, but when she met the youth's embarrassed beseeching glance, she blushed, drew her robe over her face, and slowly left the temple. Outside shouts of command and retreating footsteps were heard. Hitherto Metellus had paid little heed to female beauty: the more rugged outlines of the masculine form had seemed to him a worthier subject of artistic representation; friendship was more to him than love; now for the first time a fleeting suspicion of what love was, or might be, rose in his mind, and, as he felt with astonishment, supplanted the image of the dead youth which, hitherto, had moved beside him like a mournful shadow. A faint yearning to yield to it stole over him, the thought of an inexpressible joy assailed him, and he told himself that to be loved by a woman with deep, womanly passion must be a wonderful, rapturous thing, something very different from friendship, disturbing, torturing in the midst of its ecstasy.

But these feelings vanished when he left the temple; he smiled at his strange visions and strove to sustain his former scorn of women. As, while absorbed in thought, he had completely lost his way, he ventured to ask it of a barber who stood in front of his shop shaving a portly merchant. The man gracefully moved his razor over the plump cheeks of his customer, who leaned back comfortably in his chair, and without interrupting his important business, gave his advice to the stranger.

"So you want to go to the Tiber district?" fell from the voluble speaker's lips. "Yes! That 's a fine neighborhood. There are a great many Jews, and the houses are said to be very dilapidated; one of them fell in ruins a week ago. But you can live cheaply there if you don't mind stairs. The rooms are unfurnished, or at most have only a few bugs. Will you please turn your head a little toward the right, Crassus?" he said, interrupting himself, " there, that 's just right—so you want to go to the Tiber district, my friend? Yes, wait a minute, I can describe it to you best in this way—Narcissus, the salve, the depilatory salve! The African dog doesn't hear again." These words were addressed to an Ethiopian who was brushing the hair of a curly-headed boy at the back of the shop. The officious barber had just seen his daily customer, the young dandy, Mummius, coming down the next street. The fop, who always had to be served at once, approached, redolent of perfume, with his locks artificially curled, and called for pumice-stone and depilatory salve to keep his arms smooth.

"How are you, my lord?" said the barber, respectfully; "you look as fresh as a young plum, though a trifle pale—aha! Is my guess right—you were at Consul Piso's banquet yesterday evening?"

"What do you know about it?" murmured the dandy, contemptuously, but the barber did not allow himself to be disconcerted.

"Some entirely new salves have just come from Babylon," he said. "May I show them to you? Oh, their perfume, their perfume! Nectar is dung by comparison."

The fine gentleman received the barber's humble attentions with dull indifference, meanwhile staring steadily at the artist to disturb his composure, in which he succeeded. At last he sat down and gazed at Metellus with a look which said plainly: What is that dolt doing here? The sculptor, irritated by the expression, now determined not to go at once, and answered the haughty gaze with one still more disdainful until the coxcomb averted his eyes.

"Haven't you any news of what is going on in the city, Junius?" asked the dandy.

"Nothing that I can think of just now," said the barber, thoughtfully, rubbing the fat merchant's head with both hands.

"What insolence not to have any news when I come," cried Mummius, in genuine wrath. "I'll give you two stories with which you can entertain your customers, you stupid man."

"Oh, pray tell us quickly," said the barber.

"First order your slave to cut his nails," replied the young aristocrat; "he scratches my skin in rubbing me. Take the brush, rascal, and dab my chin. Gently, gently, do you hear? But what does this mean, the fellow is using a salve which he knows I detest," he exclaimed in the utmost indignation. The slave pleaded in excuse that he had made a mistake in the box, but nevertheless received a kick. Metellus, who was in the act of going, made a pretence of examining the salve boxes as if he intended to purchase one, by way of an excuse for remaining longer. Then after the right salve had been found, the dandy leaned back in his chair and ordered the slave to rub every hair off his chin and arms between two pumice-stones, during which process he often interrupted his story with an oath or a sigh when, through negligence, his tender skin was pinched.

"Just think what a joke," Mummius began in a listless tone, "the pedagogue Nigrinus was our guest last evening. His office is to rear the Consul's children and to teach them the precepts of the Stoics. He declaimed with dignity and feeling against the increasing luxury in food and drink. We agreed with him in bewailing the drinking and stuffing, but thrust one goblet after another under his gray beard. This 'poison of mankind' as he chose to call wine, proved so irresistible that at last he could utter his maxims of wisdom only with a faltering tongue. One of the girl flute players with whom Pompeius, the tribune of the legion, was flirting, had fallen asleep on the cushions, and I played the trick—I can't help laughing now when I think of it—of tying the worthy tutor's long beard to the flute-player's curls. When the teacher of virtue closed his eyes, he sank, without noticing it, on the beauty's breast and, when the latter woke, you ought to have seen with what fury she beat the snoring man when she found that she was fastened to him."

The barber laughed immoderately. "He can train his boys to be worthy Romans," he said, and eagerly lauded the inventive talent of his customer. Metellus marvelled equally at the dandy's jest and the laughing barber.

"Well? And Nigrinus?" asked the latter.

"The blows affected his stomach," replied the coxcomb; "his food and drink were ejected; we ordered the slaves to carry him out of the hall, but he clung shrieking to the flute-player."

"Magnificent! Will you permit me to repeat the story? And now for your second piece of news?" asked the obsequious barber.

"My second piece of news is this," replied the other, yawning. "Nero was beaten last night."

"Nero? The Caesar?" stammered the barber; and the fat merchant turned his head in astonishment, which nearly cost him his life as the blade of the razor was at his throat.

Metellus put down a salve-box he was examining and felt disagreeably affected by the news, he did not know why.

"How did it happen?" asked the hairdresser, now really interested. " Nero? Beaten? Oh, pray tell me about it, my lord."

"You know that Nero likes to wander through the streets of Rome as soon as night closes in?" said the fop in a drowsy tone, which betrayed the wine he had drunk the evening before.

"Of course!" replied the barber. "The divine Caesar is fond of disguising himself and playing his pranks upon the citizens he meets."

"Which are often very rough ones," laughed the dandy. "A short time ago he tossed in a blanket a distinguished poet, who was returning from his patron's banquet; a week ago he had a lover stripped of his clothing and tied to the door of his sweetheart's house; a certain Flaccus, who had disappeared, was found dead in the cloacae"—Here the gentleman interrupted himself, groaning, and violently cuffed the slave, who had accidentally rubbed the salve into his mouth instead of on his upper lip.

"Do you suppose you must feed me?"

puffed and panted the angry man, spitting the salve from his mouth; "fie, how it tastes! like the harpies' mire; water, bring me water, I 'm choking!"

The barber rushed forward, beat the slave about the ears with his towel, and cleansed his customer's mouth, offering at the same time a thousand apologies.

"You moved your head," he stammered; "the dog did not notice it— will you never learn dexterity, you black beast?—oh, pray, my lord, calm yourself—it was the very best of salve, made of oil of roses, myrrh, laurel, nothing but the choicest ingredients. Pray go on, tell us more of the story, don't keep us waiting. You talk so well, my lord, Virgil's verses do not flow more smoothly."

40

The slave stood trembling. Metellus desired nothing more ardently than to hear the continuation of the story of Nero's beating—Was it possible? Had the gods determined to destroy him? Had his hand unintentionally—Was the enigma of the flight of his boon companions explained? Anxious forebodings were beginning to oppress his soul. Meanwhile Mummius's mouth was washed and cleansed.

"Oh, pray go on, my lord," urged the barber, who could no longer restrain his curiosity.

"How is it possible, how can a mortal lay hands on the Caesar— true, the Caesar often deals very roughly with his victims, but is it not an honor to be beaten by the imperial hand, to be spit upon by the imperial mouth? Who would not submit and praise the gods for it?"

"We Romans, it is true, have long been accustomed to regard the insults inflicted upon us by the throne as a favor," said the coxcomb, grinning; "but in the provinces there are still a few simpletons who will not perceive what an inexpressible honor is bestowed upon them when they are belabored by the Caesar's fists and flung into the cloacae."

"True, true, there are many simpletons," sighed the barber, dusting the portly merchant. "So a provincial dared to attack Nero?"

"He is said to have given him a severe blow on the nose," answered Mummius.

"The nose?" asked the barber, "the nose, which lends the face its dignity? Well, if this provincial is caught, his nose will be driven into his insolent face with hammers. Oh, ye gods! To bruise Nero's divine nose!"

Metellus who, had it been possible, would have listened to this conversation with more than his two ears, could no longer, in his anxiety, play a silent part in the barber's shop. Though terror almost paralyzed his tongue, he asked—to obtain certainty—in what disguise Nero had wandered through the streets on this occasion. Every one turned toward the speaker, who had so abruptly broken in upon the conversation without cause, and it did not escape the attention of Metellus that they noticed his agitation and pallor. Turning away, he pretended to watch the throng passing in the street. A pause ensued.

"Stranger," said Mummius at last, scanning him intently, "Nero's favorite disguise is to wear the mask of Apollo."

Another pause followed. Metellus's eyes were fixed in a glassy stare upon the floor; he saw what he had done, the gods had evidently determined to destroy him, he had insulted the Master of the World, struck him, though unintentionally, with his own hand. What should he do now? Fly? Implore Nero to have mercy? The youth's knees began to totter, perspiration oozed from every pore, he leaned against the wall, it seemed as if the room must fall in upon him. At last he succeeded in conquering his excitement.

"Ah, h'm!" he said carelessly, approaching the door, "I am indebted to you."

Flushing deeply, he noticed that the dandy whispered something to the barber, to which the other answered in a low tone: "That would surely be doing the Caesar a service." Then, as he reeled out of the shop with the hurry of desperation, he fancied that some one behind him was calling for a lictor.

CHAPTER V

IN Nero's palace, whose entrance was upon the Via Sacra, it was still almost as silent as if night had not passed away, though the sun, for the last four hours, had gilded the Caesar's statue, whose laurel-crowned head towered aloft in the central courtyard. No sounds from the streets desecrated these halls and corridors; the courtiers who were waiting in the ante-rooms scarcely dared to whisper, the slaves who were preparing the early meal glided timidly over the inlaid marble floors; the palace guards who, with spears resting on their bare arms, paced gravely to and fro before the tapestried doorways, were on the watch to prevent any loud word from disturbing the Emperor's divine sleep.

Every stone, every pillar, every ornament expressed power and splendor; the urns on the walls of the ante-rooms, the benches in the corners of the dining-halls, the portraits, the statues in the dusk of the tablinum, seemed to refer to the man who was still sleeping behind the magnificent Babylonian hangings of his chamber; the jet of water pouring from the cornucopia of the Neptune in the atrium talked only of him in whose hand the universe rested as a toy; the dancing fauns on the walls, the nymphs on the floor, the masks on the ceilings, appeared to speak solely of him, the creator of this magnificence. The blue morning sky scarcely dared to look down through the open roof to mirror itself in the rain-basin of the peristyle and lend the marble its glittering smoothness. The gods were not more honored, more dreaded, than he who still lay asleep on the purple cushions of his lion-footed couch. Those who wished to pay the Caesar a morning call had already gathered in the atrium, whose walls and ceiling glowed with frescoes and glittered with gilding. A slave, carrying a tablet, went from one to another to take down the names, but the Senators and patricians looked as if they had assembled to attend a funeral rather than to pay a morning call.

A soldier—the Jew Rufus—was pacing up and down on guard at the back of the atrium where a curtain separated it from the tablinum. He gazed respectfully at the nobles who were talking together in whispers or glanced watchfully around, concealing their uncomfortable feeling of anxiety. And who among these knights and Senators whose togas were reflected in the polished marble floor, as if they were standing in water; who among these clever flatterers, striving so eagerly to force a smile of devotion; who among these often envied courtiers is sure of the ruler's favor? Who could say that the thunderbolt of displeasure might not threaten him this very day? Is it worth while to have togas rustle over the mosaic floors of the imperial halls, to be permitted to touch the statues in

42

the imperial atrium, and cool the ambitious brow in the silvery spray that blows from the fountain through these apartments, if one dare not say for a single moment: I can think what I please, I am sure of my life! The splendor everywhere visible on walls and ceilings seemed like a mockery to the trembling friends of the greatest of earthly sovereigns. The cold smiles of the statues mocked their peril, their brilliant misery.

Rufus looked up at the square patch of sky which laughed through the ceiling of the room. A dove was hovering in the infinite azure, its white plumage mirrored in the impluvium. Rufus sighed heavily as he saw the flitting dove, the symbol of liberty, above the golden prison; but the splendor had intoxicated him also. He envied the trembling patricians who concealed hearts throbbing with anxiety beneath purple-bordered togas. His soul knelt before the magnificence surrounding him; every stone on which he stood seemed worthy of adoration, and the proud, independent man, though convinced of the transitoriness of all earthly grandeur, scarcely dared to breathe; he would have changed places with the courtiers, though he knew that the executioner's sword already hovered over several of them. The waiting patricians stood in different groups. The bearded Burrus was near the entrance. His friend Seneca approached him, and both were soon engaged in conversation.

"How times have changed," said Burrus, the captain of the guard, to Seneca. "How differently Nero formerly received his friends. I fear that we Romans will yet see the day when we shall tremble before him as we once did before Caligula, and that the lusts and horrors of a Tiberius will again become terrible to the world in my former pupil."

"Who can look into the future? Who can anticipate the blows of a beast's paws?" said the sage, with drooping head. "I never liked the Caesar's affability. I foresaw the sleeping tyrant in his artificial smile. Hitherto, he has known how to wear the mask of gentleness with tolerable skill; the light column of smoke still adorns Vesuvius, but a distant peal of thunder is announcing the approaching eruption."

"He attends the Circus without concealing himself, as he formerly did," Burrus went on under his breath. "He often falls into the most furious fits of passion in his mother's presence, and, in abusing the gentle Octavia, defies her wishes."

"The death of Britannicus is a settled matter in Nero's mind," said Seneca. "He would divorce his wife as quickly as possible, if he were not compelled to fear the populace; and I am afraid that the cloacae could already tell of many a shameful deed performed under cover of the night."

"He darkens his good works," Burrus went on, "and makes himself a laughing-stock with his wretched singing; I would forgive his writing poetry, but to appear in public would disgrace the whole empire, and I know from his own lips that he is thinking seriously of it. If we could only dissuade him. Believe me, I have often watched him when he sat in the Circus watching the gladiators, the dying, and his expression revealed his whole soul. It is the gaze of the young tiger, accustoming himself to blood."

"And only waiting for the opportunity to shed it," whispered Seneca, but interrupted himself and silenced Burrus by a glance, for the slave with the tablet had approached to write the names of several men who were strangers to him.

"Did the Caesar have a refreshing sleep?" asked Seneca, smiling.

"The Emperor is still resting," answered the slave, hurrying on.

"Beware of speaking too loud," warned the philosopher; "there is always one more informer than we expect. For instance, I do not trust the handsome actor yonder, Bathyllus, though he always inquires about my last philosophical essays. See how he watches us!"

Burrus's harsh tones had really attracted the attention of the group standing by the impluvium; their eyes were turned toward the pair.

"Unfortunately," replied Burrus, "matters have reached a point when our opinions of things must be expressed by silence rather than speech. That dissolute actor, and yonder zither-player Terpuus are the Caesar's most intimate friends, and we—you, the philosopher, and I, the commander of his soldiers—are hateful to him."

"Hateful? Probably not quite hateful?" said Seneca, glancing timidly at his friend.

"Yes, hateful," answered Burrus, positively. "Andromachus, the Emperor's leech, gave me a hint yesterday. He said: 'Burrus, you often suffer from throat trouble. Never have it again, my friend; the Caesar ordered me to provide you with "an infallible cure."'"

"That is death," replied Seneca, "the dark bridge to happiness. My Burrus will not tremble to cross it. For my part, I value this last refuge as the best gift of the gods to mankind; if we lacked it, life would be the most cruel torture. But what did Nero say of me?"

"Do you wish to know?"

"I entreat you to tell me."

"I do not like to say unpleasant things. Ask Andromachus."

"What could alarm the sage?" replied Seneca, with a dignity which concealed his anxious curiosity. "I entreat you to speak!"

Burrus reflected; then, to deceive the listeners, muttered as if mentioning some indifferent subject,— "Seneca ought not to display his wealth publicly," Andromachus said. "The Caesar's strong-box is sometimes low, and—it might be worth while to become Seneca's weeping heir!"

The philosopher trembled.

"I will offer him my treasures," he stammered, almost losing his footing on the smooth floor; "oh, ye gods! If he has my gold, he will not desire my blood."

Burrus could not help smiling at the sage's sudden loss of calmness, and turned to Tigellinus, who had just entered, letting the curtain fall behind him, and was surveying the assembly. Burrus greeted him; Tigellinus returned the compliment, and, looking at Seneca, remarked,—

"Why is his brow so wrinkled by thought? Is he composing a new tragedy in the Caesar's ante-chamber?"

"Yes," replied Burrus, "a tragedy in which he will play the hero.— Is there anything new at court?"

44

Tigellinus remained silent.

"He has ordered Locusta, the poisoner, to come to the palace," he whispered at last in Burrus's ear; "some dark deed is to be done."

"Who is to suffer?"

"That is unknown."

"To you? What could be unknown to you r

"We may hear and see, but have no tongues. The clever man would guess."

After these words Tigellinus looked Burrus steadily in the eyes.

"Britannicus!" murmured the other, scarcely above his breath.

Tigellinus contracted his eyebrows, smiled strangely, and passed on to the group standing near the impluvium.

"Caesar has not yet left his couch," he said, accosting the zither-player; "perhaps Terpuus can tell us the reason that the divine Nero is so late in granting us the happiness of his presence."

Terpuus, Nero's favorite of the hour, twisted his gold ring around his finger to allow the bystanders properly to value the Emperor's gift, and then answered superciliously: "Terpuus knows Caesar's reasons, but he does not tell them."

The other members of the group looked at Terpuus with timid reverence.

"My friend Terpuus," said Tigellinus, coldly, "I wish you understood how to speak the truth as well as you can play the zither; but, by Zeus! I have never yet heard a false note and never a true word come from your lips."

"Tigellinus—" Terpuus began furiously.

"Hush!" said the former, "you are the favorite, you are permitted to sing to the Caesar while he is at table, to teach him to play the zither, and yet—what a disgrace, you chosen one, you favorite—and yet the reason that Nero takes a longer night's rest than usual is unknown to you."

Well," replied Terpuus, contemptuously, "let us hear what you know."

My friend," observed the Prefect of the Praetorians with courteous contempt, "if Nero complains of headache to-day and has a bruise on his forehead, say that this is the reason he still conceals himself among his pillows."

"Nero—a bruise on his forehead?" passed around the circle; and soon the tidings that the Lord of the Earth had been struck by an impious hand were eagerly whispered through the ante-chamber. Actors, zither-players. Senators, Aediles, knights, and praetors discussed, with faces of the deepest sorrow, the terrible event of the profanation of the crowned brow; but Tigellinus whispered to honest Burrus: "Just look at these cringing hounds! Yet there isn't one of them who really regrets that the Caesar has received this blow."

Soon after the beautiful youth, Britannicus, appeared in the ante-room. He was followed by the Caesar's court-fool, Vatinius, who tried to attract the attention of the company by going through all sorts of comical pantomimes imitating beheading, drowning, etc., as he walked behind him. Conversation ceased. The dwarf jester glided from one to another, laughing as he whispered: "The bull is garlanded for the sacrifice; strike, O priest; do you see the sword of Damocles hanging from the ceiling?"

Britannicus tried to speak to the singer Menecrates, but the latter retired as soon as decency would permit; the same thing happened with all the others whom he approached. All shunned him or looked another way. Only valiant Burrus, when he noticed the embarrassment of the courtiers, approached the downcast Britannicus, who had retreated into a lonely corner, and fearlessly commenced a conversation with him to which the others listened curiously. In the course of this talk, Burrus ventured to utter a warning, but the youth shook his head gloomily and replied: "Fly? Whither? Where would not my step- brother's hand reach me? The world belongs to him. His grasp stretches from pole to pole."

"Then you intend to wait quietly until the lightning strikes you?" asked Burrus.

"We will not think of the future," replied Britannicus, pressing the old warrior's hand; "Orcus will beckon to us some day, what matters it whether soon or late?"

The curtain was drawn back and Petronius appeared, walking haughtily through the ranks of the waiting throng, without vouchsafing the slightest greeting, as if he were alone in the apartment. All eyes turned toward the director of festivals, the Caesar's indispensable counsellor, the only man who could say that he possessed some degree of influence over his master's caprices,—an influence which he owed to his active imagination, tireless in devising new amusements, unexpected scenes, and the indifference and harshness with which he removed everything that could vex or disturb his master. The courtiers watched him enviously, but bowed timidly before him. He approached Rufus, who was pacing to and fro on guard, and when the latter informed him that no one was permitted to enter the inner rooms, Petronius showed him a wax tablet, whereupon Rufus instantly retired from the entrance.

Careless of the courtiers' astonishment, Petronius hurried through the glimmering marble halls to his master's sleeping-room. Here, too, he had to show the wax tablet to the Praetorian sentinel; then he asked for the valet, was announced to the Caesar, and, soon after, the slave lifted the gold- embroidered curtain to admit the waiting noble into the splendid chamber whose walls, with their brilliant bas reliefs, glittered like the moist interior of a polished shell. Statues of Venus and of Eros surrounded the ruler's couch, deep purple curtains fell in rich folds around the swelling pillows, a lion's skin lay on the mosaic floor whose gay figures were reflected in the smooth walls, while the springing columns of a candelabra scarcely seemed to touch the costly floor with their vulture claws.

The Emperor's bed was empty; the pillows lay scattered on the floor; just as Petronius entered Poppaea Sabina, with a startled cry, disappeared behind the curtain of the adjoining room. A few seconds later the Caesar came out of his bath-room at the left of the chamber.

Bowing profoundly, the courtier asked if the gods had blessed his master's sleep. Nero, wrapped in a purple woollen coverlet, was half supported, half carried to a chair by two slaves, who dried his arms and feet, still fragrant from the perfumed bath. The slaves, with practised skill, rubbed the monarch's limbs, while a handsome boy of fifteen held a silver salver, containing his breakfast. Beside the chair lay a lyre, on the round table with goat-feet were scattered rolls of manuscript; and the Caesar, after greeting Petronius, pointed to the written sheets saying: "My new epic, 'The Fall of Troy.'"

Petronius took one of the rolls with as much respect as if it had been found in the sacred archives of an Egyptian temple, and read aloud,—

"'When the Tigris enters the Persian domain it vanishes deep in a yawning chasm.'"*

[* Literal quotation.]

"Admirable!" he said, replacing the roll and casting a worshipping glance at Nero. "Oh, my Lord, you possess a power of language, a mastery of rhythmical form, worthy of the study of all coming generations."

Then he expatiated still more minutely upon the beauty of the poem, until his listener at last interrupted him.

"I think it is very admirable," said Nero, with affected modesty. "The verses came to me. Later, when I must have Hector killed, I intend far to surpass Homer. The Greek could rely on his imagination, it is true, but I will study reality."

"How do you mean to do that. Lord?" asked Petronius, drying Nero's hair and assisting the slaves, who were now rubbing the Emperor's body with costly ointments.

"Very simply," said the Caesar, yawning; "I will bind a slave to a chariot, and have the charioteer—with Hispanian stallions—drive at a gallop four times down the length of the Circus Maximus."

"Oh, then your work cannot lack truth to nature," said the skilful flatterer, assisting the Caesar, who occasionally corrected with the stylus a passage in his manuscript, to put on a flowing morning-robe.

"The mirror!" he commanded; and, when it was held before him, he looked at himself, arranged the folds of his robe, and ordered the laurel wreath, which always lay ready, to be placed upon his curls.

"Can Virgil have looked more like a genius?" he asked, and as the valet, who had just put a silver pin in his mouth, delayed his answer a moment, he cast a glance at the terrified fellow which vividly reminded him of the Sardinian mines.

"Oh, I did not sleep well." sighed the illustrious poet, seizing the goblet on the silver salver. "Art, Petronius, Art wearies my delicate soul. Pardon my speaking so low, my singing-teacher has forbidden me to strain my voice. Slave, where is the oiled leek? Look, Petronius, I am permitted to eat nothing except a little oiled leek this morning, in order to give my voice the necessary softness. Oh, Art, Petronius, I sacrifice myself to Polyhymnia and Melpomene."

"Art, my Lord," replied Petronius, with almost imperceptible irony, "is indeed the cause of your exhausted nervous system; but I know another source of your evident indisposition—it is not only Polyhymnia who destroys your health. An earthly woman, Octavia—"

"I know, I know what you are going to say," whispered the Emperor; "you mean—h'm! Do not spoil this beautiful morning so early for me with that hated name. My friend, give this Assyrian donkey a kick," he interrupted himself, pointing to the slave, "I don't wish to exert myself to-day; the dog has offered me fruit for breakfast, and he knows how much it injures the throat."

Petronius drove out the slaves, and then returned to his lord and began to explain the reason for his early visit. But Nero was not in the mood to listen quietly. He made all sorts of signs to the slave who entered to tell him about Locusta's brewing of poison, and when Petronius asked in surprise whether this notorious poisoner was in the palace, he answered smiling,—

"Certainly, I want to invent a new dish for one of my relatives, toward whom I am very well disposed; you know I understand something about the art of cooking."

Then he inquired about his rival, the singer Datus, and when Petronius said that he had elicited the most rapturous applause from the populace, Nero became extremely uneasy, sharply criticised the artist's execution, shrank when Petronius mentioned the praise of this or that musical connoisseur, declared that the Romans had no ears, asked several times whether the Caesar's voice was not far more beautiful, and when Petronius continued to describe the delight of the Roman people, said: "Datus will try his voice within a week upon the frogs of the Styx."

Petronius had now put the Emperor into the mood he desired; Nero's face was flushed, his deep-set eyes flashed, his base, sensual mouth was compressed. True, in spite of his excitement, he subdued the loud, almost shrieking tone he had just used, and asked to have his singing-master summoned, that the latter might remind him to spare his exquisite voice; but he could not wholly calm his inflamed blood, and shouted angrily to a slave who came to say that Locusta's poison, which had just been given to a ram, did not have the speedy effect expected. "Tell the woman I will flog her with my own hands, if she does not—" here he interrupted himself, pressed his kerchief to his lips, and murmured almost under his breath—"if she does not know how to make the poison strong enough to kill a man in two seconds."

The slave left the room, and Nero wailed that he was growing hoarse, he would certainly be hissed if he sang in the gardens the next morning before the populace. Petronius thought that the right time to explain his plan to Caesar had now come. First, with the Caesar's approval, he dismissed all the slaves; then, looking behind the curtain at the door, he convinced himself that no one was listening, and then in cautious words reminded the sovereign of the street scene of the night before, the pugnacious provincial, and when he perceived that the Emperor was by no means much angered about the bruise on his forehead inflicted by the stranger, but laughingly admired himself as the hero of a comedy of Plautus, Petronius said: "The comedy, august Caesar, will, at your request, receive the addition of another act. Do you remember for what object I summoned Metellus to the palace?"

Nero did remember; the courtier's words, uttered with unusual emphasis, evidently made him more serious, his brow darkened, and casting a timid glance around him, he asked: "Is he already here, this—what is his name?"

"Metellus, you mean! I have sent some slaves with a litter to his lodgings; they will bring him unseen to the palace. I hope he will enter your atrium in half an hour."

"Why does he come so publicly?" asked the Caesar; "would it not have been better to bring him before me secretly?"

"The more openly we conduct the affair, the less suspicious it will appear to the world," replied the other. "The motives of the conspiracy against Octavia's virtue will remain hidden from every eye; but the tool himself must move about the palace as freely as possible."

Nero nodded assent, sighed, rose, and approaching the statue of Venus, seemed wholly absorbed in gazing at it. Petronius did not venture to interrupt him. At last the Emperor turned hastily toward a draped picture which stood on the floor in one corner of the room; a jerk tore the concealing veil from the frame, and a woman's gentle face appeared. The painting, a work of Amulius, represented the Empress Octavia. A diadem adorned the noble brow; the eyes, with their slightly reddened lids, seemed as it were spiritualized by tears, and this expression gave the face a certain severe grandeur, a stern, repellent loveliness. "I have wept, but what do you care for that?" the lips were apparently saying to the spectator.

For a brief time the royal actor, Nero, forgot himself, and dropped his mask. He had scanned the picture with gloomy, timid eyes, half averting his face as if he was afraid to come too near it, as if those melancholy eyes disturbed his soul; an unintelligible power in this portrait spoke to the man, usually so unfeeling, a power which, instead of compelling reverence, inspired hate. Yet he soon regained his usual mood. Influenced, even in this fateful moment, by his diseased imagination, he paced up and down the room as if he wore the cothurni, showing by his gestures that it pleased him to regard the whole serious matter as an interesting tragedy.

"Yes, Petronius," he said in a hollow tone, "I must reach a decision at last. You are right. See, I feel a horror of this face. Can I tell why myself? She has a scar on her ear, which offends my sense of beauty; her nose is too stern, almost unfeminine in its contour; the countenance looks lifeless, like something that belongs to the nether world, but that is not the reason it is hateful to me. When Claudius gave me his daughter, I congratulated myself until my yes rested on Otho's wife. From that time I felt a loathing of Octavia's everlasting virtue and childish diffidence, and I realized that only what shortsighted fools call vice can possess permanent charm. Oh, and how sweet is my amber-haired smiling sin, my Poppaea!"

49

He hastened to his writing-table, hastily scrawled the word "amber-haired" on the papyrus, and said, "An apt expression, it can be utilized." Then, counting on his fingers, he hummed the Alcaean rhythm, and at last approached Petronius with the gesture of a poet who is deliberating.

"I have considered your plan of releasing me from this woman," he went on in a theatrical tone, "and must pay it the tribute of my approval. It is the only way in which I can rid myself of Octavia without arousing the wrath of the Senate or the populace."

"Yes, my august Master," Petronius assented, "the stratagem of war which I have proposed will cast all the guilt upon Octavia's head and present your divorce to the people as a necessary step, commanded by the gods; nay, it will even invest your dignity with the lustre of justice."

"But in what way is your tool, Metellus, to be made useful to us?" asked the Caesar.

"Very simply," replied the courtier. "First, we must receive him among your attendants. As the youth is a stranger in Rome, no one knows him, and that he, too, knows no one, will greatly aid our designs. No man is better adapted to tract the notice of the Empress than this gay, childlike artist nature; no one can be more easily deceived or more readily expose himself to suspicion than this inexperienced, awkward youth, who regards the world as a young priest of Isis gazes at the mysterious heavenly lights which he understands as little as the teacher who pretends to know them. If Metellus feels no anxiety concerning the future, if we can make the palace a comfortable home to him, an opportunity of bringing him into Octavia's society will soon present itself. For instance, you can apparently become reconciled to Octavia,—a task worthy of your histrionic talent," added the shrewd courtier, interrupting himself, as Nero shrugged his shoulders. "I say you can feign a reconciliation, speak to her more kindly, act the lover, and we others, meanwhile, will admire your artistic gift of dissimulation. You will order from this Metellus a bust of Octavia, for you love her so ardently that you desire to perpetuate her face. He will begin the work; I think from that time it ought to be easy for us to accuse the pair, as soon as they are left alone a moment by the slaves, of mutual love, no matter whether the charge is true or false. You know the world always believes in evil more easily than in good."

Petronius had scarcely finished speaking when the door-curtain of the next room rustled. The startled courtier grasped his dagger, but a woman's figure, whose neck and bosom were veiled by fair, loosened tresses, emerged from behind the purple folds, and, before Nero could turn, Poppaea's white arms embraced him.

"Forgive me, my Master," she said smiling, pressing her round cheek against Nero's, "I could not help it, when I fled into yonder room I heard your whole conversation."

The Caesar, pleasantly surprised and glad to break off the grave conversation, which wearied him, bent toward her, whispering: "Well, what does our Helen say to the plan we have been discussing?"

"The wish to express my gratitude for it lured me from my hiding-place," replied Poppaea, feigning an emotion which heightened the charm of her impassioned face; "oh, my Master, how wise you are to rid yourself at last of that pattern of tiresome virtue, Octavia. How much more freely we can enjoy our happiness!"

Feigning shame and devotion, the crafty woman sank down on the couch, covered her neck and shoulders with affected haste, and directed a yearning gaze at Nero. The latter stroked her " amber hair " and, having become her unresisting slave, tried to kiss her lips, which she withdrew from him. Her way of coquetting with her loosened locks was fascinating even to Petronius, though he could not help smiling at the Emperor's love-making.

"No, no, my Master," said Poppaea, struggling, "no, no! I will be chary with my charms now, for I sometimes feel what a sinner you have made me. Think! I deserted my husband for your sake, I won your love from your Octavia, and I tell you, you shall not kiss my lips again until you can call me your lawful wife. Our relation weighs heavily upon me— Octavia—oh, that virtuous Octavia, I fear you still love her better than you do me." She rose to retire. The Caesar, fired by the beauty's dishevelled charms, strove to comfort her, to draw her down into her seat again; he did not care whether Poppaea's modesty was affected or real, nay, the sham diffidence attracted him more strongly than the genuine, and he sat down beside her, protesting, with faltering lips, over and over again that Poppaea should take the place of his present wife, as soon as the latter could be put out of the way. Poppaea did not disdain to take refuge in tears, that she might still more inflame her lover's passion, meanwhile talking perpetually, about Octavia's virtue, bewailing her own sins, calling herself a base wretch, lamenting her husband, who had been sent to the provinces, longing to return to the lonely man, and thus putting Nero into the mood of theatrically aesthetic compassion, which is more akin to pleasure than to pain, and rather stimulates passion than soothes it.

Petronius reminded Nero of the visitors waiting in the atrium, but the Emperor asked: "Why do these people have legs except to stand in the atrium?" then clasped Poppaea in his arms in the most blissful mood. When she at last threw herself at his feet and implored him to cast her off, restore her to virtue, and reconcile her to her poor husband, the farce produced such an impression upon the royal comedian that tears flowed from his eyes and, fairly enraptured, he exclaimed: "What a tender artist-nature I possess! see this noble Sabina, Petronius! Alas! Octavia's fall moves me to tears, I will commemorate it in an ode."

Although he now sent for the zither to improvise a tragic melody, he issued several orders in a low tone to a slave who came in at the same moment to inform him that Locusta's poison had now gained sufficient strength: "At supper," they heard him whisper, and, after the slave had retired, he said smiling,—

"If any little accident should befall my dear brother Britannicus at supper this evening, have the kindness not to notice it."

While he was drawing melancholy notes from his instrument, Poppaea secretly questioned Petronius about Metellus.

"What is his figure?" she asked.

"Rather small than large," replied Petronius, under his breath.

"Handsome?"

"Delicate, fair, an Adonis who seems created to make women's faith waver."

Poppaea glanced up tenderly at the courtier.

"They say that Octavia is very virtuous," she murmured, "men's beauty will not win her."

"That is not necessary here," whispered Petronius; "if we can even cast a shadow of suspicion on him, our game is won."

"Poor boy," said Poppaea, with sincere compassion. "I am sorry that he must be sacrificed and abused for this Octavia. But you will not kill him?"

"The toy might easily chance to break in the giant's hand," replied Petronius; "but if it is possible to save him, your wish, oh, mistress, shall be fulfilled."

"Oh, yes! Save him, beauty has a right to live. Besides he is so wholly innocent in the whole matter, isn't he? Oh, I must see him, speak to him."

"The fair Poppaea is already conjuring up an imaginary Metellus, I see," murmured Petronius, smiling; "O Cupid, I see thy shaft."

"Do not blame me," she answered, "but stay, Nero is laying the zither aside and writing. Only one thing,—we must manage to surprise the pair, Octavia and Metellus, in a situation which will at least give us the semblance of right. This I demand—to justify my relations with Nero in the eyes of the people."

"I shall not lack spies," replied the director of festivals.

When Poppaea left the room to arrange her toilet for the morning, the Caesar ordered the folds of his robe to be draped, and announced that he would receive the visitors waiting in the atrium. Among then), during the last hour, was the sculptor Metellus. The young man felt extremely uncomfortable in this company of aristocrats, some of whom took no notice of him at all, while others cast contemptuous glances at him, and drew back in embarrassment near the entrance.

When, unable to think what he should do or where he should go, he rushed in the greatest bewilderment from the barber's shop, a. grinning Ethiopian met him at the door of hi lodgings, pointed to a litter which stood waiting, and, in very courteous terms, invited him to enter it. The terrified youth summoned up his courage and, drawing a long breath, asked what was wanted with him. The slave dispelled his fears by assuring him that they wished to employ his talent at court; and, as Metellus desired to bring his destiny to some end, even though an unfortunate one, he took his place in the litter, forcing himself to banish the future from his mind.

He was thus conveyed to the palace and conducted to a room where new, clean, nay handsome garments lay ready for him. When he had taken a warm bath and refreshed himself with the food set before him, his natural cheerfulness returned, and he asked himself: "Metellus, what is to befall you? What will the next hours bring?" The slave had assigned this room as a lodging; he was to remain here until the work (doubtless a statue) for which he was wanted, was completed. The apartment faced the gardens; the tops of the pine trees reached to the marble balcony; far and wide rose-bushes and trees most tastefully mingled with the dazzlingly white forms of marble statues.

The slave placed several dishes on the marble table, and Metellus, unaccustomed to play the master, spoke pleasantly to the old Syrian, greatly embarrassing the man, who had never heard such kind words. While conducting the youth across the courtyard, the old fellow had sometimes attempted to patronize him, meanwhile informing his smiling colleagues by all sorts of gestures that he had a perfect novice in charge. Now, when "Beryll" was alone with the youth and became more and more convinced that Nero's new favorite had not learned to command, he penitently changed his conduct and became confidence personified. He officiously closed the large green curtain which covered the pillars of the broad window, and volubly gave all the information desired.

"We had a hint given us," he said among other things, "that we were to serve you with great readiness. You are certainly on the brink of making your fortune; but beware—the thresholds of these rooms are slippery, and many a man has fallen who supposed he was standing firmly. But I'll say no more, for here the air has ears."

At last, after numerous questions, bows, and signs of humility he left the chamber.

"The thresholds of these rooms are slippery," murmured Metellus, drawing the green veil back from the window and letting the sun gild the ornaments on the walls again. The words had made him grave; a feeling as if he were in a magnificent prison stole over him when he thought that the vast palace with its troops of servants surrounded him. The consciousness of being served was oppressive to his unspoiled nature; he had been constantly tempted to take the platter or the cup from the slave's hands. When he looked around his room everything bewildered him. The gilded pillars seemed to cry out, "You do not belong here;" the splendid couch, with feet like gilded vulture's talons, had so stately an air that one might fancy it would be deeply insulted if anybody tried to lie down on its pillows.

Metellus's eyes grew sorrowful; his features expressed the melancholy peculiar to youth, and which is not free from a tinge of poetic affectation. In reality he did not know why he should be sad, but he endeavored to feel depressed, and he succeeded. Was the blue sky with its whispering tree-tops an object which invited sorrow? Did the song of the birds in the shrubbery outside sound mournful? Did not the distant roofs of Rome, above which rose green leafage and the dazzlingly white pediments of temples, present a thoroughly cheerful spectacle? And yonder lake which, surrounded by statues, lay glittering like silver in the sunshine—could one really think of nothing while gazing at it, except the death to be found in its waves?

Metellus had reason to be very well satisfied with his situation; Fortuna had favored him marvellously; it would have been the right time to thank Fate, to cherish hope. Perhaps it was the very excess of comfort that led him to place himself, with a feeling of defiance, in the position of an unfortunate man. Hark! How mournfully a turtle-dove cooed yonder, how sadly the pines rustled.

Yet his mood did not prevent him from scanning himself carefully in the round mirror which, upheld by a metal faun, stood on the dressing-table. Nay, it must be confessed that he rejoiced like a child, or rather like a Greek girl, in the Egyptian linen which draped his limbs, and passed his hand again and again through his locks, perfumed with fragrant salves, amid which rested a gold-embroidered fillet. He himself noticed, blushing, as he often glanced into the mirror, how the outlines and coloring of his face had been improved by the manner of arranging his hair; how the symmetry of his limbs was enhanced by the delicate folds of the toga; and yet, though his artistic sense of beauty was gratified, he seemed to himself so contemptible in this finery that he would gladly have left the palace at once. But the prospect of being spared all anxiety about earning a support, and especially of being able to pursue his profession undisturbed, and also a slight touch of youthful love of adventure, induced him to wait. He was still engaged in finishing his toilet, to which he usually paid little heed, when old Beryllus entered, and loudly praised his master's beauty. Metellus angrily stopped him.

"Silence, old man," he cried; "this finery tortures me. I should like— to tear these garments from my body."

He actually seized the fillet, but the terrified slave grasped his hand.

"Nero will receive you in half an hour among the morning visitors in the atrium," he said. "Be careful to make a good impression."

So, in half an hour he was to stand before the Lord of the Universe ! Before the man whom he had insulted! Then it was indeed necessary to appear as well as possible. Like all young people, the sculptor considered his manners flawless, and in his own mind believed that he need not fear a meeting with the gods; yet he was very glad that he had still half an hour in which to prepare himself for the Emperor's possible questions. It was his custom to help himself through unpleasant moments either by reading Virgil, or by playing on his flute. When he looked in his travelling pouch for the roll of Virgil he could not find it; he must have lost it in his flight from the barber's shop; so he seized his flute. Believing that his heart would throb less anxiously in the open air, he left the room to seek a shady nook in the park.

It was now almost noon. The dark green foliage of the cypress-trees towered noiselessly into the deep azure of the sky. All the leaves were shining with sunlight; it seemed as if the sun had hung golden balls on all the branches, flowers, grass-blades; even the birds were silent, only the cicada uttered its drowsy song in the bushes. The youth covered his dazzled eyes with his hands; the unusual dress burdened him; the sultry stillness brooding over the motionless tree-tops and well-kept paths inspired a mood of solemn melancholy. Before him glittered a pool, in whose waters several statues were reflected. He could scarcely look into the sparkling ripples, and his eyes ached when he fixed them upon the white images of the gods, which stood there in their peculiar loveliness.

He sat down dreamily on the high stone curb of the pond, just opposite to a Venus who was holding the apple toward a more distant Mars, raised his flute to his lips, and began to lure from it an inarticulate melody. Fear of the audience so close at hand passed away, the stupor of slumber stole over him. From yonder dark grove, he thought, a faun must soon leap forth, gaze timidly around, and dart toward the nymph who was lying asleep in the grass. While these fancies flitted through his wearied brain and dispelled the anxieties of the actual world, he lured melting notes from his flute, moved his fingers daintily, and, in this attitude, with bowed head, presented an extremely charming, idyllic picture. His eyes grew more and more weary in their expression; he sank slowly down from the stone upon the grass, and soon fell asleep with his cheek resting on his arm.

As he lay thus, with a childlike smile on his red, half parted lips, he resembled an Endymion; the flute was pressed to his breast; the clear, still noon-day shone around him.

Suddenly he started from his slumber—the creaking of the gravel had roused him—and looked around him with dull eyes; the silent gods still stood in their places, the glittering sunlight still flashed upon the water, yet he had dreamed that it was night, the dark night of Orcus, and, in the half slumber which preceded his waking, it had seemed as if a head had peered forth from behind the cypress wall, a face that was not wholly unfamiliar to him. But the cypresses towered aloft as before, nothing moved. He half raised himself, turned his face, and now saw that he was not mistaken; a woman stepped from among the trees into the open space and, smiling pleasantly, said:

"I heard your flute-playing, boy, and disturbed your sleep. I hope you are not angry with me?"

She flushed slightly, as Metellus, striving to find words, gazed into her grave, noble face. At last, lowering his eyes and blushing still more deeply than she, he said softly,—

"I know you, I saw you kneeling in the temple of Zeus."

Now he ventured to glance up at her, and thinking he perceived that her thoughts were no longer with him, but dwelling upon a sorrowful past, he dared not interrupt her silent reverie; but his eyes rested rapturously on the

slender, girlish figure, admiring the grace with which her white arm supported her mantle. Again, as in the temple, a weight burdened his breast when he imagined how those arms could embrace, what it must be to rest upon the bosom over which the folds of the robe swept so mysteriously.

"Do not look so sad," escaped his lips; "the gods know how to aid."

To conceal his embarrassment, he now sprang from the ground, and as she made no reply, went on in a tone of forced gayety: "You must be the Empress's favorite slave—are you not? For no one is so beautiful as you—"

55

and suddenly, as if carried away by a passion incomprehensible to himself, he advanced nearer to the beautiful dreamer, tried to clasp her white arm with his fingers, and tenderly stroked her cheek.

"Fair slave," he had barely time to stammer, when a wrathful look from the woman whose reverie he had interrupted flashed upon him.

"Profligate!" fell in almost inaudible tones from her blanched lips, " you will be told who I am;" and clenching her hand as if for a blow, she stood before the deeply alarmed youth. Her lips moved as if she were about to speak; then she turned and went toward the palace, from which her attendants came to meet her. Metellus watched her walk through the shrubbery, as if in a dream; he thought that she was covering her face with her hands as though to conceal tears. He looked after her like a criminal condemned to death, and almost on the verge of weeping, threw himself on the ground, propping his head on his hands. A stupor seemed to leave him, the tension of his nerves lessened, and the shameful consciousness of having completely forgotten himself robbed him for the moment of all self-control. He fancied he still felt her arm, so soft, so warm, yielding to the pressure of his fingers, still heard her voice, saw her flashing eyes; he was absorbed in the consciousness of her presence, he saw her narrow brow, the swelling curves of her bosom, and this consciousness blended in painful contrast with the feeling of shame. At last, when his thoughts began to grow calmer, he resolved to shun this woman who had dared to call him a profligate. But who was she? A slave in the palace? Was he to allow himself to be insulted by a slave? What did he care about her? Let her call him what she pleased, what did it matter? When she clenched her fist, he ought to have laughed at her and boldly embraced her. But he had little time to give vent to his defiance; Beryllus came running toward him to summon him to the audience.

"What is the name of the slave-girl who just came out of the palace ?" asked Metellus.

"Slave-girl? What slave-girl?" replied the old man, drawing the half-resisting youth onward. "Make haste, the Emperor is just entering the atrium."

So the artist was forced to thrust aside every thought of the beauty, and his eager way of pursuing every new impulse rendered this tolerably easy.

Soon after he stood blushing on the threshold of the atrium, where, with mathematical eagerness, he counted the stones of the mosaic floor and felt that anxious heart-throb of expectation which permits us to take no accurate survey of our situation. One courtier who addressed him received a rude answer by no means appropriate to the circumstances; another who attempted to banter him met one of the haughty glances which spring from embarrassment, and are so becoming to a handsome young face.

At last, surrounded by lictors, the Caesar appeared. A laurel wreath, skilfully arranged upon his hair, concealed the scratch on his brow from every eye; and our hero, who had dealt the blow, recognized the "Apollo" of his nocturnal adventure only by his broad chin and deep-set eyes. Metellus was probably the only one among the courtiers, who hastily formed a semi-circle, that gazed fearlessly into the cruel, shifting eyes of the sovereign. The Caesar moved slowly through the ranks of his servants. Every shade of trifling and levity had vanished from his bearing; gloomy, iron seriousness rested upon his swollen brow, and his eyes looked dull, yet in their depths glowed a light which seemed to gloat over the fear of his subjects. Doubtless many a pale- faced man thought that it would be more endurable to be locked into a cage with a tiger than to remain in the despot's presence.

A chair was placed in the centre of the apartment, into which the tyrant, with a sullen face, was about to sink, while the others stood in a wide circle around him. He flung the cushion at his body-slave's head, and called for a softer one. At last he took his seat, at last the cushions were arranged to his satisfaction. How often in such an hour the words exile, dungeon, death, had fallen from the Emperor's lips as carelessly as chaff drops from a torn sack.

In a low, feeble voice Nero now asked various questions, but carefully avoided any discussion of government affairs. He inquired about his mother's health, and, in the same tone, asked whether the new lions had come from Libya. The smiling Seneca, who sought to soothe him concerning Agrippina's health, received an answer which plainly showed that he would prefer less reassuring news in future. The Prefect of the Praetorians was ordered to arrest a certain art critic who, two days before, had fallen asleep at a banquet while the Emperor was reciting one of his poems. All present heard the command with a shudder. He was especially gracious to Britannicus, assuring him repeatedly of his favor, so that he would almost have deceived him concerning his intentions, had he not known, like all who were acquainted with Nero's disposition, that such exaggerated friendliness must be interpreted as signs of his approaching destruction.

As the courtiers, silent and trembling, stood around his chair, watching the dreaded tyrant's every look, Burrus who, as his former teacher, could venture more than the others, uttered a few words in behalf of Octavia, who, he said, was grieving her life away in her own apartments. The Emperor made a hasty gesture of refusal which disarranged the folds of his mantle. As Tigellinus bent down to smooth them Metellus, who stood near, could not refrain from assisting him. Advancing in his shy, childlike manner to the Caesar's chair, he changed the draping according to his artistic taste, scarcely noticing the murmur of astonishment and terror which ran through the ranks of the courtiers, or the many lips that curled in contemptuous smiles. Nero, however, in whose ear Petronius had whispered a few words, accepted the service of the youth, so inexperienced in court etiquette, very graciously. Smiling at the embarrassed sculptor, he said to Tigellinus: "My friend, this artist knows how to make me resemble an august statue better than you do." Then he turned to the assembly.

"Burrus," he said, "I should be glad to be reconciled to Octavia.

Stern Burrus, let me tell you that your Emperor also desires this agreement, and has already taken the first step toward it. This young artist was recommended to me by Petronius, I wish him to carve Octavia's statue."

Nero dismissed the company earlier than usual on the pretext that important government business awaited settlement; but in reality he was expecting some Grecian envoys, whom he had invited to a banquet, and who wished to present to him the crown of victory of the zither-players of Greece. Scarcely had the monarch left the atrium when the courtiers surrounded the favored artist from all sides, congratulated him, and assured him of their changeless friendship. How he had managed to win Nero's heart so quickly no one could tell, but they did not ponder over the matter long. They called him Favorite; predicted a fortunate future, and even those who, at his entrance into the atrium, had turned haughtily away now bowed low, protesting that as soon as they saw him, they perceived marked evidences of genius on his brow and in his bearing.

Metellus received these compliments with a radiant face, stammering confused disclaimers; and when a wealthy Senator, with exaggerated complaisance, placed his entire fortune at his disposal, he was modest enough to request only a few thousand denarii. The portly Senator, secretly so enraged by the misunderstanding that, fearing a stroke of apoplexy, he ordered his slaves to bring him cold water, nevertheless smiled graciously, and ordered a bondman to pay the desired sum as soon as possible. Metellus took it so much as a matter of course that he did not even consider it necessary to thank the rich miser.

When he reached his own room, his first act was to jump for joy. How rosily the future smiled upon him, how beautiful was the world, how kind were the people in it! And where was Nero's wickedness, of which he had seen nothing, yet which people could not paint in sufficient enormity? Had not this slandered man given him shelter, work, bread, nay life itself, though he had offended him?

Yet in the midst of this rapture of joy, a grief, hitherto unknown, suddenly assailed him,—a grief which it would probably require a lifetime to banish, but recurred like an intermittent fever; a grief which had a certain resemblance to joy and increased whenever his eyes rested on the dancing nymphs who smiled upon him from the walls. Perhaps his condition of joyful excitement contributed in filling his imagination with the yearning that so easily deepens at the sight of female forms. The very word "woman" or "girl" awakened strange emotions, and he could not imagine that there was ever a time when he had scorned the whole sex and preferred his friend's society to any other. Yes, a woman's smile was very different from a friend's, woman's timidity inspired more devotion than his friend's harsh, laconic frankness, an indescribable mystery surrounded her soft, pliant figure. As yet these emotions did not centre upon any special woman, but hovered around the whole sex, and weighed like a burden upon his soul.

But this mood, too, gradually passed away, and when the slave entered to conduct him to the Empress, his cheerfulness again burst victoriously through the misty confusion of his thoughts. Smiling as if intoxicated, he followed old Beryllus through the halls and corridors of the palace, and did not wake to real life until the latter, drawing back the curtain hanging before a door, said: "Enter, you are already announced."

Metellus heard from behind the curtain the plashing of the fountain that was pouring its jet into the basin. A light spray fell upon him as he entered the cool, dim twilight. He stood with downcast eyes in the dusky apartment, feeling, without seeing, that he was in the presence of a woman, the rustling of whose garments reached his ear. A woman! This was the consciousness that made his face flush as if he had profaned a sanctuary, and forced him to lower his eyes. Not until a man's voice said: "This is the young artist, my august Mistress, whom your husband commissioned to carve your bust "—did he venture to raise them.

But if Charon or the three-headed dog of the nether world had appeared, his face could not have blanched to a deeper pallor nor his breathing become more labored than now when, raising his eyes, he recognized in Octavia the Empress, the slave-girl whose charms he had been unable to resist in the park. How could he have taken this woman for* a slave! Where were his eyes! Did not every feature express dignity and majesty, while her large eyes diffused a melancholy radiance over the whole face?

He stood as if he expected every moment to be driven from the palace; his ears were strained to catch the first word from the beautiful woman's lips, but it was long before they uttered a sound. The Empress seemed perplexed; she had glanced at him with a look of mingled indignation and fear, and, to conceal her embarrassment, whispered a few orders to her maid. Then she seemed striving to summon up her anger. Her lips sought for a stern rebuke, and a line formed in the brow; but the frown vanished and the harsh words were not spoken. Again several uncomfortable moments passed. At last she summoned courage to ask: "What is your name?" endeavoring to display in her manner a majestic coldness, in which she succeeded so ill that the consciousness embarrassed her, and, angered with herself, she tried to conquer it by repeating more harshly: "What is your name?"

Metellus heard nothing except the falling of the fountain. Even the Empress's question had to be twice repeated to him, and he had scarcely attempted to pronounce his name when unconsciously the low exclamation: " Pardon!" escaped his lips, while at the same moment he sank slowly, reluctantly to his knees, as if the sense of his guilt bore him down. Petronius, for it was he who, standing beside Octavia's chair, had presented the artist, fixed his keen eyes upon those of the Empress, who, touched by the youth's sudden, humble kneeling, was struggling for composure. The beauty, the childlike submissiveness of his drooping figure, touched her strangely; for several minutes she gazed at him as if lost in thought, and only released herself from the spell by a violent effort.

"Rise, Metellus," she said, in a tone wavering between command and compassion.

59

"Noble lady," Petronius began, "this is really a strange, surprising scene—"

But the Empress, hastily summoning all her strength of will, interrupted his astonished questions with an almost stern voice that forbade any interference.

"I had left my attendants in the palace," she said very gravely, "to read my Virgil in the grotto of Neptune undisturbed. A stone struck me, and when I looked around, this youth was hurrying from behind the shrubbery, very much startled to find that, instead of the sparrow which he had intended to drive away, he had hit a woman. This is the story of our acquaintance, Petronius."

Metellus rose, and his grateful glance expressed so much to the inventor of this fable that she was compelled to assume a still sterner expression. Petronius coughed and smiled behind his hand; whether he believed the story or not could not be decided.

"I do not venture to oppose my husband," said Octavia, "or I should most firmly request that he would not have me modelled. I have never taken pleasure in works of plastic art, and have no desire to see myself as a statue."

Metellus shrank as he heard these cold words, he did not perceive what this composure concealed. Nor did he see the smile with which Petronius answered that he did not believe the Emperor would give up having his wife's bust made.

"Well then, be it so," replied Octavia; "my husband knows that I am his slave in all things."

She rose with dignified calmness, saying that the artist might commence his work the next day, dismissed both men with a gracious wave of the hand and as she turned away, again cast at Metellus, who was passing through the doorway, one of those half wondering, half haughty glances which the youth knew not how to interpret, though they absorbed his imagination. As soon as Petronius and his companion had left the room, the young Empress threw herself wearily upon the couch by the basin of the fountain which, shaded by all sorts of leaf-plants and palms, and surrounded by a delicate glittering spray, afforded a pleasant refuge during the noontide heat.

The fountain seemed to be talking to itself; the same refrain issued from the jaws of the marble lion. "Hypocrisy, hypocrisy, hypocrisy!" This was the word that murmured and rustled through the dreamy magnificence of this apartment, at whose rear the leafage of the park glowed in the most brilliant sunshine between the pillars of the royal chamber; but here a cool twilight prevailed, through which the gilding on the walls and ceilings cast faint reflections.

An old slave-woman was busied in cleaning the plants and dusting with a peacock's tail the statues which adorned the basin, a task which she performed sullenly. At a gesture from the Empress, she began, somewhat sulkily, to unfold the roll that lay on the table and commenced reading aloud an essay by Seneca. The words fell coldly and monotonously on the marble walls of the room; both substance and delivery were as chilling as the marble itself. The fountain plashed merrily as if mocking the hollow-sounding phrases about virtue: "Hypocrisy, hypocrisy!" it murmured ceaselessly.

Octavia sometimes closed her eyes or repressed a yawn; she was evidently occupied, not with the philosopher's thoughts, but with her own. To whom could she confide them? Whom could she trust? She could confess her sufferings only to herself: the world that surrounded the girl of twenty was as hard and unfeeling as the walls of this apartment.

Yes, yonder fountain had a right to its sarcastic laughter. What did this luxury of existence, the title of Empress, bestow upon her? The parrot yonder in its gilded cage was happier than she; she would expect those marble statues to have warm hearts in their bosoms sooner than the courtiers who obsequiously surrounded her. True, she loved Britannicus, but how rarely she was permitted to enjoy the pleasure of his companionship. The Caesar did not like to have the brother and sister associate, his suspicious nature kept them apart. Besides, she knew that her brother's days were numbered, that snares were set for her own life, and her foes only waited or an opportunity to make her disappear in some unnoticed manner from the stage of life.. This certainty of her fate, the consciousness that she only lingered in the upper world like a shade forgotten by Charon, lessened her interest in her brother's destiny; she regarded him as one of the departed, whose death had already been mourned and on whose funeral urn the hot cheek might sometimes be cooled with quiet resignation. She really never pondered over her own situation; she lived like the shepherd in the mountains who has become accustomed to sleep on the edge of a precipice. She did not know the meaning of love, fidelity, devotion. Nero, whom she had once loved, she learned to despise on their bridal night. Even then she had repulsed his mad caresses, and she was the only person who before that time had recognized the brute beneath the youth's winning exterior. She had uttered words which she knew that he could never forget; and whenever he had made advances to her, she had treated him with such cold contempt that his love was finally transformed into implacable hatred. Her sole comfort and refreshment she found in her favorite authors, and her mind, estranged from life, had ventured even to the works of Plato. The young Empress especially admired the writings of Socrates, and many of the words of this wisest of mortals echoed in the evening, before she lay down to rest, like a prayer in the recesses of her soul. Her passions had received so little sustenance, had been so intimidated by her husband's conduct, her father's death, her mother's life, that her nature was believed to be gentle, which was by no means true. Beneath the apathetic coldness Fate compelled her to display, slept glowing yearnings for life. The quiet composure which she had acquired by the study of philosophy and poetry had often been shaken by the daily spectacle of a profligate court, although her refined nature turned with loathing from all dissolute orgies. Her character could truthfully be called pure and noble, but her yearning for

happiness had often whispered: "Enjoy the remnant of your existence "—
and only a certain aesthetic modesty, and the circumstance that as yet she
had met no one who was capable of inspiring her with lasting regard, had
prevented her from yielding to these whispers. It was one of her
peculiarities to create, by her vivid imagination, a swiftly formed ideal
image of the persons whom she met,—an image whose radiance, after a
brief period, was destroyed by inexorable reality.

So, hitherto, she had been cured of one enthusiasm by another; all
had proved vain delusions; the head of Jupiter had always changed into a
grinning faun. She had now grown more distrustful, it is true, yet what can
the voice of reason do against the captivating charm of imagination? Even
the most bitter scorn of mankind, which at times ruled her mind, did not
release her from her delusion.

While still absorbed in her reverie, she felt two brown arms
suddenly embrace her. Her favorite slave, Meroe, an ugly, idiotic Egyptian,
had glided up to the couch during the reading, and tried to play one of her
usual foolish tricks by dealing her mistress a blow on the shoulder to kill a
.fly. This slave-girl, with her hanging lips, flat nose, and perpetually
cheerful, mindless expression, could venture to do almost anything.
Octavia pitied the undeveloped, good-natured creature, was often amused
by her meaningless chatter, and sometimes permitted her to see her tears.
Then she at least had one human being who asked the cause of her sorrow,
and, when she made no answer, began to weep with her without knowing
why. Meroe sank down on the floor, pulled at the fringes of the cushions,
and clasped her mistress's hand, while, with the other, she pressed her
long hair to her thick lips.

"How beautiful he is, isn't he?" she whispered, while the old woman
went on reading Seneca.

Octavia started from her dream, looked at the Egyptian in
astonishment, and asked: "Whom do you mean?"

"Oh, I watched," the slave-girl answered.

"I was standing there behind the curtain, and it seemed as though I
was in the temple of Isis and the priestesses were beating the kemkem, and
my senses were intoxicated by the blue clouds of incense floating around
the gay pillars. Oh, how happy I was, my Mistress. Oh, how beautiful he is,
more beautiful than Osiris, and how manly, yet gentle, his voice sounds. It
is like the night wind rustling the papyrus reeds by the Nile. Do you hear
how it murmurs; do you see how the heron flies with steady wings above
the waves?"

Octavia understood that the slave-girl meant Metellus, and,
blushing, stroked the poor fool's hair back from her forehead.

"You are right, Meroe, he is beautiful," she murmured dreamily,
gazing down at her.

"And good," whispered the Egyptian.

Octavia nodded, and held her hand in the jet of the fountain, so that
the fans of the palms quivered under the splashing drops.

"And, Mistress," the slave-girl went on, "he looked at me, his eyes flamed like the mirror of the Nile when the sun floods it with fire, and a burning thrill ran through my limbs as if the hot breath of the desert had touched me—"

"At you?"

"Yes, when I was standing behind the curtain he noticed me," said the girl, smiling and, striking her nude, hideous bosom, she continued: "Oh, he loves me! I feel it here, here—"

The Empress could scarcely help smiling as she heard this artless confession, but with her amusement mingled a sense of bitterness that startled her. Yet she forced herself to make a pleasant answer.

"Aha! Then you might soon have a wedding," she said; "I'll give you a red veil, and order flute-players."

"You saw it too, didn't you," cried the girl, greatly excited; "you saw that Sechet, the goddess of love, favors us?"

"Of course, of course," replied her mistress, compassionately; and this assurance threw the poor fool into such a rapture of joy that, unable to find words, she kissed the Empress's hand again and again, often rolling her eyes upward to sink into a reverie. It was one of Meroe's pet fancies to believe that somebody was in love with her. This delusion could never be dislodged, and she changed the object of her affEction every week. Sometimes it was a soldier who sought her; sometimes a slave, frequently even a patrician official. No doubt the fool sometimes suspected that she was being made the butt of coarse jests; but this did not prevent her from continually falling in love, or from loving most ardently the very men who most inhumanly insulted her.

Octavia closed her eyes; she did not hear the words of the reader or the plashing of the fountain; she suddenly felt transported to the gardens and, for an instant, beheld, as if in a dream, the sleeping youth, the dazzling sunlight shining upon the water in the basin, the tender touch of his hand on her cheek; then she started up, sighing,—the sunlight had vanished, the cool dusk made her shiver, the fountain plashed monotonously. She gazed wonderingly around the chilly apartment, blushing as vividly as though some watcher had known her secret thoughts.

Now she tried to listen to Seneca's wise maxims, and for a time succeeded, until gradually some strange, diverting idea began to associate itself with every precept of the philosopher. Her own thoughts mingled with his, just as the ornaments twined about the masks of the wainscoting. More than once she raised her head toward the azure opening in the ceiling, or watched the play of the sunbeams in the water in the basin of the fountain with a sense of pleasure, an expansion of the soul which, hitherto, she had never known. The brilliant blue above the dusky room, the dancing gold on the ripples in the basin, suddenly roused in her a longing for the pleasures of life which, as she saw herself barred from them on all sides, wakened an emotion nearer to tears than to smiles. Meroe's words: "How beautiful he is!" were still echoing in her ears, when the

63

reader stopped, a slave entered the room and announced that the Caesar would visit her immediately.

The Empress rose slowly, and, though she mentally asked herself in great perplexity how it happened that Nero, who had so long shunned her, suddenly again sued for her friendship, nothing could be detected in her manner except the apathetic indifference which she had intentionally endeavored to assume. Was he weary of Sabina? Or was his kindness the surest sign of her approaching destruction? Yet Octavia knew that he dared not harm her, so long as she remained the favorite of the people. Her female attendants, who were much excited by the rare event of a visit from the Caesar, were ordered, with a sternness very unusual in her, not to prepare in any way for his reception, not even to put on better garments. She herself did not move from her place and, though a feeling of anxious fear weighed upon her heart, the expression of indifference, more offensive than open scorn, did not leave her features for an instant.

The curtain at the door rustled back, two guards appeared, and the Caesar, attended by a numerous train, slowly approached the threshold. He wore a very simple flowered mantle, for he had heard that artists usually neglect their personal appearance, only his hair, on which the laurel wreath rested, had been carefully curled. A smile of assumed graciousness rested on his fat face; but when his wife rose with cold dignity from her couch, the smile gave place to an almost foolish expression of timidity and distrust.

The courtiers formed a group, and the Caesar advanced toward Octavia, who awaited him with downcast eyes, as if in a half dream. Perhaps, for the first time in his life, this god upon earth experienced a feeling of embarrassment, and, extremely perplexed by the new sensation, turned toward Petronius. The latter, however, took a malicious pleasure in remaining silent, and Nero, dissatisfied with himself, awkwardly began to stammer a few questions to Octavia, asking how she lived and whether she wanted anything,—perhaps a new litter, new slaves, a better bath, choicer viands.

Octavia shook her head at each query, and not until he finally asked in what way he could serve her did she raise her large eyes to his, saying: "By permitting me, undisturbed, to mourn my father's death."

Nero, who had always been classed with the murderers of Claudius, started, evidently struggling to maintain his composure, and, repressing his rage with difficulty, said to those who surrounded him,—

"I came to offer her my hand in reconciliation; you all see how she receives me."

Burrus, who stood nearest to Octavia, bent toward the woman sitting with so indifferent an air.

"August lady," he whispered, "use the opportunity to save your life; his intentions are kind; be gentle, and you may reconcile him."

Then, turning to the Caesar with a pleasant smile, he said aloud: "Do not leave your wife in anger, oh, Caesar! She will fulfil your wishes if you ask her to do so."

64

All eyes were bent upon Nero, who instantly perceived how greatly he might profit by Octavia's defiant silence and pose as a martyr to feminine caprices.

"Well then," he answered with feigned humility, "you know, Octavia, that I once knew how to value your beauty, and that it would make me happy, on every account, to win your heart, at least as far as decorum commands. Let us at any rate appear before the Roman people as husband and wife."

Nero turned to Petronius.

"If she promises to obey me," he whispered, "I really feel disposed to give up the whole plan which was to cause her destruction."

Petronius started. Although well aware that Nero was uttering a falsehood, in order to deceive even his most intimate friends and increase the excitement of the scene, he thought it possible that Octavia's beauty might again exert its former power of attraction over the Emperor's unstable heart. His object was to place Poppaea upon the throne; Octavia must be overthrown at any cost, and now her position appeared more secure than ever. Nero, who was immensely pleased with the theatrical pathos of the situation, resolved to render the comedy still more effective. He now turned to his train, and, coquetting with his negligent attire, intimated that he had no more ardent desire than to be permitted to press the kiss of reconciliation upon his wife's lips. But when Octavia perceived his intention, she involuntarily clenched her hands, and rose as if to seek refuge in flight. All expected to hear some scathing reply from her lips, and the Emperor was already preparing to receive it with noble resignation by seeking to give his features the expression of an innocent sufferer. Octavia, however, as soon as she noticed this look on her husband's face, resolved—difficult as the task might be—to outwit the crafty hypocrite and conceal her scorn.

"My husband," she said, with unmistakable sarcasm, "my husband, what need is there of any tokens of affection from you; I know that you love me. Is not the attention you show by ordering my bust a proof of it? Oh, I understand how to appreciate this evidence of your regard, although, to speak frankly, nothing is more distasteful than to see myself as a marble ghost. Yet since it is your wish to possess me doubly,—dead and alive,—I will make this sacrifice for your sake. Yes! How could I longer resist such devotion! Come! Let us show the Roman people that we live in the most affectionate harmony, and that you are very far from wishing to divorce me for the sake of another. I know that is slander."

If it had been difficult for her to dissimulate, the embarrassment and wrath visible in the Caesar's features now repaid her for the effort. Had she met him with repellent pride, as she had so often done before, he would have emerged this time from the conflict as victor; but he was not prepared for this amiable malice on the part of the haughty sufferer. A spiteful glance, which she returned by a contemptuous smile, rebuked her boldness in spoiling the imperial actor's beautiful farewell scene and embarrassing him in the presence of his train.

"See that the bust is finished soon," he answered sullenly; "do you hear? I want it quickly—"

Here he interrupted himself, and, as his rising wrath at the failure of his farce must have some outlet, he shouted to the slave who stood nearest to him, and, without any apparent cause, dealt him several blows as he left the room. On reaching the threshold, he supported himself on the shoulders of some freedmen, and called to his wife that he would have their mutual reconciliation announced in the "Daily Informer" of the Roman people; but she must attend at once to the modelling of her bust, as he intended to have it placed in his sleeping room with great ceremony, and had already composed an elaborate piece of music for the festival. Then, bending toward Petronius as he passed him, he muttered,—

"See that we have proofs as soon as possible; my patience is exhausted."

Petronius attempted to reply that several months must elapse before the end could be reached; but Nero retorted: "I will wait no longer than the Saturnalia. Your head is precisely as firm as my wife's."

Petronius compressed his lips, and remained silent.

When the room was empty the Empress, radiant with the consciousness of victory, kissed her slave Meroe, who, having no understanding of what had happened, received the caress with a silly smile. Octavia felt that she had given the Caesar this answer under the influence of a higher power. Without fully realizing it, she imagined that an apparition to which she forbade herself to give a name, had witnessed the scene of Nero's humiliation with her. Her whole being still thrilled with the strange perception that his spirit was standing at her side, expressing his approval, which she accepted with a smile.

"Did I act worthily?" she would fain have asked him; "did I please you?" True, as she leaned back on her cushions and closed her eyes, beneath whose lids tears were stealing, her throbbing heart told her that she had enraged the lion and defied his paws to deal the destroying blow; but with this consciousness of approaching death blended a sense of quiet happiness. She felt so safe; she knew that her funeral pyre would soon blaze, and thus felt secure. Something hovered around her, she did not reflect what it might be. Was it the perfume of an individual, the subtle aroma exhaling from the personality of a beautiful, beloved human being which intoxicates us, and, even against our will, we inhale more and more eagerly until it becomes like the breath of life?

Toward evening, the leech Andromachus visited the Empress. The sun was casting its crimson radiance through the opening in the roof into the sleeping room; outside the pines were rustling in the breeze before the window, and their broad tops were suffused by the tints of the sunset sky. The physician's eyes looked grave, as he felt Octavia's pulse, and said,—

"There is something going on; beware, august lady."

Octavia nodded. The leech released her arm, stepped back frowning, and continued:

"I wished to speak to you."

She smiled mechanically, her thoughts were evidently elsewhere.

"Will you listen to me, august lady?" Andromachus began again.

"Pray go on," she replied.

"Perhaps I am interrupting you—if I have come at an inconvenient time—"

"No! Stay! Speak," the Empress answered the hesitating man. "I am absentminded, am I not? But pardon me."

"I have to give you the last greetings of your brother Britannicus," said Andromachus, very gravely.

"He is dead," cried Octavia.

The leech bowed his head.

"He is dead," murmured the Empress, dreamily. Andromachus tried to say a few consoling words to the mourner; but she gazed fixedly into vacancy, without heeding him, and did not appear to need consolation. The physician left her. In fact, she scarcely did need consolation. She had expected her brother's death for years, and now that it had come and she was entirely alone, she felt free, independent, strong. Doubtless she was angry with herself that she had no tears, nay, that a passionate yearning for unchecked pleasure strove to stir within her soul; but she would have deemed herself less heartless had she realized more distinctly that this impulse was the same emotion experienced by the animal -fighter who carouses and loves to-day, knowing that the blood- stained arena awaits him on the morrow. She felt that now, for the first time, it was her duty to sip the neglected joys of existence. She had mourned for her brother while he lived, why should she lament him now that he was released? No tie bound her; Orcus summoned her early enough; there below she would grieve with her brother; here she must hastily gather a store of happiness to take with her to the sad shore.

Such were her thoughts when, that same: night, she stood beside the body of the murdered man. The sight of the beloved form had awakened, instead of grief, a strange feeling of defiance in the bosom of the desolate girl. She rebelled against the gods who had never been gracious to her; she longed to grasp by force the happiness which they withheld.

Britannicus lay in the spacious hall, as was the custom, on a tapestried bier, with his feet turned toward the door. The face which in life had been so beautiful and gentle was now distorted; the expression of suffering was fixed upon the livid features. A lamp hung above, whose dim, bluish light fell mournfully upon him, leaving the rest of the apartment in darkness. The night- breeze, rustling the cypresses outside, sometimes fanned the flame of the lamp to a brighter glow, sometimes almost extinguished it, then gliding over the marble floor swept over the bier, stirring the locks and fluttering the white toga of the corpse. But it could lend no movement to the rigid features, only the ends of the toga waved as if they would fain bear away the lifeless form.

Octavia stood motionless; she longed to be like her brother, yet she wished to live; she envied his repose, yet feared it, disdained her fear, and at the same time would fain have had eyes see her that were far away. The rustling of a garment roused her from these conflicting thoughts; her heart stopped beating, but the eyes that gazed into hers were not those she expected; Agrippina, the murderer's mother, stood before her, with her figure drawn up to its full height, the wrinkles in her face looked waxen in the flickering light.

"Poor girl," whispered Nero's proud mother, "the lion has taken his first spring; you will be his second victim."

She clasped Octavia's hand.

"Oh, would that I had never borne him; he laughs at us; he revels while we are weeping, the monster. Let us be friends," she added. "The unhappy bear their grief more easily when united; we will defy him. Or, no, not defy him; we have both renounced life."

"If you have done so," replied Octavia, with a bitter, angry smile, "I have not. I shall now begin, for the first time, to enjoy it. Who will blame me, since I was always compelled to mourn? If I must sleep as he does, I will first intoxicate myself. They say that we forget down below—I will not; I will live there on what I have enjoyed here."

The lamp flickered as if in pain; sometimes the hall was perfectly dark, sometimes flashing with light. Agrippina did not understand the young Empress, as, shivering, with a strange smile on her flushed cheeks, she wrapped herself in her mantle. Then she closed her eyes and her parted lips quivered over her white, clenched teeth.

That very night the funeral pyre of Britannicus blazed upward to the star- strewn sky.

CHAPTER VI

METELLUS was very well content with his life in the palace. In his simplicity he overlooked the vice that surrounded him, and clung to the beauty which was offered. He set great value upon the flatteries of the courtiers, and did not perceive in the least that there was anything extraordinary in the favor bestowed upon him by the Caesar, as they asserted; to him, this favor was extremely opportune, but it seemed perfectly natural. True, it happened more than once at table that he did not know how to eat some dish, begged a slave's pardon, or helped himself sooner than etiquette allowed; but what mattered these little annoyances, which evoked the laughter of the court? They were far outweighed by the favor of the Caesar, who systematically trained him to be a gourmand.

"What do you think, Metellus," Nero sometimes said, "suppose we should try a new invention? Purple snails boiled in wine; that must be delicious!"

Metellus modestly gave his opinion. The goddess of the culinary art avenged herself bitterly for the contempt with which hitherto he had regarded her gifts by forcing him, when he had finished his meals, to confess with shame that, while eating the choicest delicacies, he really had thought of nothing except that they tasted remarkably nice.

The idealist had quickly accommodated himself to the customs of the court; he even learned to bow, and often succeeded in not interrupting a speaker; only one thing was difficult,—to flatter without cause. He noticed that all who surrounded the Caesar possessed great skill in this art, applauded him frantically whenever he spoke, listened to his every breath, watched him incessantly to find an opportunity to utter a word of praise, and, if he sneezed, commended his health to the gods. He also perceived that an omission of these tokens of approval might, under certain circumstances, become dangerous; yet he still blushed as he stammered his morning greeting, and, when asked to express his opinion concerning any of Nero's artistic performances, usually uttered phrases whose awkwardness showed their lack of sincerity.

"My friend," Petronius once said to him, when they were leaving a banquet at which the youth had vehemently condemned the Romans' love of fights between animals, "my friend, you have won the Caesar's heart, it is true, but beware. Truth is enjoyable only when it is new, and it very soon grows rusty."

"But isn't it an abomination," replied the artist, heated by the wine he had drunk, "that sedate men, even cultivated women, find pleasure in such spectacles? Did not Sophocles write for the Romans?"

"My friend," rejoined Petronius, more kindly than ever, "help yourself over such reflections by means of satire. That is now our consoler, our religion. If you wish to say spiteful things to guests at table, smile as pleasantly as possible while doing so. Rely upon it, they will think you have flattered them."

"I don't understand that," replied the son of the Muses.

One day the artist found the Caesar busied in copying in clay the head of a Venus by Praxiteles. Nero asked him how he had succeeded. Metellus muttered a few unintelligible words, took the modelling stick from the Emperor's hand, and began to re-shape the whole bust. Nero's face darkened more and more as he saw his work vanishing under the sculptor's hands, and only the presence of mind of Petronius succeeded in averting the gathering storm. The clever courtier declared Metellus's work to be the Emperor's, and vowed that the artist had not changed a single line.

Another time the Emperor wished to be drawn with the expression of an enthusiastic singer on his face.

"But, Metellus," he said, glancing into the mirror, "could not this curve of the lips be changed?"

He passed his hand across his broad nose as he spoke, to indicate that he did not wish to see the lips, but the nose, idealized in the likeness. Metellus, to the universal horror of those who were present, declared that the broad nose could not possibly be changed, that was exactly what gave the face its characteristic expression. Again the Caesar's eyes sparkled maliciously, and again it was Petronius who protested that the Emperor's nose ought not to be altered on any account. Metellus was perfectly right, it was an ornament to his whole face; every Roman was proud of this feature of his sovereign. The others assented, and Nero believed the majority.

"I am no longer pleased with the youth," Nero had said to his director of the festivals; "it is time to use the tool, that we may get rid of him as we dealt with Britannicus."

At the end of a month the day at last came when the Empress sat to the artist for the first time. She had adorned herself as magnificently as possible, then, before he entered the room, removed the jewels and, after reflecting a short time, put them on again. A change, which she vainly endeavored to conceal from her attendants, had taken place in the young sovereign. Octavia, who was formerly so resolute, had become undecided, a variable manner of life, a carelessness in everything and to every one had now become the habit of one once so determined. She neglected the gods; some mental conflict often seemed to absorb her so completely that the external world scarcely existed. Already she had three times declared that she was ill, and thus deferred the sittings. Whenever Metellus had asked for one, he had always been refused; yet she longed to meet him, to fill her monotonous existence with his companionship. She knew from her philosophers the transitoriness of all worldly pleasures; but she wished to test these pleasures, and yet, before yielding to her passionate impulse, she was forced to conquer her aesthetic sense of modesty, her whole training, and this was more difficult to the delicate natured woman than she had imagined.

But a month is a long time to a youthful heart, and so the artist's imagination had become considerably cooled in regard to Octavia's charms. Besides, he had met at the Emperor's court far more beautiful women who made a very different use of their attractions, whose boldness often repelled him, yet, nevertheless, occupied his thoughts. Only their effrontery, the dances which unveiled every physical charm, prevented his taking any serious interest in these beauties. So it was not strange that he was tolerably composed when, preceded by a slave bearing a mass of clay, he entered the Empress's apartments. He was clad in a plain, sleeveless garment, smiled in a somewhat embarrassed way, and bowed rather awkwardly, but began to use the modelling stick on the soft substance without any signs of confusion.

Octavia gazed at him with a feeling of disappointment. She had not supposed that his mind would have been so little freed from the indifference of youthful innocence; had that scene in the garden left no deeper traces?

Childlike people very speedily forget the expressions of their unconscious variations of mood; yet this very innocent security formed a fresh attraction. Did he not feel that she had wound the rope of pearls through her dark locks that day on his account? Had he no eyes for the grace with which she tried to move? Alas! She had never learned coquetry, and could make no impression with her modest ornaments.

Metellus did not utter a single word while at his work, but gracefully pressed the clay with his beautiful hand, and sometimes glanced hastily at his model's profile. Poor Meroe sat at her mistress's feet, watching the sculptor, whose calm absorption greatly awed her, in silent rapture. Often, while changing a faulty line, the youth's lips moved as if he were reproving himself, and his face often brightened when he succeeded in obtaining the right contour; otherwise he did not seem to be aware of the presence of any other person in the room; he kneaded the clay with the same indifference as if he stood before a marble head.

During the preceding days, the Empress had adorned the youth's image from her own imagination, decked it with every mental charm, and expected to enjoy Olympus upon earth during her quiet life with him. She did not intend to be to him—what indeed she was only in name—the Empress, and now his behavior did not harmonize in the least with her expectations. How passionately her heart had throbbed last night, when she imagined that she again saw him kneeling before her, that she spoke to him kindly; what chaste embraces the god of dreams had bestowed upon her; how she had fancied herself relieving the burden that oppressed her soul by revealing it to his sympathizing one,—and now she scarcely dared to say a word to him!

Like all high-born, but inexperienced women, she had expected that he would serve her ardently, melt under her eyes, feel happy if she extended her hand to him; nay, she had cherished the fervent wish that he would conquer her scruples, put an end to her struggles, fulfil her eager hopes; and now he was completely absorbed in himself and his work. Yet she yearned to find one drop of happiness in the bottom of her cup of life, ere happiness on earth for her was over. The poor heart must indeed resist; but the man's strength must conquer this resistance, and if a true love seized her soul she felt that she would listen to the kind gods, and that they would approve; now the gods had again deceived her, her thirsting soul must continue to languish.

She sat lost in thought, with her tearful eyes fixed intently upon the ripples in the basin of the fountain, pondering over her wasted life, and longing for the hour which would end all these hopes, conflicts, and passions. The patch of blue sky above the basin had gradually flushed with the hues of sunset; Metellus wished to finish his model's brow before it grew perfectly dark. The task began to defy his talent, for it was not easy to catch the expression in this woman's face; already he had failed thrice in producing the individual look that pervaded the whole countenance, and wrath at his lack of skill was visible in his frowning brows and the vehement movements of his hands. The flush on his cheeks and the restlessness of his glowing eyes also indicated his extreme dissatisfaction with himself.

He was so anxious to gain honor by this work; his august patron must be convinced of his talent.

Suddenly he exclaimed angrily: "That won't do; higher! Hold your head higher!" and, without waiting for his command to be obeyed, he approached Octavia, seized her somewhat rudely by the chin, pressed his other hand upon her temples, and lifted her head. At first, when the loud words interrupted the stillness of the apartment, the Empress seemed startled; then, as the youth's beautifully formed arm moved directly before her eyes, she felt as if cold steel had passed through her bosom, and sat motionless and rigid; the careless manner in which he handled her head, as if it belonged to a wooden doll, filled her with a strange humility.

Metellus felt the tremor of her body, saw her press her chin hastily downward to try to check the heaving of her bosom. He was still holding her chin in his hand, and, as Octavia raised her large eyes with such a submissive, wondering gaze, he awoke from the fever of work which had completely absorbed him. Flushing deeply, he faltered an apology, letting his arms fall at his side, and, in this attitude, stood motionless for a moment, like a beautiful statue. How strangely he felt, as if under the influence of a sudden spell, when this royal woman covered her glowing face with her little hand, as if to conceal it! A sweet compassion overwhelmed him as he thought that his heedlessness had caused the terrible embarrassment which, with the most intense anxiety, she endeavored to hide from his eyes. As he returned to his clay model, he felt as if he had tortured the gentle Empress, who was still struggling with her emotions. How pallid and corpse-like her face still looked; terror clutched his heart-strings. "What have you done?" cried a voice in his soul. If he had killed her, the pang in his breast could scarcely have been keener.

At last Octavia recovered her composure, and told Meroe to bring a cup full of water. The slave, who took all the sculptor's glances to herself, rose to obey the order; but her mistress called her back; it was not necessary, she might stay.

"How do you like the palace?" asked the Empress, after a pause, in a low, timid voice, trying to assume an indifferent expression; and a weight fell from his heart as she spoke.

"Oh, very well!" he replied, sitting down and playing with his modelling stick. The beautiful woman's agitation had had a contagious effect upon him. Now that she had recovered her calmness, he felt how the brief moment of tension had exhausted him, and struggled wrathfully against a physical discomfort hitherto unknown; even the control he was compelled to exert over his voice, which sounded harsh, he angrily resented.

"Poor boy, so you like the palace?" she repeated, and her voice sounded so gentle, so sympathizing as it uttered this " poor boy." Why shouldn't I like it?" said Metellus. Why, oh, august lady, do you call me poor?" I pity you because you are obliged to learn the abominations of this court life so young," replied Octavia.

"Oh, your husband has been sorely slandered," cried Metellus. "I am grateful to the Emperor, nay, I love him, for he fosters Art. I serve him gladly; it is false that he does not love you, as the Romans say. They gossip so much in the taverns and the barber-shops. You ought to see your husband more frequently—"

"Tell me about your parents, your home," interrupted the Empress,

72

evasively; and Metellus began to describe his birthplace. Hurriedly, as if he was afraid of awakening homesickness by dwelling too long upon details, he related what first entered his mind, and then broke off abruptly.

"I wish that I had known your mother," said the beautiful sovereign, when he paused.

The opening in the ceiling had grown darker; the water in the basin was blood-red; crimson spots flecked the gleaming walls; the objects in the rooms could scarcely be distinguished,—pictures and statues were assuming vague outlines. Both were silent. Octavia still gazed, as if listening, at his beautiful face, whose chin was yet beardless. His brow, in which a line of pain was visible, drooped mournfully. At last she broke the pause.

"You are longing for your home, poor boy."

"Oh, I am not so faint-hearted," replied Metellus, smiling. "Rome is beautiful too."

"But here you have no heart that sympathizes with you," she said.

"Have you such a heart?" he asked.

"No," she answered. There was a harsh tone in her voice.

"Then mine shall feel with you," he answered as frankly as if he were saying something perfectly natural. Octavia had bent her head, toward him with a beautiful curve of her slender neck. The delicate arms were sharply outlined against the background of the black chair.

"Do you wish to be interested in my fate?" she asked, half smiling, half sadly.

"Surely," he exclaimed almost gayly, "you please me. Mistress. You are not like the other ladies in the palace, not bold and forward. But tell me, why do you often look so sad? It seems to me you have no cause for that here."

"Poor boy," murmured the Empress, sorrowfully, "many things are hidden from you. May the bandage never fall from your eyes, poor boy."

"No! Do not call me that," replied Metellus, shaking his head. "I am not unfortunate, and it hurts me when you say so."

"I like to see you when you are sad, Metellus," she said softly, as if to herself.

The youth glanced up at her with a happy smile, was about to speak, then paused, blushing, and remained with his eyes bent upon the floor until she rose. She was moving toward him to give him her hand, but paused, and again gazed at him with one of those looks which convert the eyes into an embodied soul, one of those deeply sympathizing looks in which love speaks when it can find no words.

Metellus, who had also risen, caught the last quivering reflection of this glance, then gazed after the retreating figure, noting how gracefully her dark locks fell over her dazzlingly fair neck, sweeping to the slender hips like the mane of a noble steed. A sensuous yearning, ennobled by tender devotion, overpowered him until the curtain at the door fell behind her white robe. That deep look had touched him strangely. No human eye had ever before rested on him thus, stirring his heart to its inmost depths.

She must be very unhappy, he began to think. Oh, if looks were only words, he reflected, still haunted by those eyes. What did she wish to tell me? I know, and yet I fear that I am deceiving myself.

Just as he was leaving the room, a shapeless creature, whom hitherto he had not noticed, came stealing to his feet. It was Meroe, who was trying to attract his attention, as he had not seen her in the dusky room.

"What do you want, Meroe?" he said kindly, as she held up a date to him.

"Take it," she answered, grinning. "Eat, my friend."

"No, thank you," he replied. But the fool would not desist, and offered him successively a piece of an old comb, a ring, a necklace, a small image of Osiris, which as she drew them carefully from her pocket, he pleasantly refused. But Meroe did not allow herself to be discouraged, probably thinking that her lover was faint-hearted. She began to play ball with the date, to exhibit her grace to the best advantage, in which her half-brutish manner and shrill laughter were so repulsive to the object of her tenderness that he tried to leave the room. But she clung around his knees, lavishing inarticulate words of love upon the startled youth, who was too compassionate to treat her harshly. At last Petronius, who appeared at the entrance of the room, released him from his disagreeable situation.

"Oho! Metellus is practising the art of kissing," said the courtier, laughing.

"How do you obtain admission to the Empress's apartments?" asked the artist, surprised at his sudden appearance.

"Oh!" replied the other, evasively, "I wanted to summon you to the Caesar. He has invented a new beverage which he calls Nero's cooling drink.* You must help him try it."

Petronius had hoped to surprise Metellus in a tender conversation with a very different person, and, in order to at least be able to give his master some tidings of the pair, he asked: "How do you like the Empress? Is she not a beautiful woman? And you, lucky fellow, have an opportunity to linger in her presence as long as you choose."

But the watchful questioner was mistaken if he had hoped to catch any remark from the young man's lips which would aid in his ruin. Metellus avoided making any comments, and when Petronius, to attain his object, finally assumed, in a very cynical style, the part of a tempter, the artist harshly stopped him. The courtier laughingly proposed to win him the favor of the deserted Empress, representing that her virtue was by no means proof against every assault, nay, even attempting to cast a certain mysterious halo around her by allusions to former love-affairs.

"You do not know her," cried the sculptor, indignantly, "and are unworthy to take her name on your lips."

The crafty noble answered soothingly, but, as a shrewd judge of human nature, perceived by this causeless anger that his victim's heart was no longer so indifferent as before.

"My dear fellow," he said smiling, "I don't understand why you should be so excited. A young man has a wish, nay, a right, to enjoy life, and he is a fool if he is too cautious in his choice. Wary in words, bold in deeds. Day smiles on us but once, and the shades no longer love. Venus is welcome, wherever we may find her; or do the kisses of a slave differ from those of an Empress? To reject a woman's love is a crime."

"There is no question of love here," said Metellus, with sullen sincerity, "or what are you thinking of Octavia and me?"

Oh, pardon me," Petronius hastily replied. You misunderstood my words. I do not think about your relations at all. What affair is it of mine? Besides, if you should admire Octavia—who would blame you? Certainly not I, and you can rely upon my silence."

"I need no confidants," said the youth, proudly.

"Who knows, my good fellow, whether you may not some day need one? The air which blows through these halls is not as pure as that in Tibur. Here we breathe oppressive perfumes. Here the marble is slippery, and it is also cold, unfeeling, and very hard. Perhaps the time will come when you will be grateful for a tender word, a kind bosom, an honest counsel."

Petronius cast a side-glance at the youth. Both, without noticing where they were going, had reached the palace-gardens, whose dark trees towered upward against the pale night heavens, and whose shrubbery shone with a golden light beneath the moonbeams. As the crafty spy saw the young man's honest face, uplifted with such childlike innocence to the moon, as if the golden disk floating between the summits of the pines could shed light upon the tangled labyrinth of his life, a passing emotion of pity affected him.

"It is a shame," cried a voice in his hardened heart, "a shame that this fresh, pure soul must be ruined, but it will be; who can live in the society of a Nero and keep his virtue?"

Yet the vague words of the director of the festivals had roused the emotions slumbering in the breast of Metellus, given his ardent soul purpose and direction. He understood his own nature more clearly; and, when he brought Octavia's form before his imagination, he felt as if a soft, warm rain was falling upon him. At least this was the general impression produced by her face, her voice, her manner.

"Love for a woman is a strange thing," the courtier went on thoughtfully, and now he described the joys of love with a charm glowing with hidden sensuality; yet he admitted the rights of Psyche beside those of Amor so fully, that even a rigid moralist could have censured, at the utmost, only certain careless sentences. His words groped their way on, winding themselves about their hearer's mind like the meshes of a loathsome spider's web. As the shades of night lure wild beasts from their dens, these vague, subtle words awakened all sorts of wishes and desires in the unsuspicious youth,—wishes and desires that wondered at themselves, yet gradually felt at ease in the gloomy atmosphere. Metellus • knew that he ought not to listen to these words; more than once he tried to interrupt the descriptions; but the poison gradually stupefied his senses and robbed him of strength.

"The spell of Venus falls some day upon every one," Petronius concluded; "it will come to you also, and you will be wise not to struggle against the yoke, for you will thus only thrust the barb deeper into your breast. We no longer all believe in the gods, it is true; but no one ventures to doubt the divine power of Venus. It burns more hotly than the glowing iron with which the cowardly gladiator is forced into the arena; it tears deeper wounds than the claws of the tigress. Friendship alone can afford comfort in such cases, and, Metellus, you will find a friend— as you have already felt—in me. Give me your hand, and promise to be frank. I will aid you where and as I can."

Metellus made no answer, his heart was too full for words; but he mechanically grasped the proffered hand, his face still shadowed by the beautiful, artless expression which gives the eyes a wondering, dreamy gaze. As in his helplessness he looked up into the winning face of the courtier who was pressing his hand, he forced back his tears and summoned all his courage.

"If you wish to listen," he began, "perhaps I might tell you some things. I do not know, oh, Petronius, what has befallen my heart to-day. I must have some one in whom I can confide."

Petronius concealed a smile, as he heard the confession. Listening intently, he bent down to a clump of box and pretended to drive away an insect that was glittering there.

"I hear you, my friend," he said as indifferently as possible; "just see that fire-fly, how it shines among the leaves—" The fool must surely betray himself now, he thought.

Metellus gazed wearily up at the moon which was just appearing below a thin bank of clouds, illumining the distant pool and the white marble statues.

"Yes, I will tell you," he murmured.

Petronius had no more ardent desire than to have Metellus complete his confession, yet he did not venture to urge him, so he merely passed his arm around the youth's shoulders and again kindly entreated him to trust him. But the helpless expression which he now saw on his victim's face touched even the cold heart of the courtier, and when Metellus, with downcast eyes, whispered that he could not force his lips to utter what he desired to confess, the old satirist suddenly felt a sort of reverence for this purity,—a reverence so new to him that it almost aroused his anger.

"You do not belong at court," he exclaimed in a harsh tone; "leave it."

Metellus looked at him in surprise. Then, regretting his words, Petronius laughed, pretending that he had uttered them merely in jest. He really felt relieved when a slave appeared to summon both to the palace. Upon the terrace- like roof of an outbuilding, behind pillars garlanded with flowers, reclined Nero's guests,—a very motley company of dancing-girls, actors, and singers. Tall candelabra sent flickering flames upward toward the night-heavens and flooded with their dull red glare the whole party of revellers who, flushed with wine, tossed, half-clad, on their cushions. Busy servants filled the goblets Empress Octavia

with Spanish wine; beautiful boys, dressed like girls and smiling affectedly, passed wreaths and dishes; pale Greek women lay intoxicated on the floor or mischievously struggled to escape from their lovers' caresses. Wine flowed down from the round tables; crushed roses, goblets, ornaments, fragments torn from dresses floated on the sullied marble; and from the shadow of curtains and cushions peered faces smiling hideously, or repulsive giggling greeted the ear. The whole scene was shrouded by the murky red smoke of the burned Arabian gums; this incense veiled the dripping pillars and the revellers' figures with long, heavy clouds which swept like a mist between the candelabra and the tables. Metellus felt no inclination to share the banquet; he stood near the door, gazing gloomily at the extremely picturesque spectacle; the night-breeze blew the stupefying smoke toward him; a slave-girl fanned the fire on a silver tripod and flung on fresh fuel. The smoke poured more densely around the half nude forms and the flower-wreathed pillars. Thus the gods reclined upon clouds at their banquets. Meanwhile Petronius had reported the result of his investigation to the Caesar. Nero nodded, well satisfied.

"The fruit is ripening," whispered Petronius; "we can soon shake it down; leave the execution to me, oh, Caesar; you shall be content."

Then, turning to Poppaea, he added mischievously.

"Cherish no hope, fair lady; the boy is an enthusiast, and Octavia's virtue seems to enthrall him."

"I will set my nets, Petronius," replied Poppaea, smiling, "we will see who first catches the beautiful game."

Then, trying to attract Metellus's attention by the language of her eyes, she said to Petronius,—

"Just see how gloomily he gazes into vacancy! By Zeus! He is handsome, and I grudge him to the proudly virtuous Octavia, He is too beautiful to be permitted to remain innocent."

The courtier smiled languishingly like a satyr from whose grasp the nymph has escaped; but Poppaea seized some roses that lay before her and flung them so skilfully over the heads of the revellers that one struck Metellus on the forehead. He looked up and, recognizing the person who had played the prank by the side-glances she occasionally cast at him, he averted his face with intentional persistency.

The whole scene was repulsive to the youth; yet its demoniac charm gradually allured his imagination. He resolved to go, yet closed his eyes and remained. When Poppaea sent a slave to invite him to sit beside her, he could not, in his conflict with himself, decline. Approaching with a sullen face, he sat outwardly indifferent, but inwardly greatly agitated, beside the beauty, who ordered a wreath of fresh roses to be placed on his hair, and wine to be set before him. It was the first time in his life that he had been so near a woman. He said little, and indignantly repelled all advances. True, when she rested her arm on his, he could not prevent his pulses from throbbing more violently, or his imagination from painting Octavia's charms in more glowing hues; but he always withdrew his hand from her clasp with the slightly contemptuous smile which might have been taken for a reluctant surrender, and gave the impression that he constantly desired to go and only remained through courtesy and a slight weakness of character.

Poppaea talked incessantly, sometimes telling the latest news of the Circus, sometimes the last Roman scandals, tried to make him laugh, and finally reproached him for his silence, meanwhile leaning so heavily upon his shoulder that it was almost impossible for him to rise, while her breath, laden with the fumes of wine, disturbed him strangely. Nero, who had gone away to make his voice more flexible by an emetic, now returned. Its effect was still visible in the pallor of his fat cheeks, which thereby, in contrast with his reddish hair, assumed a peculiarly repulsive hue, like raw flesh. So, bearing his lyre on his arm, he walked through the ranks of the revellers, his ample cloak hanging in disorder around his clumsy limbs. He would declaim the "Niobe," he shouted; whereupon a breathless silence ensued.

Then he appointed the critics of his artistic performance, humbly addressing them as his masters, upon whose just verdict his life would depend. They must be lenient judges, rejecting everything accidental which might appear in his work. The judges encouraged the doubter, whose timidity was sincere, by reminding him how often he had proved his talent.

Standing between two candelabra freshly supplied with pitch, he began to recite the poem, which he had composed himself. His voice was sharp, but praise could justly be given to his verses, as well as to the dramatic expression of his gestures. One portion, with which he was especially pleased because it described the tenderest maternal love, he repeated, going into such a rhapsody that, directly after the first verse, an unfortunate incident occurred. While making a bold gesture with his arm, he overturned one of the candelabra, whose flaming pitch almost burned the guest nearest to it. Nero went on as if nothing had happened, while the cushions were blazing, and the trained applauders did not cease clapping their hands madly. Many who were present afterwards asserted that Nero had upset the candelabrum intentionally upon the couch where lay his rival, the poet Lucan, whom he bitterly hated.

As the slaves now began to cleanse the marble floor, Metellus found an opportunity in the universal confusion of escaping from his seat beside Poppaea and going to his own room. After removing his garments, he sat down at the table on which the lamp was already shedding its dim blue light over books, rolls, and sketches. Poppaea's love-making, which this time he had perceived more distinctly than ever before, inspired a momentary self-loathing; he felt humiliated when he looked at his arm, which, for some time, had rested upon hers, a tremor of disgust ran through him, and, to escape it, he hurriedly turned to his books. To cool his fevered blood before he went to sleep, he selected some of Horace's odes, but, unluckily, while searching for the book, Ovid's "Art of Love" fell into his hands. He had hitherto known nothing of this work; it was not among his own volumes, and must have been placed here secretly.

So he began to read, while the moon peered over the tops of the pine- trees through the folds of the curtain, and a night-moth circled like a warning spirit around the bluish flame of the lamp. Often Metellus laid down the book and fell into a reverie. The satyr-like boldness with which the lover is counselled selfishly to lead his mistress's heart astray, repelled his mind, which had not yet learned to make shrewd calculations in love. "No," cried a voice in his heart, "Ovid never knew love, else how could he advise lovers to feign tears." Yet, sometimes, when thinking of Octavia, he could not shut from his ears an evil whisper that he ought to use the maxims of the writer.

So, propping his head on his beautifully formed arm, he sat staring at the flame, unconsciously pushing the wick with the plectrum of a lyre which he held in his hand. The breeze sometimes bore from the park the distant sound of the carousing courtiers, and gradually Metellus was overpowered by a melancholy which oppressed him all the more deeply because, hitherto, he had been accustomed to regard life from an entirely different standpoint. His existence seemed utterly purposeless; he felt as if he was in the midst of the sea, with no support anywhere. He no longer believed in the gods, and doubtless he would soon be unable to believe in men; for he feared that he should learn by experience on what a feeble foundation the nobility of human nature rested. The fact that he must undergo these experiences filled him with indignation against himself, and yet he lacked the moral courage to give this indignation the ability to exercise a regenerating influence upon his heart. The paralyzing consciousness that vice might possess power over him shadowed his soul like an evil dream which we cannot shake off, yet which, in our dozing state, we know that we only need make a vigorous effort to dispel. According to the habit of youth, he soon put a plaster over the sore spot in his soul, and, with the skill of self-deception, his thoughts glided away from all that was disturbing to his comfort. Only often, while reviewing his life at this court, a strange chill ran through his limbs, all sorts of vague forebodings oppressed him; and though until now he had not perceived the mire under the gilding, the serpent under the flowers, he had had an uncomfortable feeling that everything around him was not exactly as it should be. His conversation with the Empress had increased his doubts, robbed him of the careless youthful thoughtlessness of his former life, nay, almost given him the deliberation of mature years, at least at times.

The wick of the lamp was half consumed when the slave entered, and announced Burrus,, who appeared immediately after, leading a boy by the hand. He apologized for disturbing him at so late an hour, and then said: "This lad would not stop begging to be taken to you, until I consented." The boy knelt before Metellus, entreating the artist to let him stay with him.

"He clung to my cloak as I was going down the Via Sacra," said Burrus, "declaring that he was your slave, and had lost his way in Rome."

"You saved my life once, when they were going to throw me to the wild beasts," said the little fellow. "Oh, take care of me now; don't leave me to starve. I have been searching all over this great Rome for you three whole days; yesterday I saw that you were living in the palace."

Metellus now recognized the boy whom, while wandering through the streets at night, he had hidden in the niche of the wall while the band of Christians was being taken to the Circus. He told Burrus the incident, and then asked the lad's name.

Stephanus," he answered quickly. Well, Stephanus," replied the artist, "I like you. You shall be my slave, and you will not fare badly with me, if you are obedient."

The boy gratefully kissed Metellus's hand, and squatted on the floor, watching with half parted lips every movement of his master. Burrus approached the artist.

"Young man," he said, "let me speak a few words to you in confidence."

Metellus looked up inquiringly.

"I do not know why you can so suddenly call yourself the Emperor's favorite," the general went on, with a troubled look, "I will not think that vice binds you to the Caesar's heart."

Metellus blushed and turned angrily away, his features assuming an expression of haughty indignation. As he stood thus, an image of youthful beauty and noble wrath, Burrus's eyes rested on him with pleasure; he offered him his hand, but Metellus did not clasp it.

"I did not wish to offend you," said the soldier; "I do not believe that you are one of the venal souls who come to Rome to be the tools of the rich. Your face inspires me with confidence, and I will venture to speak frankly to you. Whatever may be the cause, it is a fact that the gods have given you great power over Nero's heart, and old Burrus entreats you not to misuse this influence."

The general's voice trembled as he uttered the last words, his face flushed, and he fixed his eyes upon the floor.

"I am no freedman, but a free man," said Metellus, still indignant.

"Well, my friend," replied Burrus, "as you have obtained some power at this court, use it to protect the good and to ruin the evil. Above all, avoid imperilling the virtuous, whose fair fame is so easily sullied." The last words were uttered with a strange vehemence, almost as if against his will; he seemed to wish to add something more, and now bent his head, whose brow wore a troubled frown.

"Is any one in peril?" the artist asked involuntarily; and Burrus, who had subdued his excitement, answered that the Empress's life was in danger.

"The Empress?" cried Metellus. "Why do you bring foolish rumors to destroy my peace? No one's life is more secure than Octavia's."

When the youth now heard that Nero himself desired his wife's death, his blood boiled, and he called Burrus a slanderer.

"Alas," said the latter, without showing any sign of ofFence, "that I should be the one to destroy your happy youthful dreams."

Then he gave the youth a picture of court life, described the mortal terror of all who came in contact with the Caesar, showed him a glimpse of Nero's character, and intimated that he, Metellus, was only balancing like a rope-dancer on the swaying line of imperial caprice.

"You see only the front of the picture," he added; "but there is an unpainted, ugly back, and I should like to warn you against the companionship of several courtiers. But, above all, be on your guard, I emphasize this a second time, not to sully the reputation of the good."

Metellus shook his head; he had not heard the last warning, his mind was dwelling on the unprecedented news,—Nero wished to get rid of his wife; he was incapable of understanding anything else for the moment.

"I will never believe it," cried the unsuspicious youth; "that is high treason. The Emperor may have faults, but you exaggerate them to ruin him. I honor the Caesar as my patron, and no one shall venture to turn me against him."

In vain Burrus tried to show him that Nero did not love his wife; in vain he hinted that people at court were beginning to gossip about his more familiar intercourse with Octavia,—the young man did not understand him and at last exclaimed that he would go at once to Nero and speak to him about the matter. When at last, as the artist praised Petronius's friendship, Burrus called the courtier an old profligate and hypocrite, Metellus angrily told him that he must leave the room, and the general, glancing compassionately at the angry youth, retired.

"They want to rob me of my confidence, make me a misanthrope," murmured Metellus, approaching the open window; "but men are not so bad as they are represented—are they, ye eternal stars?"

He raised both arms to the glittering star-strewn sky, and, in spite of his resolute clinging to the beautiful and the good, a pang of anxious fear thrilled his breast like a foreboding that the time was not far distant when he would be forced to bury his youthful ideals. He did not wish to believe in wickedness; and though Burrus's words had sowed fresh doubts in a heart already corroded by distrust, it was so much more comfortable, so much pleasanter, not to see ugliness, or at least to excuse it by a little expenditure of neighborly love.

True, Nero, when he reflected seriously, was not what he should be; Octavia was unhappy; while Petronius was talking, one felt convinced of his sincerity, when he ceased speaking, one felt ashamed of having listened to him; Poppaea could please no pure-hearted person; the rest of the Caesar's train were of little worth; the singers, actors, zither-players, and dancers were undoubtedly swindlers; the inhabitants of Rome, especially the stoics, dandies, barbers, tavern-keepers, and slaves by no means suited the ideas of an honorable man; but there were probably exceptions, and perhaps the dealings of all these people appeared more reprehensible than they really were. Or did Burrus wish to deprive him of the Caesar's favor? What did he mean by saying that he must not imperil the virtuous? Had he not always respected virtue? No, Burrus was a slanderer; Petronius meant honestly by him. How much more pleasantly the latter's words had sounded; how evident it was that Burrus desired to bring him into a quarrel with Nero! Such were the thoughts contending in the artist's troubled mind; but before he had reached any definite conclusion, he felt some one clasp his hand, and a boy's voice asked: "What is the name of that star, twinkling so brightly over yonder temple?"

Metellus looked down into the beautiful, innocent face of his new slave, passed his hand over his waving black hair, and said,—

"I am no astrologer, my Stephanus; perhaps it is Cyllaros."

"Oh," cried the lad, "please tell me if it is shining over Greece."

"I cannot tell you even that," answered the youth, "but it is possible."

The boy's head drooped mournfully, and his master asked him why he was so sad. The lad shook his head. "I do not know," he answered.

"You do not know?"

"No."

"That is strange!"

Then both were silent,

"Oh, my lord," Stephanus suddenly exclaimed, raising his large, timid eyes, "can you take me to Greece?"

"Greece is far away from here, my friend," said Metellus.

"Far away from here!" murmured the boy, in assent, gazing dreamily at the stars as if he could discern in them the mountains of Hellas.

"Why do you wish to be taken to Greece?" asked the master.

But Stephanus made no reply, and, after some time, said in a low tone: "I am hungry."

Metellus ordered food to be brought; and the lad eagerly drank the milk, while Metellus watched him silently, still pondering over the warning he had just received from Burrus, The grace with which the slave handled the dishes attracted his attention, and, in the midst of his serious reflections, he could not help suddenly bursting into a laugh, as he saw the boy eating so eagerly, especially as Stephanus, after every mouthful, looked across at him as though to get permission to go on.

"Stephanus," he called.

"Yes, my lord?"

"Why do you always breathe through your mouth, instead of through your nose?"

"I don't know, my lord," said the boy, smiling. This way of breathing compelled the little fellow to keep his lips parted, giving his face the expression of dreamy yearning which we admire in the Greek statues, and which now filled the artist's heart with delight.

"How old are you, Stephanus?"

"Fourteen, my lord."

"Where do your parents live?"

"I don't know my parents," he answered carelessly, without showing any sorrow. Metellus, moved with compassion, asked in what country he was born; but Stephanus could not tell him, though he spoke with strange emotion of a rich, mild land, with cool groves, numerous temples, and lofty, cloud-capped mountains. There he had rested on beautiful meadows among the goats, and an older friend had played to him on a reed-flute; but never at noon-day, when the sun rested so stilly upon the woods, when the goats slept, and only the fountain murmured, for at that hour, his friend had told him, they must not wake the sleeping Pan. Oh, it was so beautiful when the shepherds in their shaggy garments met to sing songs for the prize of a cheese or a cup of wine, and the shepherds had so often contended about him and kissed him, while the little kids frisked merrily about.

"And do you know nothing at all about your parents?" asked Metellus when he paused. The boy shook his head.

"I will be your father, Stephanus," said Metellus, holding out his hand; "will you love me very dearly?"

"Oh, I do love you," said the boy, rushing to his master, patting his cheeks, and smiling so sweetly that Metellus, deeply touched, kissed his parted lips.

"You do love me?" asked Metellus; "why do you love me?"

"I will not tell that," replied the boy.

"You will not tell?"

"No."

"Come, tell me!"

But he could not be induced to speak, and pressed his lips tightly together, breathing, for the first time, through his nose. Metellus jestingly shook him, and threatened him, laughing, with blows.

"You will not hurt me," cried the boy; "beat me, if you wish."

The artist released him, protesting that he might expect it, which, however, the boy did not believe.

"I am sleepy," he said after a time, and, sitting down in a chair, watched his master over the back, as the latter turned the pages of a book.

"But you will give me a reed-flute, if I serve you well, will you not?" asked Stephanus suddenly, yawning.

"Ah, now I know why you love me, you rogue," replied Metellus; "you think I will make you plenty of gifts?"

The boy smiled; and his master promised him a reed-flute, which seemed to delight him, for he sometimes fingered his lips as if he already possessed the instrument.

Gradually Stephanus became less and less talkative, and only nodded wearily when his master looked up at him from his book. There was something wonderfully trusting in this nod; but soon he ceased to make it, and when, after an unusually long interval, the reader turned toward him, he found that he had fallen asleep with his head on the back of the chair.

Metellus laid his Ovid down, carried the sleeper carefully to the tawny lion-skin which adorned the marble floor beside his couch, and threw himself wearily on the cushions. After extinguishing the lamp, he gazed a long time at the delicate features of the child stretched upon the floor, over whose beautiful limbs the moonbeams were weaving a silvery network. He also scanned, with the eyes of his soul, the countenance of the unhappy Empress. Were the words of Burrus true? Did the shadow of the nether world already rest upon that noble brow? He resolved to track out the secret. Yet never had he felt so content as at that moment; no mournful reflections should steal into his heart now. He experienced genuine paternal affection as he thought that here at his feet rested a life which was dependent on his love, his favor. A weight like a heavy coat of mail fell from his breast, when he remembered that perhaps in the wide world there might be a noble woman's heart that beat for him, shared his weal and woe. "Thou bearest within thy soul the greatest protection against the malicious power of Fate," he said to himself; "what can be wrested from thee henceforward?" How gladly he would have thanked the gods for the happiness they had bestowed upon him, but he no longer found them when he sought them; they did not respond to his call. Outside in the gardens their pale images glimmered in the moonbeams; but they were lifeless masks; they smiled indifferently, unsympathizingly, majestically, in the silvery light.

Stephanus muttered a few Greek words in his sleep; Metellus asked what he wanted; but the lad did not rouse from his slumber.

"The poor boy will freeze," said Metellus, pushing his pillow under his head and wrapping the purple coverlet of the couch over his graceful limbs.

CHAPTER VII

A FEW days after the incidents just related, a little group had gathered on the portico of the stately reception-hall overlooking the palace gardens. The Empress was reclining upon a couch which, shaded by a purple awning stretched from several trees, stood half under the branches of the little grove of lemon trees, half under the gilded columns. Her face looked brighter to-day than ever before; one might almost say that her eyes sometimes glowed with fervid passion, and only very rarely a shadow suddenly fell upon her brow. Then she gazed absently into vacancy, but soon roused herself forcibly from her melancholy mood and tried to glance about her with a smile.

Seneca, Andromachus, and Burrus were seated around her couch; while in the centre of the company, with his back turned to the dark yew-hedge, stood a young, long-haired, very lank personage, clad in a somewhat shabby toga, reading aloud his first work,—Odysseus.

At first all listened attentively; Seneca sometimes expressing his pleasure by a nod; only the slave-girl Meroe, who, as usual, was lying at her mistress's feet, instead of attending to the divine sufferer, occupied herself in catching the flies which took refuge in the cool twilight of the colonnade from the scorching heat of the sun in the gardens.

The delivery, of the drama, which was distinguished by admirable choice of words, but suffered from prolonged monologues and very weak delineation of character, lasted a long time; Andromachus began to yawn slightly, which he tried to conceal by skilful movements of the hand; Burrus looked very sullen, and was mentally execrating Seneca, who had promised to afford the party an intellectual treat through the long-haired dramatist; the Empress after the fourth scene had listened only occasionally; Seneca alone held out, apparently finding great enjoyment in the bombastic words. He was the young poet's patron, and had aided him to obtain the honor of reading his work to the Empress.

The latter had readily given the honored philosopher, who eagerly praised his protege's talent, permission to present the youthful genius. The long- haired writer heeded neither Octavia's wearied looks, nor the muttered oaths of Burrus, which he probably received as signs of approval, but thundered forth his trimeters in a voice which, owing to prolonged use, was growing somewhat hoarse. When any specially pathetic passage occurred, he ventured to lift his glowing eyes over the edge of his manuscript to note the effect of his verses; and if the Empress, startled from her reverie, nodded with her wonted graciousness, the happy youth threw his head back proudly, or swept his wiry hair away from his forehead with his hand. Andromachus, to keep off drowsiness, was already counting the gilded ornaments on the pillars; Burrus had caught the contagion of his neighbor's yawning,—when at last the poet, raising his hand, took a somewhat deeper breath in order to prepare worthily for the approaching catastrophe. The Empress availed herself of this opportunity to cut the bewildered declaimer of verse short with the exclamation: "Magnificent, very beautiful!" True, a glance from the interrupted author, who even believed that he detected her in a yawn which the ejaculation was intended to conceal, rebuked her.

"Very beautifully expressed," cried Octavia, somewhat embarrassed, and quoting, "'Thou art the torment of Cupid, the gods, and men.' Very beautiful!"

"No—'thou art the happiness,'" corrected the irritated poet, but it was of no avail. The spell was broken. Burrus instantly chimed in, declaring that the effect of the drama was too concentrated to enjoy it all at once; an interval of several days was necessary to prepare for the proper appreciation of the second part. Seneca expatiated in detail upon the beauties of the lines they had just heard, and was warmly supported by Octavia.

"You have bestowed a very pleasant hour upon us," she said graciously. "Your sentences do not lack depth, and your comparisons are very learned, borrowed from the teachings of the gods."

The happy dramatist, greatly flattered,, smiled; and Andromachus used his privilege as a physician to request the Empress to have some food set before the young man, whose delicate constitution had evidently suffered from the delivery of his impressive verse. Octavia assented to this suggestion; so the poor dramatist was obliged to pocket his manuscript, which, when cold roast meat and wine were offered to him, he did by no means reluctantly. He even smiled and condescended, with much dignity, to make the remark that he had distributed the food of the gods and received in return the good things of earth. He took the food with the contempt of a god dwelling among mortals; and after arranging his shabby toga picturesquely, he devoted himself to the viands as eagerly as if for three days nothing but words had passed his lips.

The Empress asked one of the slave-girls for Metellus, and, in a low tone, bade her request him to spend the afternoon in her society. Then she beckoned to Burrus, and while the hungry poet was absorbed in the pleasures of the table, conversed eagerly with the soldier. Burrus perceived very plainly that Octavia constantly endeavored to bring up her favorite subject,—the traits of Metellus's character; but he avoided it with the tact which all frank people involuntarily display toward secrets. He secretly regretted that he had told his mistress the day before something about his visit to Metellus; but as this could no longer be recalled, he intimated by brief answers, and looks of annoyance, how tiresome the whole matter was to him, and how earnestly he desired not to be honored with an insight into the heart of the august lady.

Octavia put her questions very cleverly, and with smiling ease, as if she expected to hear only pleasant answers. It was evident that she was watching eagerly for some remark the sculptor had made about her. Meanwhile, she knew how to cloak her ardent curiosity with feminine dissimulation; the more her heart flamed, the more quietly she spoke of indifferent matters, till, with marvellous sophistry, she suddenly turned the sentence to her main topic. Burrus could not follow these leaps, nay, even evasion was becoming difficult enough. When his sovereign mistress asked what reply Metellus had made when he heard that her safety was endangered, the rough warrior looked another way and intimated that the news had disturbed the boy—he always intentionally called him the boy— very little.

"I cannot believe it," cried Octavia, at this information. "No! He is interested in my fate!"

"I think you are mistaken," answered Burrus, wrathfully; "the youth —lives in the present, and troubles himself neither about the gods nor you—"

"The subject of our conversation is no longer a boy," the Empress contradicted, blushing; but Burrus muttered something about "beardless lad."

"It does not matter whether he wears a beard or not," answered Octavia, with flashing eyes, in a louder tone than before; "the beard does not make the man, Burrus, nor even give him intellect. But I know that Metellus is interested in my fate, and no one shall rob me of this consolation,—or can you give me proofs of the contrary? True, if you could do this, you would be my enemy—"

"You forget yourself, noble lady," whispered Burrus, gazing in alarm at the agitated Empress, whose eyes were beginning to fill with tears.

"I forget myself?" she said laughing nervously, "and why should I not forget myself? What have I to lose? Do you suppose I conceal that I feel for this youth—" she stopped abruptly as she met the old soldier's glance, which had suddenly become fixed and imperious, and looked around her as if waking from a dream, while her lower lip quivered violently. She had incautiously revealed the secret of her heart; yet this caused her only a fleeting sense of confusion; but the thought that the man on whom it was bestowed could have remained indifferent to the news of her expected destruction suddenly filled her soul with a dreary sense of emptiness, oppressed her bosom with the weight of unshed tears. It seemed as if she had now lost herself, and in self-pity must utter a compassionate " woe is me!" over her life. After a long pause, Burrus broke the silence.

"I hope we had no listeners," he said quietly; while his royal mistress was trying to calm herself. Apparently to aid her in regaining her composure, Burrus told the news that some new Greek pantomimists had appeared at court, and yesterday, when they played Paris and Helen, the Helen, by the Emperor's orders, had worn a mask bearing the features of Poppaea Sabina. When censured for this, he said: "Pshaw, my wife must be satisfied with the title of Empress."

"What has befallen our Mistress?" interrupted the talkative Seneca, who, standing at the other end of the hall, had been watching the conversation between the two.

"What? So depressed, august lady, and just now you were so gay?" he continued, approaching the couch with Andromachus; "what has happened?"

"I was telling the Empress about Poppaea," said Burrus, harshly.

"Ah!" replied Seneca, fixing his eyes on the floor; while the dramatist, who was still eating, looked toward the group. Andromachus exchanged glances with Burrus, cleared his throat, and, as was his habit, frowned.

"Our Mistress knows," he began earnestly, "how highly we esteem her, regarding her as the one pure star shining in unclouded radiance above the mire of this court life. Our Mistress knows how important it is for us to be able to hold her up as a contrasting picture to profligacy and wickedness. The better class of the Roman people need you, oh. Mistress, to refresh themselves by the sight of you when, on the brink of despair, they ask the gods in horror whether fidelity, purity, nobleness of nature are only meaningless words on earth. That is why we stand before your throne to sustain you on it as long as possible, and to remove every danger which threatens your august existence. For the sake of the Roman people, our Mistress will avoid every step which might be misinterpreted and lead to her downfall."

Andromachus had emphasized the last words strongly, and Burrus added with a tremulous voice: "How easy it is for a spy to make things appear suspicious. At this court, the executioner's axe is formed from the mist of conjecture."

All were silent; the Empress still held her blushing face bowed; each knew what the other was thinking, but no one expressed it in words; Burrus and Andromachus exchanged meaning glances. At last the royal woman slowly raised her head; they could hear her panting breath as she closed her dazzled eyes.

"Do you really believe that I am necessary in this world, necessary to the Roman people?" she asked.

"With you the last prop of the noble minded will be broken," said Andromachus; "what will our people think, to what will they cling in their distress, if even you—" he paused, and Burrus finished the sentence in a whisper: "Can no longer be held up to them as the ideal of chastity?"

Octavia shuddered.

"I am still mistress of my acts, I hope," she said in a low tone, but with repellent haughtiness, then, looking up at Andromachus, added: "Tell me how the city and the court judge me, what is said among the people."

Andromachus, fearing that he must touch upon the painful and delicate details, was silent; and the Empress, instantly conjecturing the cause, said with a defiant emphasis: "Have you nothing better to do than to listen to the gossip of the taverns, the stories of the Circus? They are the source of all your wisdom, all your suspicion. Do not come to me again with the oracular speeches of slaves or the philosophy which my husband's weary dancers ponder over at their banquets. You think you understand me; but you are utterly mistaken."

Enraged that, in her lofty position, she could have no secrets, she threw her fan upon the floor, and tears filled her eyes as she struggled to find words. She was forced to approve the warnings of her friends; she knew that they were doing their duty as loyal, honest men, and this knowledge angered and wounded her. Her friends had read her soul, perhaps had listened to the voices of the people, and only made just remonstrances that she must control herself, must be more than mortal.

To be loved once at least before her death! Might she not wish that? Was she to be denied what was permitted to all, merely because from it might be forged the axe which would give her forever to Orcus? Because spies watched her every step? Must she be forbidden to obey the impulse of her lonely heart, which, for the first time, had found a heart? Yes, it would have been beautiful to love and to be loved, but it was also beautiful to stand like an unsullied marble statue amid the corruption of this age, an emblem of all goodness, a second Lucretia, upon whom even the most venomous scandal could not cast a single drop of poison. What should her choice be? There was yet time to avoid the man for whom her still inexperienced heart yearned. Then every temptation would vanish, and she would stand worthy of adoration. Nay, mortals had often been transported to a place among the gods; perhaps the same fate might be allotted to her ? A lofty thought! Worthy of resigning earthly joys for its sake! As, absorbed in this conflict, she raised her eyes to Andromachus, she met his pitying gaze, and rising from her cushions with a sigh, like a person suffering from physical illness, she held out her little jewelled hand to the physician. No one except Seneca noticed the almost jealous expression on worthy

Burrus's face; no one saw how fiercely he gripped his sword-hilt between his fingers.

"There comes our friend," exclaimed Seneca, as Metellus walked down the hall toward them.

Octavia averted her face as soon as she perceived him, but quickly turned toward him, again surveying him with an admiring glance. Every movement stirred her soul; there was a charm in the melancholy droop of his head which thrilled her whole being; yet she was forced to maintain her imperial majesty when she would so gladly, casting aside all restraint, have appeared a simple woman.

Metellus came forward carelessly, as usual, without heeding his surroundings. When he had entered the circle, he noticed that all were silent, and felt that they had probably been talking about him. At the same time he saw the dramatist, who sat with dilated eyes, the image of terror and amazement. If his hair had not been so long, it would certainly have bristled on his head as he perceived that Metellus, whose glance at first had been absent, was now looking at him more closely; . but he might console himself. Even had the artist recognized him as the beggar who, during the night that he wandered through the streets of Rome, had stolen his last denarius, he would at most have smiled over the stoic's present metamorphosis. But he did not know him, which fact made the poor poet, in his joy, drink several cups of wine.

Octavia's struggle had ceased at the first sight of her favorite. Andromachus saw, with regret, how unreservedly, almost casting aside her imperial dignity, she gave herself up to her feelings, begging the artist to draw his own likeness with a few strokes by means of a mirror held before him. A slave-girl brought the glass, and the royal lady's manner of giving it to him had a shade of defiance, as if she wished to say: "Let them talk as they please, I love you!"

Metellus, on receiving the mirror, looked at his patroness a long time with the wondering timidity which pure natures feel in the presence of a strange, overmastering passion, and then asked why he should draw himself. Octavia evaded the question, and when Metellus, with his innocent want of tact, still continued to gaze at her, she began to be uncomfortable in the presence of those who surrounded her. She avoided the look, which seemed to ask: "Unhappy one, what do you want to do with me? Why do you disturb my peace?" She felt the gaze as steadily as the sleeper feels the noontide sun, and meanwhile had the painful consciousness that her noblest friends were displeased with her. When she remembered what lofty support the conversation of Andromachus had often afforded her soul, she was seized with an emotion of self-contempt; when she saw the frowning brow of her teacher, Seneca, she felt with shame how little honor she was now doing to his wisdom. She would gladly have avoided Burrus's sullen face too.

Scarcely a word was spoken while Metellus sketched before the mirror, and the royal lady carelessly watched him; an uncomfortable silence brooded over the group, which was interrupted only by the smacking of the poet's tongue as, though already half intoxicated, he continued to drink.

The artist sketched with a rapidity that showed he would rather have studied some other face than his own. He was wholly unconscious of his surroundings, and more than once was tempted to lay down the brush and ask the Empress: "Is your life really threatened?" Though he did not see her, he felt her presence surrounding him like a perfume; and the possibility that death might snatch her from him lent her fresh charms in his eyes. He did not know whether he loved her, and pondered over the matter the less because he had very vague ideas of love.

"It must be extremely difficult to draw by the aid of a mirror," said Octavia, at last, to break the silence, which had gradually become as oppressive as a block of glowing marble. The poet rose as he heard the question, and, waving a goblet gracefully in one hand, staggered toward the group.

"The credit of inventing this mode of taking portraits," he said with a somewhat stammering tongue, "belongs to us Greeks. It was a woman named Jaia, who first thought of painting herself before the mirror."

Then, precisely as if the question had been addressed to him, he discussed Art, praised those who honored it, condemned others, and dilated at length upon his theories of painting, which he could do the more undisturbed as no one contradicted him, and Seneca was the only person who listened. He had by no means finished the first part of his discourse when a slave came rushing in.

"The Emperor," he cried breathlessly, "the Emperor is coming, with zither- players and mimes."

In fact the voices of a large number of people, engaged in eager conversation, were already heard approaching the hall from the garden. Metellus was continuing to sketch; but Burrus snatched the sheet and flung it hastily behind a pillar; then while the others hastened forward to meet the Caesar, he tried to make the Empress understand by significant glances the necessity for taking the step. The artist had clenched his fists when the drawing was torn from him, and was on the point of demanding a reckoning with his enemy, who measured him with reproachful glances. But Octavia cast a beseeching glance at the wrathful youth, whose clenched hands relaxed, while his angry features regained their former composure. Nero's appearance also instantly put an end to the quarrel.

Preceded by two lictors, the Caesar, with rustic pomposity, led the procession, which consisted of flute-players, zither-players, and mimes, and was followed by Petronius and Poppaea Sabina. Nero had wound a toga around his body in clumsy folds that made him look almost like a rotund oil-jar, roses hung over his brow, and his fat hands fingered his hips. So, with a half- boyish, half-theatrical manner, he strode towards his wife as clumsily as an Egyptian stone colossus, smiling at her with his fat face. At first he pretended to be surprised to find the Empress here, and only a few detected the cheat, for, as a skilful actor, he acquitted himself admirably in the character he had assumed.

90

"Pardon me, if I disturb you," he said, pointing to the gay party, who bowed low before the Empress. "I wanted to afford myself a little amusement. Some excellent actors of pantomime have arrived from Greece, admirable artists! It is fortunate that you happen to be in the gardens. Let us try their skill together. I think you will not object if they delight our eyes with a play." Octavia bent her . head in token of assent, while Metellus, leaning against a pillar at the back of the hall, surveyed the scene. The Empress would gladly have avoided the play, nay, she already had a suitable apology on her lips; but though she despised her husband, his presence exerted a certain constraint, a power over her nervous system, as though she was on the verge of confronting the outbursts of some incalculable power of nature. She could not help obeying him, and it was a singular fact that, since the death of Britannicus, her husband's character was beginning almost to awe her. The influence emanating from this man was like the alarming paralyzing effect of an approaching thunderstorm. It was not because she feared him; the rascally skill in dissimulation, the easy unscrupulousness which he had displayed since the murder, robbed her of her former firmness. Not only she herself, but every one since that day, had seemed, in the Emperor's presence, like flies whose wings had been torn off by a cruel boy.

Smiling patronizingly, thoroughly content with himself, the dreaded sovereign sat down beside Octavia; the others grouped themselves about the hall; and his smile, as he now ordered the play to begin, was as kind as the operator's who, cutting into his patient's flesh, says: "Only keep quiet, my friend, you will soon be better!"

"What long-haired flag-pole is that?" he asked, turning to Octavia, as his eyes fell upon the poet, who had been trying to attract attention by all sorts of striking attitudes and frantic gesticulations. Seneca informed him; and Nero, who liked to have authors patronized at his court, ordered the poor parasite to approach him and addressed him as " honorable colleague." The long- haired dramatist, almost breathless from rapture and embarrassment, bowed repeatedly; the Caesar inquired about the drama, and, although he must have seen that the fellow was not fully in possession of his senses, treated him very graciously, respectfully, nay, almost humbly, and even extended his hand to him, saying: "Only continue, my friend; the laurel grows for every brow. I hope you know that I myself sometimes serve the Muses. What do you think of my 'Niobe'?"

The Caesar evidently waited with anxiety for the opinion of his colleague, bent his head to catch his answer, and, when the verdict was naturally very favorable, intimated that he had made the acquaintance of a discerning man. The poet, cleverly taking advantage of the opportunity, now colored his praise more highly, and Nero, who could receive a great deal in this line, listened intently, motioning to the others not to interrupt the speaker. The dramatist was scarcely dismissed, when the imperial poet, with a sigh of relief, whispered to the prefect of police, who sat beside him: "Try to get possession of his drama. If it is good, burn it; if it is bad, spread it!"

Meanwhile two mimes, very beautifully formed youths, had taken their places before the dark yew-hedge, while two flute-players and a zither-player stationed themselves at the left of the spectators. A herald called: "Aeneas and Dido will be danced."

The exquisite figures of the dancers were charmingly relieved against the dark foliage, above which arched the deep blue sky; the sun shone on their anointed, perfumed limbs, lending them the shimmer of marble. The one who personated Dido was barely eighteen, and, as he tied on his mask, every one noticed that it bore, by accident, a resemblance to Octavia's features. How Metellus, when he perceived this, envied the dancer, who, as the flutes now strove to imitate the rumble of a thunderstorm, darted off, scarcely touching the ground. The other, who was somewhat older, carried a quiver of arrows and a spear. Soon he, too, rushed into the dance. Dido shrank back; the music grew more melting, the dancing less rapid. Softer and softer grew the harmonies; the movements of the youths followed the yearning tones; they no longer danced singly but together, while the language of their hands became more eloquent. The lad of eighteen represented Dido's timidity admirably; she repelled and lured at the same time, encouraged and restrained. Aeneas embraced her; the pair stood motionless a moment, graceful as statues, then she released herself and fled; he pursued, and she, swaying to the sweetest tones, paused full of trembling expectation. Aeneas timidly approached, laying his hand upon her arm. The spectators were excited to the utmost, for the scene which now followed described the conquest of the cold beauty with a keenness of observation and grace of motion, an artistically refined sensuality, which not only supplied the place of words, but expressed more than they could have done. Their fingers, especially, took the place of thoughts; and when at last Dido yielded and Aeneas kissed her, endless applause burst forth, in which Metellus also joined.

The Empress had watched the play with fixed eyes, as if she wished to shake off its enthralling spell; Metellus's soul, on the contrary, had received, as if by magic, revelations concerning the nature of love. He now knew what he desired; the music had whispered what love was; the feigned ardor of the dancer had kindled his courage, transformed the modest boy into a bold man. His fevered glance met Octavia's fixed, startled eyes; she felt the youth's gaze, yet did not turn her head, but sat as though cast in bronze; and Nero was forced to repeat his question how she liked the play a second time, before, rousing herself as if from a stupor, she replied that it had by no means pleased her taste.

During the whole performance Petronius had not lost sight of his victims, Metellus and the Empress, and his observations seemed to have satisfied him; for when the Caesar rose, he nodded as if in confirmation.

Nero asked to see the portrait bust of Octavia which had been commenced. The Empress, still absorbed by her own thoughts, motioned to her slaves and was about to retire to her own apartments; but Andromachus, pressing his way through the group, whispered to her that she must stay, this hasty withdrawal might give opportunity for all sorts of interpretations. With compressed lips, downcast eyes, and pallid face, she stood beside her clay bust, which, meanwhile, had been brought, steadying her trembling figure by resting her left hand on the back of a chair, while her husband, smiling pleasantly, pointed out the beauties of the bust. He undoubtedly perceived his wife's agitation, for his smile revealed unusual satisfaction.

"Just see this line!" he said to his courtiers; "how beautiful it is; with what youthful grace it runs into the neck; and what sweet melancholy rests upon this brow! Yet Art has but stumbled lamely after nature; our sculptor must confess that he will never catch the beauty of the mouth."

Then, turning to Metellus, whose eyes were glittering with a feverish lustre, he asked, suddenly assuming a foolish, waggish expression, whether the neck was really quite so long in the original? And when Metellus, not noticing the movement which ran through the group of spectators, replied that perhaps it might be shortened slightly, without violating fidelity to nature, Nero answered in a good-natured tone,—

"Oh, yes! We will shorten it a little!" With these words he withdrew, after kissing his wife's brow, in which he skilfully acted the part of a languishing lover by means of sighs and glances.

Octavia also retired to her apartments without casting even a single glance at Metellus. After reaching them, she paced up and down several times like a prisoner, a prey, for the first time in her life, to anxious fear. It was long ere she succeeded in again calming her troubled soul. She stilled her panting breath, forced herself to move quietly, and learned the advantage which mental training could afford in the fateful moments of life; for, to her own astonishment, she succeeded by reflection in explaining the dull movements of blind impulse.

The Emperor's last words seemed to intimate that she would not long enjoy the light of the sun, and although prepared for death, the cold sentence had pierced her warm heart like a sword, robbed her for the moment of all self- control. Besides, she suddenly began, she knew not why, to fear Metellus. She had no suspicion of Nero's plans; she did not guess what he intended to accomplish through the young man; but the play just witnessed, which had described in such vivid detail the madness of love, had showed her, as in a mirror, the consequences of her passion, and she shrank in terror from herself. What could long remain concealed at this court? And if her love should become known, the Emperor would have found a safe means of justifying his deed of violence to the people; that he was trying to obtain this method she did not think. She feared Metellus, not only because he might be the cause of her death, but her delicate nature shrank from a closer union with him; the dance of the mimes, pleasing as it was, had dragged love down to the level of human nature, and this human love, of which, hitherto, she had thought only as if it were a dream, disgusted her. What had encouraged Metellus, disheartened her, made her fly from the young man as a sinister power, revealed him to her as the hideous soiler of her pure soul. And yet she loved the lovable fellow! Mortal terror, shame, and yearning blended so strangely in her soul, each of these feelings increased by the demands of the other, till at last the feminine one. conquered, and she was overpowered by the delirious rapture against which neither reason nor education avail, since it springs from a source that is unintelligible and supernatural.

"What shall I do?" she asked herself. "Let me touch his lips but once, then the headsman's clutch can tear me from the light of day." She had thrown herself on the couch with her face hidden on her arms, and suddenly started up as she felt a warm breath upon her hair. Meroe was bending over her mistress, and, as comedy so often blends with tragedy in life, Octavia, in springing up, struck the good creature violently on the chin with the jewelled ornament in her hair. The girl, with the drollest grimaces, tried to hide her pain; and her mistress, giving herself up entirely to her feelings for a moment, embraced her attendant. She did not weep; the muscles which bring tears quivered, but they did not flow.

Meroe played with her mistress's hair, and, half smiling, half angry, gripped her wounded chin. Why did Octavia cling to her so?

Why did her lips move without uttering any words? She relapsed into her usual childish mood, began to sing a lullaby, and then talked in a tone of rapture about Metellus. But she was greatly astonished when Octavia, hastily controlling herself, stopped her.

"Why mustn't I talk about him any more?" she asked in a half singing tone. "I dream about him so much at night, I can't help thinking of him all day too."

But her mistress answered,— "Silence, it wearies me."

"Ye gods, how pale you look to-day. Mistress," she murmured. "Shall I bring your red Babylonian rouge? And your eyes are so red, I will fetch the white Egyptian salve."

Octavia nodded, and sat motionless while Meroe was bringing the salves.

"What is it, what have you here?" she exclaimed when the slave-girl began to arrange the boxes on the table.

Only the rouge," laughed Meroe. The rouge?"

"Which you wanted."

"Wanted? I?" asked her mistress, and ordered her to take them away.

"Then put on your new robe," pleaded Meroe, "or will you take a bath?"

The Empress shook her head.

"Well, then, I will sing you an Egyptian love-song."

But Octavia refused this too.

"By Osiris, we will disguise ourselves and walk through the streets of Rome," the talkative girl proposed.

"No, Meroe, be sensible," said her mistress, reprovingly.

"Not that either?" cried the slave-girl. "Then I'll send for gladiators; we will see bleeding and dying men."

"Do not summon the dead too soon!"

"What, Mistress?"

"Be sensible, Meroe," said Octavia, gravely; "do you not know that your mistress must soon die?"

The word "die" sounded strangely to the slave-girl; she looked bewildered, and as Octavia, startled that it had escaped her lips, remained silent, the Egyptian laughed merrily.

"Die?" she cried. "By the Nile! I never saw you as you seem to-day. An Empress die! That is impossible. Die! How funny!" And she clapped her hands, still laughing. The sound hurt her mistress, though she bore the foolish girl no grudge for it; it represented the lack of sympathy of the world.

"Go," she said, fixing a stern, reproachful glance upon Meroe; "that is wicked, that is altogether too absurd."

She did not know herself what she had said, and, at any other time, would have been shocked at the absence of meaning in her words. But nothing better occurred to her; her brain was so hollow, so empty and an icy dagger seemed buried in her breast. But her mistress's reproving glance had amused rather than saddened Meroe. After a pause, during which the girl had been turning her forefinger in the rouge-pot, she pressed it on the end of her I nose, saying,—

"Die? What is that? • I know how a dead person looks, but not how he feels."

Then she again laughed, this time at her red finger, and hit upon the idea of painting half her face scarlet with the rouge, declaring with a yawn that the dullness was killing her.

"If I were like this child," thought the Empress, noticing that the girl, turning away from her, drew something from the folds of her robe, and held it close before her eyes. As her contemplation of the object lasted an unusually long time, Octavia's attention became attracted,—a suspicion arose in her mind, and she demanded an explanation.

Meroe, startled from her reverie, instantly slipped the article into the folds of her robe, and turned with a crafty smile.

"Guess who it is," she said. Her mistress wished to go to the bottom of the matter; a little dispute arose, and after much roguish hesitation, Meroe drew out the piece of papyrus containing the half-finished sketch of Metellus which Burrus had torn so rudely from the artist's hand.

"See, it is he," cried the girl; "it is his face, I found it behind a pillar in the audience-hall."

Octavia repressed her excitement, that she might gain possession of the papyrus without arousing suspicion; but all her eloquence would not induce Meroe to surrender her treasure, which she declared Metellus had put behind the pillar intentionally, that she might discover it She refused even the ornament that was offered, pressed the picture to her lips, and danced up and down the room with it, humming the commencement of an Egyptian love song.

After Octavia had watched the happy girl for a time almost with envy, a plan entered her mind which might possibly relieve her from the suspicion resting upon her, and restore her to her former position in the eyes of her friends. Scorning all secret paths, she had often been forced at this court to enter devious ways; enforced companionship with vice had brought even wise Seneca's head into controversy with his heart; Octavia therefore deemed herself sufficiently justified, if, as a woman, lacking every weapon, she sought refuge in strategy. Even the bravest love life, or, at least, sometimes fear death; in Octavia's breast a sudden sense of fear drove out every other consideration. "Escape for the moment!" cried a voice in her heart. "Let Meroe keep the picture, and hang it, if possible, in her sleeping-room. Any love-affair will be forgiven her; she will avert suspicion from me; and what, after all, is love? Can I not do without it? Am I not sufficient for myself? Do I need the sympathy of another? Time will help me calm my captivated imagination; and dost thou even know, oft deluded heart, whether thou art not again deceiving thyself? Thou seest a god in this man! Who knows what thou wouldst think of him in a few months? How many a praetor whom thou didst believe to be a man of lofty qualities, afterwards proved himself a base adventurer; how many a noble countenance was but the mask of selfish designs!"

Ordering a stylus and papyrus to be brought to her at once, she wrote a long letter to the Emperor, in which she entreated him to give up the completion of her bust, and send the young artist away from the court, as the latter's conduct was not exactly what she desired. Was it not better for him, as well as for her, that he should leave the palace? Reading the letter over, she was startled by the undue harshness of its expressions; she hastily corrected a few sentences which suggested a relation between the sculptor and one of the Empress's attendants, but could not resolve to send it in this form, and tore it up, ashamed of the feminine cowardice which had dictated it. Yet she resolved never to see Metellus again, and, whenever he appeared before her mental vision, to subject him to inexorable criticism and pitilessly destroy every bewitching charm that imagination strove to weave about his image.

When Burrus visited her, later in the evening, he found her apparently mentally aged. She was dining alone, served by a single maidservant, in the solitary, spacious apartment. The candelabrum faintly lighted the table, leaving the rest of the room in darkness. Behind her stood her major-domo, to whom she sometimes addressed a careless question. It seemed as if a corpse was dining, she took the dishes with such mechanical slowness, raised her heavy lids so wearily, appeared so utterly indifferent to everything around her. The magnificence of the floor, the gilding of pillars and furniture, which glittered in the reflection of the light, only enhanced the sorrowful effect of the scene. She ate because it is customary to eat, not from necessity. Honest Burrus watched her a long time with a gloomy face; his eyes, which had never wept, now glittered with a moister lustre than ever before. Octavia did not speak to him. The major-domo, in the dim light, was talking with a lower functionary about Sabina's toilet arts. The giggling of the two indicated that piquant gossiping tales were not omitted.

"She will soon be a fallen star, too," hissed one, and, as Burrus turned, the major-domo, to show his zeal, kicked a young slave who had fallen asleep on the floor. The little sleeper started up, exclaiming: "Has the cock crowed?" and the loud words broke strangely upon the solemn stillness of the room.

Just as the Empress had finished dining, Andromachus appeared, and glanced anxiously at Burrus, who, whispering a few words to his friend, withdrew. Andromachus went to the table, and as Octavia, pushing aside a dish from before her, looked up at him, he laid his hand with paternal affection upon the white brow of this woman of twenty. For an instant her face quivered with pain at the tender touch; then her expression grew grave to the verge of sternness, but at the same time she whispered, smiling to deceive the slaves who were present: "Your warning did not come too late; you will be satisfied with my conduct in future. I shall not see him again."

While uttering the words she had risen, perhaps to conceal her agitation. Andromachus, also smiling, although his heart was bleeding, answered,—

"I thank you. To-day's play tells me that you have the worst to fear."

Casting a suspicious glance at the dishes, he clasped the Empress's hand to feel her pulse. The latter understood him.

"Do not be anxious, I am provided with antidotes." She smiled as unconstrainedly as possible. Yet the smile barely relaxed her features a few seconds ere they resumed the expressionless rigidity of repressed passions. Andromachus remembered that Agrippina possessed such remedies; the latter had probably supplied the Empress with them. This was really the case; Octavia had carried with her for several days a little silver box filled with pills, which Agrippina had given her.

"It will be wise," Andromachus continued, glancing timidly around, "if you would thank the Emperor for the pleasure which the performance of the actors has afforded you."

As she looked at him questioningly, he added: "In order to dispel the suspicion that you guessed his thoughts."

Octavia's lips curled in anger; but she could not disapprove the well-meant counsel of her faithful friend; it had become the custom at court to meet the Emperor's plots by apparently falling in with them, in order to defer them.

"I suppose I ought also to thank him for his amiable criticism of my bust?" she exclaimed with a short, piercing laugh. A slave who entered to fan the flame of the candelabrum forced both to pause in their conversation.

"Mistress, you are making my hard task easier," said the leech, after the attendant had retired; "listen to me."

This time not only his brow, but almost his entire face was furrowed by wrinkles, as if drawn with pain.

"You know that the Caesar hates you. Well then! There is only one way of turning the thunderbolt aside, and it bears some resemblance to the expedient used by Seneca." The physician paused, scanning Octavia's face. After some time he continued,—

"Seneca offered the Emperor his wealth because he knew that, to obtain this fortune, Nero longed for his life. Yesterday Nero embraced the philosopher, declaring that never would he harm a hair of his teacher's head. That is the more credible because Seneca's skull is almost bald. You, oh, royal Mistress, now that the sight of you is annoying to the Caesar, must propose to him to banish you to some island."

"Banish!" cried the Empress, so loud that Andromachus looked around him in terror, lest some of the attendants had caught the echo of the word reverberating from the marble walls.

"And you expect me to stoop to such humiliation, you to whom I have looked up from childhood? You, my teacher?" she went on in a lower tone, drawing herself up to her full height.

"Conquer your reluctance, august lady," replied the leech. "Is it humiliation, when I appeal to generosity? Or when I outwit cunning? By Zeus, I would not advise it, were it not necessary for you to dissemble in this case. The Emperor will refuse your petition, and assure you of his friendship; he cannot do otherwise, since public opinion forces him to it. But your life will be saved by the humiliation—"

"Saved? For how long?" replied the Empress, vehemently.

"A few months at least," replied her friend, sorrowfully; "when we cherish new fears, we will devise new antidotes."

"No, Andromachus, the daughter of Claudius will not stoop to such degrading expedients," replied the wife of Nero. "Let the terrible monster do with me what he will, I will neither sue for mercy nor seek refuge in other subterfuges. How long can you escape the tiger with whom you are confined in the same arena?"

Turning away in embarrassment, the leech endeavored to convince the Empress of the necessity of his proposal; but neither the example of Seneca, nor the other arguments which he brought forward, could change the royal lady's resolution. She left the room, giving orders to admit no visitors.

"Then your friends must act for you," cried Andromachus, and went in search of Burrus.

It was about this time that Agrippina left Rome to go to Baise. When Nero's mother appeared in Octavia's apartments, the Empress at first appeared wholly inaccessible; but when she perceived that Agrippina, with a certain grandeur of character, alluded to her own speedy death, it aroused the younger woman's sympathies so deeply that the two at last parted from each other with mutual regard.

"He will send me to Orcus before you," Agrippina had said; "yet I am proud of having given the world an Emperor of Rome."

CHAPTER VIII

SINCE the performance of the play, a strange transformation had taken place in Metellus. Stephanus often saw him sitting silently in a chair, gazing into vacancy, or wandering along the garden paths with the step of an invalid. Sometimes he tried to exhaust his bodily strength by severe physical exercises, rushed as though tortured by mental anxiety from his room into the open air, and from the open air back again into his room; sometimes he lay idly, wearily, on his couch, and, forgetting the outside world, gave himself up to his thoughts. "Oh, if I had but been able to keep the oath I made to my friend," he often reflected, "I should have kept aloof from woman!"

If the boy nestled affectionately to his side, asking what troubled him, he usually received the reply that he would not understand.

"I shall understand, if you explain it to me," the little fellow answered; "I am not stupid."

"Your turn will come, too, some day," his master answered; "only have patience."

Then he embraced and kissed Stephanus, trying to believe that the love of this forsaken waif might divert his passion. Often he succeeded in turning his thoughts elsewhere; but he always felt as if he missed something. The boy, in his undeveloped nature, suspected what was occupying his master's mind, and almost felt jealous. He became quieter, more sullen; at which the artist, when he finally suspected the cause of the change, smiled.

"Come here, my pet," said Metellus; "don't be angry, you know that I am fond of you."

The boy turned sulkily away, and Metellus,, laughing, asked why he was so cross. As he received no answer, he sat down beside him on the lion-skin of the couch, and tried to talk pleasantly to him. Stephanus listened intently, and then said: "No, no; you are not telling the truth."

"What? Do I lie?"

"Are you really not lying?" asked the boy.

"How can you believe that I am?"

"Give me your hand."

"There it is."

"And you are really fond of me?"

"Very fond of you, Stephanus, you are my child, my son."

"I don't believe you," said the lad, shaking his head, "you are more fond of other people."

Metellus laughed, kissed him, and promised to get him the reed-pipe he wanted that very day.

Andromachus had tried to make friends with the artist, and, on the pretext that he noticed a nervous disease about him, advised him to leave Rome. Egypt would be the country to restore his nervous system. A ship

99

was lying in the harbor of Ostia, bound for Alexandria, and he himself would gladly advance the sum necessary for the journey. Metellus declared that he felt perfectly well. .

"At present," said the physician, "but the disease is one whose development is very rapid. Save yourself before it is too late; you know that we leeches are usually lovers of Art, I should be glad if I could preserve your life.

"Let the illness come," replied the youth, doggedly.

"And what if death should come?" asked Andromachus.

"Well? What then?" returned Metellus, shrugging his shoulders. When the physician obstinately persisted in his counsel, a feeling of defiance began to stir in the sculptor, who vaguely suspected his true motive. He answered more sharply, refused all advice, and at last became so disagreeable that the leech was obliged to leave him.

"You will regret having refused my offer," he said as he went away; and Metellus called after him,—

"What affair is it of yours?"

Greatly dissatisfied with himself, and most painfully conscious of his selfishness, Metellus had wandered through the streets of Rome one day to buy a copy of Virgil. In the book-shop he entered the publisher was talking with a young author about the market for the newest books. While, in the adjoining rooms, slaves were busily writing a work from dictation, the publisher, holding a roll in his hand, said to the very modest-looking author: "Your poems are really extremely beautiful, strong, and full of feeling; I have read no better verses for a long time; but, my friend, lyric poetry is entirely out of fashion in Rome. We want salt, not milk. Epigrams, not sweet love-songs. The sharper the satire, the better it pleases."

"I have no satirical vein," replied the young writer, sighing.

"That is a pity," observed the publisher, dryly; "but the vein will be developed when you have seen the Roman world for a while. I advise you to visit the taverns, or become reader to a rich man. That is a good school."

Then he returned the manuscript to the poet, saying again that the verses were remarkably fine. Meanwhile Metellus had been admiring the books bound in purple displayed along the walls; but when, judging the contents by the binding, he took out one of them to enjoy the wisdom of a Plato in beautifully written letters, he restored the supposed Plato, blushing, to its place. The magnificent binding contained a scurrilous story whose title was enough to repel any decent person. Asking for Virgil, he received a book whose outward appearance did not bear the slightest comparison to the wretched tale. The publisher shrugged his shoulders.

"You must write such works," he said to the young author; "then, my friend, you would not lack money from me."

The timid, hungry-looking poet shook his head and left the shop; while the book-seller, turning to the others, remarked,—

"A very talented fellow. But, ye gods, how can I help him? Critics would silence him, or tear him to pieces as a hungry wolf rends the lamb. He hasn't the money to bribe them."

When Metellus had bought the Virgil, he went to the bank of the river to see the landing of the wild beasts which had been sent from Africa to the imperial gardens. For some time he had found pleasure in stupefying his thoughts with vivid, savage scenes; only strong impressions could divert his mind from its perpetual visions and reflections. Passing through a dirty, narrow street, he felt the handle of a staff strike his knee, and, when he turned, he started back in alarm as the ugly features of a sunken-eyed Jewish woman grinned at him from the dark doorway of a house.

"What do you want, old witch?" escaped his lips, as the woman, beckoning to him with her withered finger, looked around to see if any one was watching her.

"Come into the house," she whispered.

Metellus, filled with loathing, could not resolve to accept the invitation; yet his curiosity was awakened, and he stood still. Shuffling nearer to him, she cautiously drew from her pocket a little silver box, rubbed it with her gray under-garment till it shone, then blinking roguishly at him, she whispered: "Can you guess what I have here?"

"Poison?" asked Metellus.

"Oh! For what do you take old Esther, Rufus's mother?" she gasped. "Poison? Why, yes! If you want to give it that name, it may be so; others call it by a different one."

"No, I thank you," he replied. "I have no enemies."

You are a happy man," she murmured, to have no foes. But stop a moment and look at the mixture more carefully. Are there not sweet poisons? Poisons which prolong life, instead of shortening it? H'm. What is a kiss, you rogue, except poison?"

"Let me alone," he muttered, turning to go.

"Don't scorn the old Jewess," she groaned, clinging to his cloak; "the Emperor himself sometimes asks the aid of our arts, and Poppaea Sabina prizes my cosmetics. Don't despise old Esther; I wish you well, my boy. Guess what I have here?"

Then, opening the box, she smelled its contents, and held it under Metellus's nose.

What fragrance!" she said coughing; your sweetheart's breath is not sweeter; may Jehovah's wrath overtake me if I did not brew this with my own hands and put mysterious ingredients into it."

Then, rolling up her eyes till only the whites were visible within the red rims, she sang in a shrill tone a hymn that bore a strong resemblance to the Song of Solomon, but interrupted herself at the words: "Thou art beautiful, beloved, yes, beautiful"—and whispered: "Three denarii, my master!" Then she went on singing: "Thou art beautiful, yes, beautiful as the sun." Metellus suspected that this was a love-philter. The blood rushed to his brain; his heart throbbed when he thought what happiness the little silver vessel might bestow upon him. The old woman, seeing his agitation, continued to praise the mixture, and give directions for its use, in doing which, as if by accident, she dropped the little silver box.

Metellus picked it up, thrust it half reluctantly into his pocket, and, at the same time, let three denarii fall upon the ground.

"That's right, young fellow," said the old crone, coughing, "don't forget, one half of it dissolved in wine."

Wondering at his hasty resolve, horrified at himself, Metellus was hurrying away as fast as possible, but was stopped by the appearance of Rufus, who, in full armor, was coming down the street and instantly clasped his hand.

"Have you been visiting my mother?" asked the soldier, pointing to the old Jewess; "you are wise; she is a clever woman,"

Rufus's haughty manner had changed to an almost cringing humility. He regarded the youth whom a few months ago he had heartily despised, as if he were a higher military officer, which caused the artist, who received Nero's favors without losing his sense of independence, no little embarrassment. .

"You have become a powerful man, oh, lord," sighed the soldier; "it beseems me to listen to your commands."

Metellus rejected all these humble speeches, though they began to gratify his pride; and when Rufus courteously invited him to enter the house, he accompanied him. The old Jewess retreated into a dark corner of the dirty, dilapidated room, from which she watched the two men with glowing eyes. The cracks in the walls were covered with strips of papyrus; a rusty tripod, an old bedstead, and two broken pots constituted the entire household furniture. The artist, who soon found the place uncomfortable, took his leave and went away. Scarcely had he left the wretched apartment, when the warrior, removing his armor, sank down with a heavy sigh upon the couch, which creaked in every joint. The old woman glided softly up to him, and, seeing blood-stains on the dirty woollen coverlet, started and then said in a trembling voice,—

"My son Rufus, the apple of my eye! You have again been made to feel the centurion's lash upon your back."

Rufus uttered a disagreeable laugh, while the evening breeze whistled through the chinks of the dilapidated room.

"My son, let me rub the Egyptian salve upon the stripes on your back; let your old mother apply the salve which she has made so carefully herself."

"Let them bleed, mother," he answered, using the Hebrew tongue.

The old woman glided to a cupboard in the wall, from which she took several boxes of ointment, and then, with a sorrowful face, approached her son's couch; but he did not stir.

"Rise," she said at last, "and let me bandage your wounds."

"They must bleed," he answered.

"God of our Fathers," wailed Esther, "he says: 'They must bleed;' why must they bleed if we can bind them up?"

"The wounds cool my soul, mother," groaned the son; "when I am suffering physical pain, I do not feel the pangs within. Or can you give me a salve to ease the burning of my heart?"

"I wish I could, Rufus, I wish I could," the old woman whimpered. "But tell me, why have they bruised your back; why have they beaten my son, whom I bore under my heart as honestly as any Roman woman, and nourished with my own milk?" Rufus was silent. Esther felt his thoughts as though they were her own. He was suffering under the idea of his low station; the fate of the more fortunate Metellus filled him with envy and gnawed at his ambitious soul. She crouched on the floor with a troubled heart; drawing her upper lip under her lower one, she brooded over her plans. "I will raise him," she said to herself, "I will endure the sight of his grief no longer."

Evening closed in, but both remained silent in the same attitudes. Sometimes shuffling steps echoed from the street, now filled with the disease- breeding blue mists of the Tiber. At the end of an hour Rufus rose from the couch, wrapped himself in a military cloak, and left the house. Esther knew where he was going. She had learned that he loved and visited every evening a family whose daughter's life he had saved. He himself never uttered a word about the matter; and when she sometimes questioned him about it, he seemed annoyed.

"He shall be happy," she murmured; "what is life to old Esther if her son is consuming his days in misery and yearning for power? The Romans have gods to whom they pray; well then, I will become his good goddess, who will advance him to a position near the imperial throne."

She had scarcely finished her soliloquy, when she heard voices outside the door of the house. They seemed familiar, for she smiled, and was not at all disturbed when a muffled figure entered the room. She was too much accustomed to hear the robes of the rich rustle in her poor dwelling , and when the stranger stood still in the apartment, she at once assumed the tone of a friendly acquaintance.

"The lofty visit the lowly," she said coughing. "Lay aside your cloak; I know your wishes."

The muffled figure motioned toward the door, then moved nearer, and sank wearily into a chair, which she had first dusted with the end of her mantle.

"What a long way! And the perfume in
your palace is not very pleasant, old Esther," she whispered, in a somewhat agitated tone. ** My maid brings a legion of vermin with her whenever she comes from you."

"Why does not the noble lady send her servant," answered the old woman.

"What I have to arrange with you this time has nothing to do with cosmetics, Jewess, nor even love-philters," whispered the aristocrat, carefully shrouding her face and apparently very impatient.

"Ah! you need poison this time?" said Esther, offering her patroness a cushion. "Is a rich heir to be removed from the world? What? Have you a faithless lover?"

She had moved nearer to her visitor, and her greenish eyes were trying to discover, through the openings in the mask, the features beneath it. But as soon as the lady perceived it, she averted her face.

"Don't trouble yourself, old woman," she murmured nervously. "You do not know me; and woe betide you if you recognize my person, for I am powerful."

Esther noticed that her guest was beginning to fear her, and, extremely flattered, she at once spread out on the floor—in order duly to display her knowledge—all her glasses, bottles, lamps, and mixtures, explaining with great importance the power of the various salves, most of which, she asserted, had been invented by Egyptian kings.

"Let us come to the point, old woman," said the veiled lady, interrupting the praises.

"Oh, I am always at the point," replied the Jewess.

"Shut the door," the other went on, trying to control her panting breath. "What I have to tell you must remain a secret. I want poison, it is true; but you will shudder when I reveal for whom I desire it."

"Well?"

"You must not only prepare this poison yourself, you must administer it with your own hands."

"What?" cried the old woman. "Go on, mistress,—I myself—for whom?"

"Put your ear close to my lips and listen."

Then a conversation took place between the pair, in .the lowest whispers, which lasted quite a long time and seemed to gratify Esther exceedingly. At last her noble guest rose. "Do as I have commanded," she said, slipping a purse into the hands of the smiling old woman. After the muffled figure had glided away as fast as possible, Esther stood for several minutes absorbed in thought.

"A strange coincidence," she murmured in a hollow tone. "Her plan is the same as mine, only the result is different,—the very same plan. And I know her, too," she added in a louder voice, glancing scornfully around. "I'll never make another poison, if that was not Poppaea Sabina. I know she loves the Jews. She wishes us well. And how cunning she is! Ha! ha! I see through you! You want to terrify your Emperor, that—that—he may—the other one who is in your way. But, hush! what am I saying? Did anybody hear? It is only a supposition, a little, correct supposition!"

Esther had lighted the shallow lamp whose flame illumined a vessel upon the tripod. From a chink in the wall, skilfully filled with mortar, the old woman now drew several dried herbs, limped back to the tripod over whose ashes little blue flames were dancing, and, with her toothless mouth blew the sparks into the air, at the same time cautiously crumbling the herbs into the pot. Pouring water on them, she crouched beside the tripod and watched the tongues of flame circle around the old pot. She sat motionless till it began to hum. The monotonous sound exerted a soothing influence upon her; her eyes closed; her head drooped on her lean neck;

the locks of gray hair that escaped from under her cap fluttered in the hot breath of the glowing vessel.

She had not slept long when the noise of voices in the street roused her. Starting up, she set the kettle back and hurried to the door of the house. In the street below she saw by the flickering light of numerous torches several disguised figures, who held a cloak stretched out, in which, amid peals of laughter, they tossed into the air a thin, long-haired figure, skilfully catching it again to hurl it up anew. The thin figure's limbs whirled comically, and its long locks fluttered as they whizzed through the air. It was the luckless dramatist, who was being tossed by the reckless crew till his throat tightened from fright.

"See," cried one of the long-haired poet's tormentors, "what aspiration he possesses; how he strives to reach the stars; by Zeus, he is a poet who, in the flight of his genius, no longer touches the earth." The tortured author at last begged for mercy; but his whimpering amused the maskers so much that they shouted to him that he should not tcuch the dust of earth again until he declaimed one of his poems from his height. The old woman laughed softly.

"Nero is amusing himself," she murmured; strange, strange; and here I am brewing something which could make the Lord of the World more powerless than the poor wretch he is tossing in a cloak!"

She limped back to her fire, and while pouring the greenish liquid from the pot into a a little triangular clay vessel, she reflected: "In three days my Rufus will stand on guard before the Caesar's room,—in three days. Steep till that time, sweet drink, more powerful than the Lord of the World. In three days! Rufus! In three days!" And, whispering mystic magic formulas, she concealed the clay vessel in the niche of the wall.

CHAPTER IX

A FEW days later than the incidents just related, a throng of people poured through Nero's gardens at the north of the Janiculum. Octavia's secluded mode of life had attracted attention at court, and instantly excited the suspicions of the Caesar, who feared that the plan would be baffled, and ordered Petronius to bring it to accomplishment as speedily as possible. Petronius was greatly embarrassed. How was he to accomplish the. work if the Empress shut herself in from every one's society? To compel her to appear in the world again, the arbiter elegantiarum had. exerted his imagination to the utmost in making the arrangements for this garden festival., Octavia could not refuse the Emperor's invitation and came in a richly ornamented, but closed litter.

Scarcely had the imperial train reached the gardens, just as twilight was gathering, when tall tree-trunks, garlanded with wreaths like pillars, and ending at the top in a gigantic bouquet, towered aloft into the air. At a distance only the beautifully arranged flowers were visible, but, drawing nearer, the eye perceived in each bouquet a human body. The figures were fastened in such a way that they appeared to be soaring, like gods or spirits, above the blossoms. The pleasure grounds were not yet lighted; but when Nero, reclining in his litter, asked Petronius wonderingly what surprise he had in store for him, as he did not see even a single torch, the latter, smiling, waved his hand, and instantly flames ran up the pillars, transforming them into huge, living torches. The whole horizon glowed; it seemed as if a blazing diadem was hovering from the heavens over the earth.

The spectacle aroused Nero's poetic tastes; he ordered the train to stop before a little villa, and, while his attendants' took their places on couches which stood ready, he called for music. Standing on the terrace of the villa, close to the balustrade, he gazed at the torches now burning far and wide, whose flames were reflected from the pools and whose decorations of flowers poured forth terrible groans and shrieks of agony. Turning to Metellus, he exclaimed: "You ought to paint this; it is a magnificent spectacle. See! How redly the foliage of the beeches shines; how the blaze mounts higher and higher! Those poor people! how fleeting life is— is it not? A dream, a shadow is more lasting! Woe betide us mortals! But let me hear music; drown the cries of the stifling in waves of melody!"

Then, while blood-red flashes quivered over the assembly, and the giant torches, gradually blazing higher, steeped the roof of the villa in a purple glow, he sent for a lyre. Disdaining the cushions arranged for him, he draped his toga in artistic folds, raised his arm, and, as the melting music of flutes floated from within the dwelling, he bowed his head in melancholy enthusiasm and placed his finger on his lip to warn his train that his artistic reflections must not be disturbed.

Metellus saw little more of the whole scene than a few bedizened masks with some bright spots in the darkness; a bit of papyrus drew his thoughts from the present, and filled him with torturing impatience. It had been thrust into his hand by a stranger, directly after he entered the gardens, and must contain some news of her who, up to this hour, had so rigidly avoided him, and now, having left her litter, sat yonder, with her head bent downward. Some news, some token of love at last!

The groans of the burning victims grew more pitiful; but his senses seemed numbed, now that he was again permitted to see the woman whom he had so often embraced in his dreams. Metellus often tried to approach the Empress; but when, after brushing past many togas, he at last succeeded in reaching a place opposite to her chair and attracting her attention by coughing several times, she raised her head, how her glance startled him! Her eyes, cold as the gems in the diadem on her narrow brow, rested lifelessly on him, as destitute of interest as if he were a stranger with whom she never had been and never desired to be in any relation. The look pierced his heart; yet once more he endeavored to make his presence known by advancing close behind her chair and whispering her name. She rose, with almost insulting resolution; and, without glancing around, as if utterly unconscious of his presence, she approached several of those who stood nearest, exchanged courtesies with them, and was in all respects the gracious Empress.

Metellus stood as if he did not believe his eyes. What? Had this woman loved him? Now, at this moment, when, after so long a time, he hoped to greet her, did she fly from him? Could she exchange insipid flatteries, bow, smile? His eyes, filled with tears, gazed into vacancy, and the thought that the Empress might be feigning this coldness to escape suspicion first restored life to his limbs and removed the aching burden from his breast. "The letter, read the letter," cried a voice in his heart. "It will explain."

He held the papyrus clenched in his left hand; but there was so little light in the place where he stood, and it could so easily be overlooked by every one, that he resolved to go, without attracting attention, to the candelabrum burning in the ante-chamber of the villa. Trembling with expectation, he bore the suspense a few minutes longer, and then glided cautiously toward the dwelling. Entering the brilliantly lighted ante-room, he did not give himself time to take a close survey of it, but hurried straight to the gilded candelabrum. The sheet was hastily unrolled; it contained nothing; it was merely a blank, unwritten page. What! A jest? A deception? But the artist had gradually become initiated into the usual wiles of the court; he moved close to the flame of the lamp, and, under its scorching glow, letters appeared distinctly on the white surface. "You will find me in the Grotto of Bacchus—"

This was the entire contents of the letter; but the words fell upon his ear like the summons of the gods, as he now repeated them in a low tone. His old light-heartedness instantly took possession of him. For a moment at least the ray of happiness dispelled all mists and restored the joyous short-sightedness of youth, which lives only for the present. In an overwhelming, almost childish feeling of gratitude, he compressed his lips, closed his eyes, and kissed the metal of the candelabrum, which cooled his face, while the crackling of the living torches and the sweet notes of the flutes floated to his ear. The Grotto of Bacchus, as he knew, was at the western end of the Neronian Circus; he was ready to seek it at once, and, so great was his ecstasy of rapture, that he felt by no means clear what he should do when he arrived there. Nor, in his happy blindness, did he have the least doubt that he would find Octavia in the grotto; though he must have told himself that it was by no means in harmony with her character to pursue nocturnal adventures like other aristocratic ladies. His experiences had freed him from his errors so little, in spite of many a deception, many a scruple, that he still hoped to realize the happiness which his imagination pictured. How absurd was Burrus's statement that the Empress was in danger! He hated Burrus, who wanted to deprive him of his happiness, and wished that he could show him this hatred. The pillars of flame whirling skyward in the gardens outside now cast their light into the room; but the artist was first roused from his thoughts by the rattle of the handle of a spear upon the marble pavement. Turning, he saw Rufus standing at the end of the hall before the curtain of a doorway; but the sight of the sullen-browed soldier did not destroy his composure. On the contrary, he nodded gayly to him, exclaiming: " My poor friend, must you stand on guard here?"

You are happy," replied the sentinel; don't trouble yourself."

Yes, the gods granted me happiness," said Metellus, sighing, while his head drooped as if bending under the burden of his bliss.

I am a god!" he added with a faint smile.

"And I am a dog!" fell fiercely from the soldier's lips. Metellus held out his hand to the disheartened man, and promised to aid him in his aspirations. Rufus laughed spitefully.

"Yesterday they gave me a taste of the scourge," he muttered; "I wish they had beaten me to death. Am I fit for nothing except to carry this spear, or wheel about in the ranks? Can I not smile and bow and ask: 'How didst thou rest. Lord?' Have I less brains in my skull than the Emperor's favorite fool, Vatinius?"

True, Metellus did not hear the complaints and sarcasms Rufus muttered; yet he answered as though he had been the most attentive listener.

"Yes, yes, quite right," he said absently; "I will surely help you."

"I must remain what I am," murmured the soldier; "who can aid me?"

But Metellus, in his ecstasy, made the foolish promise that he would ask the Caesar to promote the soldier. Rufus, who thought that the sculptor was mocking him, drew back a step, his face expressed angry suspicion.

"Do you need money?" asked the sculptor without noticing his indignation; "here, take some. I have plenty. Just see, a whole pocketful."

He shook out the money on a table, and, laughing gayly, left the room without waiting for an answer. Nero was still standing by the balustrade, holding the lyre, although a disagreeable smell of burning already impregnated the air. Dense clouds of smoke rolled over the terrace; sparks darted like falling stars through the black mist; the shrieks of the dying sounded fainter. Metellus, though looking carefully in every direction, no longer saw Octavia among the assembled company; and this induced him, though scarcely conscious of what he was doing, to go at once to the Grotto of Bacchus. He had scarcely left the terrace behind him, when Burrus emerged from the shadow of a dark myrtle- grove.

"Wait a minute, my friend," called the old general, "I have something to say to you." In the artist's state of feverish excitement it would have been hazardous, even for an intimate friend, to stop him. But when the half crazed youth saw his supposed foe before him, and this foe apparently intended to bar his way, mad fury seized him. He scarcely knew himself, so fierce was the clutch of passion.

"What do you want?" he panted.

"A command of the Empress," whispered Burrus; "you must fly, this very hour, that is the Empress's will."

"Fly?" retorted Metellus, trembling with nervous excitement;

"begone, old liar, or your aged bones might come into painful contact with my young ones."

Burrus tried to seize him by the cloak as he hurried on. Metellus turned, with a half brutal cry of rage, and struck his detainer in the breast with his clenched fist. True, he was ashamed of the act as soon as he had committed it, yet he rushed onward with frantic haste.

The Caesar, still admiring the flames, had wanted the cooling drink which he had invented, as the singing of several songs had wearied his throat. The golden goblet which I contained the precious liquid stood in the anteroom of the villa between heaps of snow. As the silver tub in which the cup was cooled was too large to bring out on the terrace, and the snow would have melted too fast in the hot air, the Caesar, at the end of each song, went to the villa to moisten his throat, which also afforded him the opportunity of receiving the bows and applause of the courtiers on his way. After a specially long piece, he again went to the ante-chamber, and was just raising the goblet to his lips, when a hand—the hand of Rufus, the sentinel—was thrust between the gold rim of the beaker and the imperial lips. Nero's voice failed from sheer astonishment; his eyes stared furiously at the soldier, who stood before him, tottering his spear shaking in his grasp, and his face as white as a criminals who had just been condemned to death.

"Do not drink, august Master," stammered Rufus, his teeth chattering as if he were shaken by a sudden chill.

"Wha-a—What is it?" fell from Nero's blanched lips. "Do you dare—"

Rufus was silent; no sound was heard in the room except the crackling of the candelabrum flames. The Emperor, whose broad face had at first flushed angrily, grew paler and paler as he gazed at the Praetorian's features, whose expression revealed the menace of some grave misfortune; and when the latter took from the table a small triangular clay bottle which had lain close to the edge of the silver tub, the Caesar set down the goblet with every sign of terror.

"Poison!" whispered Rufus, "a woman—in the cup—"

Nero, turning his thick neck, gazed around him as if some one had clutched his throat; then he motioned to Rufus to be silent, as if he could not endure to hear the word " poison " uttered.

"Call Petronius," he gasped at last, after making several futile attempts to speak; and, as Rufus left the room, he dragged himself, utterly broken down, to a chair, his face whiter than the toga with which he wiped the sweat of terror from his brow. Was it possible? Dared they poison him, the Lord of the Earth? Yet it was so; here lay the little vial! A few minutes more and the great artist would no longer have enraptured the world. While pondering over this, a plan matured in the brain of the inventive monarch. When Petronius came hurrying in with the soldier, Nero ordered the doors to be carefully locked, then pointed to the silver tub, feigned the most violent suffering, and, leaning back in his chair with his eyes fixed keenly on the courtier, faltered,—

"Alas! I am poisoned!" The joyful horror which flitted over

Petronius*s face at this remark by no means satisfied the sovereign, who wished to test his friend, or at least only so far as the alarm was flattering to his talent as an actor.

"Poisoned? Really poisoned?" stammered Petronius.

"Yes, you can choose a new Emperor; it is all over with me," panted the hypocrite.

Petronius stared at him incredulously.

"Whom shall we choose?" Petronius continued.

"By Pluto, you say that with a coolness—I believe you would see me go to the under world as carelessly as an old temple rat," said Nero, distrustfully; "but I shall not afFord you that amusement just yet, my dear fellow. Luckily, this faithful soldier preserved me from appearing to my good friend in the part of the dying Ajax."

Petronius, conquering his bewilderment, had assumed an expression of the most intense anxiety; assurances of sympathy flowed from his lips; and these professions were so sincere, so skilfully uttered, that the despot, who had risen from his chair, could find no fault with them, and therefore said,—

"Very well! you play your part admirably! You have learned your lesson well from me, the great actor. I am touched; by Zeus, your friendship moves my heart." Then, pondering a moment, he threw himself into a chair, murmuring, perhaps with sincere sorrow, as he gazed gloomily into vacancy: "Ye gods! Not one is honest; they are all hypocrites, all! I know it! What a fate is that of a sovereign! Woe betide us! The crown does not suit earthly brows!"

But this mood passed as quickly as it had come, when Petronius had the happy thought of lauding the marvellous skill with which his royal master had simulated the dying convulsions of a poisoned man. Nero listened in delight to the discriminating critic; and, as if gagged by this overwhelming outburst of praise, sullenly motioned to him to let the matter drop. Yet as soon as his eye chanced to fall upon the little vial of poison, the fear of death again assailed him. Gazing fixedly at it, he fingered both sides of his hips, as was his custom, in doing which he often wrapped his toga around his trembling hands, and only Petronius's exclamation: "What an artist would have died in you!" restored his composure.

"If I had drunk the potion," he said with a gesture of horror, **how great would have been the world's loss! The lips of the most eloquent poet forever silenced!" Then, carried away by his theatrical imagination, the vision of his death,—the magnificent expression of the dead face, the wreaths which sorrowing Art would place upon his bier, the gloomy funeral procession with the sound of the tubas, the superb pyre were all eloquently described, and he resolved that he would announce this attempt at poisoning to the Roman people in the Forum, and subdue their hearts by the might of his words, the power of his tears. Then, turning to Rufus, he asked for the details of the affair,

"I was standing," said the Praetorian, much excited, "I was standing before this door absorbed in thought, when cautious footsteps attracted my attention. Glancing around me, I saw the muffled figure of a woman who approached the table where your goblet. Lord, was resting in the silver tub. I kept quiet that I might discover her design, until she reached the table. There I saw her draw this little clay vial from under her robe, hold it over the goblet, and let several drops fall into it In my astonishment, I may say horror, I struck the handle of my spear heavily against the floor; the vial slipped from her hand; she ran toward that little door, and I, in pursuing her, had the misfortune to slip, with my nail-shod sandals, on the smooth marble, or I should have arrested her, though the swiftness of her retreat was wonderful."

"That is well," said the Caesar; "your reward shall be an extraordinary one. What is your name?"

"Rufus," said the soldier, visibly exhausted by his story.

"Well then, Rufus, you are sure of a country estate in Baiae." Turning to Petronius, he went on in a lower tone,— "Who do you believe is the instigator of this deed?"

"I will not venture to express a suspicion," answered the courtier. Nero went close to his side, and, in a voice which prevented any opposition, with an emphasis that was like a command, he whispered,—

"No one except Octavia would send me so early to the under world."

Petronius, who foresaw what consequences this suspicion must entail, tried, in spite of his master's frowning brow, to offer some opposition. Nero listened to his words without contradiction.

"You will take care," he said, suppressing a slight yawn, when Petronius paused, "that the matter of which you know is ended in three days. The third from to-day I must have in my hands the proofs which will render Octavia's death a duty to the people."

Petronius, perceiving that delay or opposition was no longer possible, bowed silently. A deed of violence was to be executed, that was evident to the experienced courtier. "My Master, to place this tragical farce upon the stage, I shall need your assistance in person," he said, smiling craftily, and then explained to the Emperor in detail the part which he was to assume. The theatrical character of the situation described pleased Nero, who rubbed his hands, protesting that he would play the deceived husband the better because he intended to study it in advance.

"But I shall need armed force to induce Metellus to take this step," observed Petronius in the course of the conversation; whereupon Nero replied that that was quite possible, but he wished to have the tool disappear as soon as it had been used. He made a little gesture with his hand as he spoke, and whispered pleasantly: "The boy might tell tales!"

"His death will be inevitable only in case he resists," replied the courtier, who could not conquer a certain feeling of affection for Metellus.

Caesar, complaining of being utterly unnerved, left the room. On reaching the terrace he showed his most amiable side, jested with his zither-players, and praised the cohort of his admirers. Yet he had whispered to Petronius to see that no report of the attempted assassination reached the ears of the people that, as he said, the example might find no imitators.

So he smiled and praised continually, even pardoned two men accused of having written sarcastic verses about him, saying that the verses showed talent, and talent had a right to live. He maintained this forced gayety until he was lifted with effort into the litter. The curtains were at once drawn down; he closed his eyes, and ordered himself to be carried to the palace as fast as possible; while Petronius, reflecting upon the plot to be executed, lost himself in the paths of the pleasure grounds. The clever courtier could not deny that his heart was drawn toward the youth; a tender emotion attracted him to the unspoiled I artist, at whose purity he, the refined profligate, gazed as at his long-vanished childhood. Should he warn him? That meant to forfeit the Caesar's favor! But to deliver him to the snare, seemed, as he walked on, often impossible, wholly at variance with the voice in his breast.

Turning around a clump of shrubbery, he saw in the distance a figure which, after a closer scrutiny, he recognized. Metellus was darting through the bushes. Should he stop him? For a moment he cursed his position, his relation to the Emperor; it seemed as though he saw his own son rushing to destruction, and his feet were rooted to the ground, he could not hold him back from the abyss. His trembling lips uttered the name Metellus, but the hurrying figure did not hear.

Meanwhile, wandering through the gardens, the sculptor had sought the Grotto of Bacchus. Neither the nymphs reclining around the springs, nor the women who were dancing in the groves had been able to stop him. The disguised dancers could scarcely awaken his curiosity. The torch-lit temple, from which floated sighs of love blended with the sweet melody of flutes, presented a wonderfully beautiful spectacle; the boats on the ponds which, surrounded by scaly sea-monsters, left golden furrows in the water, were an even more marvellous sight. Far above the tops of the trees, dyed copper bronze by the torch-light, the deep red hue of the night heavens marked the spot where the living candelabra were gradually dying down.

"Cherish love, oh, mortal," breathed a voice from the shining pillars of a temple crowning a hill; "soon, instead of blooming maidens, the heavy mists of Orcus will embrace you; do not let youth flit by without having enjoyed what lends youth its charm; even the graybeard likes to think of the rose-colored days that will never return, and sheds a tear for the hours when he neglected to sip joy. Cherish love, pay homage to the universal mother Venus; her yoke is gentle and garlanded with flowers."

Metellus stopped and listened with moist eyes to the sweet sounds that floated over the meadows, while the altar flamed mysteriously between the shining columns, and dark figures moved in the mystic fire. "I will ask there where the Grotto is to be found," thought the youth, who had lost his way. As he was climbing the hill, a white figure rose beside him, saying,—

"Do you wish to hear your fate, Metellus, which I have read in the stars?"

112

"Who are you? I know you," the youth answered, "you are no woman."

"Ask not who I am," replied the muffled form; "ask who you are."

"I know who I am," said Metellus, and, seized with fear, he hurried down the hill. Uncertain where to turn, he met a slave disguised as Mercury, who, in a short time, led him to an artistically arranged mass of rocks whose fantastic pinnacles the moon was veiling with a silver-green haze. It was lonely here. Far away in the distance rose the arches of the Circus; close at hand white marble forms glimmered against the black background of yews; the wires of a gilded aviary glittered through the darkness, and, from the broad canopy of the pines, the cypresses towered aloft, dark and melancholy, toward the sky.

The youth's anticipations rose higher and higher as this Mercury, smiling mysteriously, led him through a little door in the rocks which closed behind him, and he stood surrounded by darkness. He ventured to move forward, toward a spot from which echoed the wailing whispers of flutes. A peculiar fragrance, surrounding him in the gloom, stupefied his senses, and at the same time a bluish light illumined the apartment, veiling every object in a mist that awakened curiosity; and before the youth could clearly understand what he saw, he felt two arms clasp his neck and try to draw him down upon a couch. The bold embrace surprised him, and filled him with pleasant bewilderment. True, the idea of being thus boldly clasped by the noble Octavia oppressed his heart and filled it with incomprehensible sorrow; yet, as if lost in melancholy, blissful reverie, he allowed himself to be drawn down upon the cushions. As, spite of his ardent yearning, he bowed his head in embarrassment and felt a woman's warm breath upon his hair, a pair of glowing lips were pressed upon his neck, and, indignant at his own faint-heartedness, he turned, vehemently throwing both arms around the woman he loved.

But he instantly became a prey to the keenest disappointment; instead of Octavia, as he supposed, he was embracing Poppaea, who smiled at him with her craftiest expression from beneath her rose-strewn mantle. The dying gladiator, writhing beneath the red-hot iron of the inspector of the dead, cannot feel sharper anguish than now pierced the heart of Metellus; a cry which, though low, seemed as if it would burst his breast, escaped his lips; and the cruel consciousness that Octavia did not love him, overwhelmed him as though he was beaten with rods, till it seemed as though blood must ooze through every pore in his body. Poppaea saw by the youth's dull gaze what was passing in his mind, and her eyebrows contracted angrily until they met across her nose.

"Why do you suddenly start up, almost before you have embraced me?" she asked. "Does not Poppaea please you? Whom did you expect to find here? I can divine whom you expected to embrace; but I tell you, beware, that others do not discover it to your destruction."

As he did not listen to her, she whispered angrily,—"You expected Octavia here; confess it!"

She pierced his eyes with the searching gaze of jealousy; but even

113

Octavia's name did not seem to rouse him from his melancholy; and the beautiful woman went on in a louder tone:

"Oh, this Octavia deserves death, since she gives death to you. Yes, stare at me; your Octavia will send you to Orcus. I dare not speak; my lips are sealed; but one word from me would suffice to make you curse that Octavia."

As he now raised his eyes to her face a feeling of pity gradually stole over her for this pallid youth who still gazed into vacancy like a corpse. Yet, as a handsome face first reveals the deepest secrets of its beauty in suffering, the profligate woman felt a more ardent passion for him than ever before. She began to try to draw him down again on the couch at her side, using all the arts of coquetry at her command, sometimes smiling, sometimes pouting, sometimes beaming, sometimes shamefaced, as she played with his hand.

"What do you find so attractive in Octavia?" she asked jestingly; "am I not just as beautiful? Do not people praise my hair, my hand, my foot? See what a little hand I have, and, how strange, your hair is as golden as mine; the gods have created us for each other. Oh, how I admire you, how beautiful your arm is! Do not be angry with me for telling you so; love draws me on, forgive my madness—" She pressed her head against his breast; love and jealousy overpowered her; tears streamed from her eyes, and, wiping them away with her robe, she gasped hastily, as if fearing every word, amid her sobs,—

"They will kill you; you are betrayed, fly!" And, forgetting herself, she told Metellus what a net had been cast around his limbs, revealed to him that he was the moving spring of the cruel machine which had been set in motion for the destruction of Octavia,

Metellus at first heard meaningless words, stammers, sighs; gradually, in the remotest corner of his consciousness, the suspicion dawned upon him that the words to which he listened were not mere words; a mist of ideas gathered in his brain; an anxious suspense bound his thoughts; and when Poppaea ended her vague tale, interrupted by sobs and expressions of tenderness, it seemed as though some incomprehensible, nameless thing was gliding, in ever-narrowing circles, around his head.

He knew everything and nothing. As he now slowly worked his way out from under the oppressive burden of his grief, as if he were extricating himself from the ruins of a falling house, he felt with astonishment, nay, terror, that a strange despair, a half animal fury was gradually taking the place of his grief. He did not know with whom he was angry; but he was enraged, and so frantically that it seemed as if he must destroy everything near him, as if nothing but blood could satisfy him. Everything orderly and decorous grew hateful, and, in that moment bordering upon madness, his eyes fell upon the caressing woman. A sword appeared to pierce from his heart to his brain; every vein swelled; he gripped the extended hand so fiercely that Poppaea suppressed a groan as she sank back on the couch and, when she saw the strange, bright, wandering expression in his eyes, was about to call for help. It was too late.

That same night Metellus again wandered through the park, throwing himself on the ground, utterly bereft of composure, and moistening the earth with burning tears. In his wild despair, he lay upon the grass writhing like a man dying under the scourge of the executioner, and only longing for forgetfulness. Stephanus, with half parted lips, sat beside his master. He could not understand why he should lie there, with his face pressed against the dewy turf as if he wished to hide it He touched Metellus*s head wonderingly, but said nothing, and, drawing out the flute which he had given him, began to lure sweet tones from it. The first rosy hues of dawn were already beginning to tremble over Rome, the first timid twitter of the waking birds was heard among the leaves; the light morning breeze fanned the hot cheeks of the unhappy youth and played with the curls of the innocent lad. The soft notes of the flute at first sounded like mockery to the artist's ears.

"Stop that," he said angrily. Stephanus took the flute from his lips, but after gathering flowers for some time, could not resist the impulse and began to play again. Again his master impatiently silenced him.

"What ails you?" asked the boy, half crying; "may I not play the flute? You are so strange! Are you sorrowful, oh, master, or are you happy?"

Metellus hid his face on the lap of the child, feeling a sort of timid reverence for his purity.

"Play your flute, I will permit it, Stephanus," he murmured, conquering his repugnance to the sound, "but play very softly. Your master is not well."

Are you ill?" asked the slave. No," said Metellus, blushing. Your eyes look so ill," replied the boy; shall I keep quiet?"

Don't ask questions and begin," said his master, ashamed of his mood. Then he pressed a kiss on the pure lips of Stephanus; and the latter warmly returned the caress; but it seemed to startle, rather than to please the youth, whose face blanched as he averted it.

The child joyously placed the flute to his mouth.

"Listen, this is a song which I remember from my former home."

The sweet, plaintive melody, the rosy flush deepening on the foliage and the clouds, the cool morning breeze, with its dewy breath, thrilled Metellus like a sorrowful foreboding; he sighed and smiled as he closed his tear-filled eyes. Now he fell asleep, but painful dreams assailed him. His brow darkened indignantly; he rolled over on his back, muttered defiant words, and suddenly started up, groaning. Pressing his hand to his fevered brow, he faltered,— "What is this?—Is it possible?—How was it?—Did she say—"

He clasped his hands as though struggling for breath, Stephanus laughed aloud at his master's bewilderment, and asked if he had seen a goddess in his dreams. Metellus gazed doubtfully around him; he had heard Poppaea's voice in his sleep.

"Is what she told me the truth?" he murmured. "No! I dreamed it, it cannot be true; it would be too unprecedented."

Then Stephanus said that, while he was playing the flute, armed men had approached the place; he had seen their helmets glitter through the bushes in the morning light.

"Armed men?" asked the youth, still drowsy with sleep, "in this place—"

"Yes," replied the boy, "perhaps we shall see a military spectacle. Hark! There they are again, I hear their armor clank."

Stephanus had scarcely finished the sentence when Petronius appeared in the nearest gravelled path, now steeped in the blue mist of morning. Metellus stared absently at him, as he approached with a courteous smile.

"Have you a moment's time?" he asked with studied humility, which, however, did not fail to produce an impression.

"Yes, yes," said Metellus inquiringly, without stirring from the place.

"Then have the kindness to follow me."

"Why?"

"The Emperor has invented a new favor for you, my master."

"Do you address me as master?"

"You will be henceforward," replied Petronius, bowing.

The submissive tone and the words "my master" attracted the inexperienced youth, whose wearied senses denied him the service of calm deliberation. Starting up as if in a. dream, he followed the courtier, who invited him to take his place in a litter which awaited them. When both, had reclined upon the: cushions, Petronius closed the curtains. Metellus noticed the movement of the vehicle as it was borne forward, then he fancied that cautious steps, the subdued clank of weapons and confused voices fell upon his ear, but the regular swaying of the litter overpowered him with unconquerable drowsiness. He fell asleep, though he struggled vehemently against the paralyzing weakness.. Petronius lay beside him in the dusky interior, compressed his lips firmly, and gazed fixedly at the wan, sleeping features of his victim. Sometimes he pushed the hair back from his face, but the necessity of rescuing the beloved youth no longer mastered him; the habit of obedience had hardened his soul; his heart lay in his breast like a leaden weight, and a fixed expression of suffering rested on his features. At last he could not refrain from pressing a kiss upon the smooth brow of the sleeper, turned over and closed his eyes, as if to force himself to slumber.

* * * * *

When Metellus again woke, he found himself in his room in the imperial palace. Evening had already closed in; the last beams of the setting sun crimsoned the lion-claws of his couch, were reflected from the walls, and glided up the curtains which half concealed the dusky garden. The rays also flickered over the round goat-footed table at which the artist sat. The roll which he held in his hands, and read over and over again with staring eyes, glowed, and the youth's pale face was flushed under the crimson light with a deceptive semblance of vigorous health. He had found the roll on the table when he awoke; it was placed so that he could not help seeing it. Its smooth surface contained a demand which he had now been re-reading for an hour. At last he let it fall and struck his forehead with his clenched fist.

"A plot! A concerted plot!" he groaned; "and I was the tool? Fool, who wandered as if with bandaged eyes where everything was only too clear."

It was no deception, no dream; he felt the roll; it was signed by Petronius. This was the selfsame plan which Poppaea had communicated; he remembered her every word, as we recall, when awake, a nocturnal vision. The roll offered him, besides a country estate, high honors, if he would consent to involve Octavia at night in a situation which must render her fidelity as a wife suspicious in the eyes of those who rushed in. What would befall him, in case he should refuse to enter into this rascally trick, the roll did not state. Were these people with whom he associated human beings? Was the character of the persons who surrounded him evident at last? Had one been better than another? Did not selfishness, lust for pleasure, jeer at him in every form? His gaze turned in horror from the life which, hitherto, he had accepted unexamined; a horror overwhelmed him at being condemned to breathe in such a world; nothing but hideous masks, claws, and teeth confronted him; wherever he looked, he fancied that he was already wandering where he should one day arrive—in the mournful, mist-veiled nether world. And Octavia? Had he not unintentionally deceived her ? Had not Burrus told the truth? The Caesar was already weary of her! This certainty, the hatred of mankind, with its desolating chill, love with its yearning importunity, the bitter realization of the world,—all these varied emotions swept through his soul, often dashing over him like destroying waves, and stifled the last remnant of childlike nature. He put the roll down, raised it to his eyes once more, and exclaimed again and again: "Octavia, they are playing a game with us! Oh, Mistress, forgive me! Oh, forgive me, Burrus! Would that I had fled then! I shall kill her, kill the woman I love!"

Beating his breast, he sank down with his head against the hard wall, and gave himself up completely to his grief, which shook him like a giant.

He remained in this mood for some time, weeping like a child, yet no longer a child. As it grew darker and the trees outside, no longer reddened by the sunset glow, rustled in the night-breeze, he was about to rise, but a hand was laid on his shoulder; Petronius had entered unobserved. The two men confronted each other, Metellus with laboring breath, Petronius watching him anxiously.

"You have read the roll," the latter began, averting his face; "I think you will consent?"

"Oh, certainly!" said Metellus, through his set teeth, gazing at the embarrassed courtier with a look of silent fury.

"Do you consent?" the other repeated dejectedly.

117

"Oh, my admirable teacher," replied the artist, "by Zeus! your school was a good one, your plan clever! What a pity that you were mistaken in me! Why did your choice fall upon a provincial? Are there not plenty of gladiators and jugglers in Rome! Your knowledge of human nature does not keep pace with your years; you might have supposed that stupid Metellus would not suit your shrewd tricks. But take courage, my friend! Rome is large, in two days you will have found a better tool. Do not be vexed because I am unwilling to become a rascal, though the opportunity is very tempting!"

Metellus's anguish was so deep, so diffused over life as a whole, that he maintained a fair show of composure and subdued his anger.

Petronius received the bitter accusations of his victim with bowed head and lustreless eyes, as if he had expected them.

"Tell your Emperor that I despise him," the youth continued, "that is my sole answer. And now make way for me; I shall leave the palace."

The courtier did not stir.

"Did you understand me ?" cried the youth; "move aside from the door; I wish to leave this place; you are shameful wretches, with whose breath I will not mingle mine." As Petronius still kept his station, Metellus went toward him.

Then I must force my way," he cried, and regard you as a slave who is driven off by kicks."

Do you say that to me?" exclaimed Petronius, as Metellus clenched his fist.

The courtier really drew back a step, as the youth's hand clutched his arm.

"I will drive this miserable, worm-eaten courtier from the door," muttered the youth; but he had scarcely drawn aside the curtain, when he staggered back with the exclamation: "Force!" on his blanched lips. He was surrounded, captured, a prisoner! There they stood before him, in the dull red glare of the torches, like brazen columns, the pitiless tools of tyranny. He pressed his hand to his brow—captive? Was it possible? The features of the Praetorians stared at him from behind the columns. Glittering spears were levelled at his breast.

"Force," he stammered scornfully, "do you believe that you have power to constrain me? Why do ye stand there? Do gray-haired warriors become executioners? Oh, what Romans! See the brave descendants of Romulus!"

The soldiers still stood as motionless as brazen statues; the smoke of the torches drifted along their ranks and circled in black wreaths around the columns.

"I am acting in my master's behalf," replied Petronius, in an unsteady tone; "you know the Emperor's will: he promises wealth if you fulfil it; death, if you refuse."

"Death, if I refuse to injure a woman?" cried the youth, letting the curtain fall.

"Instant death," said the courtier.

118

"And can you suppose, miserable tool of the tyrant, that death would be unwelcome, after you have torn the masks from the faces of my fellow-mortals, showed me that they conceal wolfish ones, and revealed how hollow, how empty is the life of the world? Do you imagine that existence would still be desired by the man who has experienced what I have endured? I marvel that any one dares to live, not that the wise long for death. Go on, kill me if you choose."

Metellus had uttered these words with the agitated pathos which even men devoid of imagination involuntarily use as soon as their situation becomes tragical.

"I will give you time for reflection," replied Petronius; "and, as I have always had a friendly feeling toward you, I might add: you would do well to yield to power, and, instead of death, receive reward."

Metellus had folded his arms across his breast and was gazing sullenly into vacancy. It was no lie to others or to himself to say that he desired death. Life, divested of every charm, met his eyes like a fleshless skull whose pleasant smile is transformed into a sarcastic grimace. There was no more pleasure for him; even love for the royal lady had almost vanished from his breast. Petronius, to whom the whole scene, as his timid glances betrayed, was a painful one, watched the youth a few moments with dim eyes. "He really does not seem to fear death at this moment," he said to himself; "it is a pity about him," he added sighing.

Then it chanced that Metellus had scratched his arm a little against a Praetorian's spear as he took a step against the ranks of warriors, and they supposed he intended to escape. It was uncertain whether this little physical hurt occasioned a change in the artist's mood; but Petronius noticed that he turned pale when he saw his own blood flow. Shrugging his shoulders, the courtier was about to withdraw with the soldiers, when Metellus called him by name, and, much pleased, he returned*

"Be sensible, submit to circumstances," he urged; "why should you seek death?"

Metellus gazed at him with a smile of mingled superiority and contempt.

Yes, why should I seek it?" he said.

Well spoken, my friend."

This admonition from the courtier had suddenly flooded the mind of the hitherto bewildered youth with light. He saw a way of escape; a distant glimmer of hope shone upon him. Why should I not meet fraud with fraud! he said to himself. And, clumsy as he might be under the mask of dissimulation, he perceived that it was necessary to divest himself of his frankness.

"Do with me as you choose; I yield to force," he said, after considerable hesitation, trying to assume as trustworthy a face as possible.

"You consent?"

"To everything!"

"You will execute the plan?"

"What is the use of questioning?" replied the youth, who was in perpetual fear that the mask he was so unused to wear would be discovered. Petronius, with a sigh of relief, held out his hand.

"You have no other choice," he said; "you cannot transform the world, so you must let it transform you."

"Very true, my teacher in worldly wisdom," said the boy, coldly, "I am hereby giving you a proof that I do not love Octavia, as you seem to believe, and that my life is worth more to me than her honor,—are you convinced now?"

"You have no other choice," said the courtier, evasively.

"And that I may not arouse the Emperor's anger," continued Metellus, in a still more expressionless voice, "I beg you not to repeat what I uttered in a moment of bewilderment, and to assure him of my devotion."

"I will make it the business of my life to promote your welfare," said Petronius, equivocally.

"And now let me know the details of the plan," Metellus went on in an almost imperious tone, by whose firmness he hoped to give himself mental support.

"Two hours before sunrise," Petronius began in a whisper, "I will accompany you to the apartments of the Empress. At this time she will be still at rest. You will make your way to her sleeping-room, whose adjacent chambers will be filled with watchers. You need only exchange a few words, you and the Empress,—that will suffice to surprise and accuse you."

Metellus shuddered as he imagined himself in this humiliating position.

"That will not do," he retorted; "I shall need half an hour. If this play is to produce any impression of truth upon the watchers, and not that of an absurd farce, I ought to have at least an hour's time. Besides, it would be well not to send the spies into the adjoining rooms until later, after I had remained a little longer in the Empress's presence."

Metellus had spoken with unusually stern decision; Petronius reflected and, believing that the youth had relapsed into his former frankness, nodded assentingly. "I cannot help approving your reasons," he said; "you may be right. You shall have your way; hold yourself in readiness—two hours before sunrise."

With these words he left the room in a more cheerful mood than he had entered it. The mosaic floors of the broad corridors outside echoed under the tread of retreating footsteps; words of command were given; dull echoes gradually died away.

Metellus sat listening, his head propped on his hand. "I am beginning to accommodate myself to the world," he murmured; "I am outwitting the crafty; may the gods grant that I can explain the plot to the poor Empress, that she may be saved."

Then he started up, laughed furiously, and, hiding his face in his hands, was forced to summon all his strength of will to save himself from bursting into loud weeping. As he paced up and down the room with strange restlessness, often pausing and murmuring unintelligible words,

120

Stephanus entered and told him that the moonlight was beautiful in the gardens outside, but that a soldier was standing in the shrubbery.

Metellus looked out. Not a breath of air stirred the leaves of the trees; the radiance of the moon steeped the branches; an oppressive sultriness brooded over the motionless leafage. He stood there like a statue,, awaiting the second hour before sunrise, and thinking of the time when, a free-born artist, he had entered Rome, where he was now held captive.

CHAPTER X

A SMALL lamp hanging above the couch in Octavia's sleeping- room cast its faint light upon the wearied features of the Empress, who lay staring with dilated eyes at the Babylonian ornaments on the hangings of the bed, vainly trying to dispel the sorrowful thoughts which had haunted her throughout the day. Finding herself unable to succeed, she struck the metal basin standing beside the bed, but was obliged to repeat the blow thrice before the vibrating sound waked the attendant. The curtain at the door of the adjoining room parted, and Meroe, with a shawl wrapped around her shoulders, entered.

"Forgive me, I was so sound asleep," yawned the drowsy Egyptian; "aren't you asleep yet. Mistress?"

Octavia, without answering the question, asked for Plato's works.

"The volume I usually read," she said with

emphasis, as if it cost her a great effort to

speak coherently. Meroe tottered sleepily to the book-rack, curling up her bare toes at the touch of the cold marble floor.

"I don't know why there is such a stir outside to-night," she yawned, handing the roll to her mistress; "the gravel in the garden paths creaks, and there are strange echoes in the corridors. Oh, how sleepy I am!"

She stood before the bed like a reed that the wind sways to and fro.

"Sit down beside me a little while, my dear child," said the Empress; " tell me about your home."

The maid sat rather sulkily beside the couch, playing with the purple fringe of the coverlet.

"Well?" asked the Empress.

"Yes, yes," answered the maid, suppressing another yawn. A pause followed; the flame of the lamp quivered; the curtain stirred slightly in the night-breeze.

"My heart is so sad to-night, Meroe, I cannot sleep; it would be very kind to divert my thoughts by talking a short time," said the Empress, raising herself on the pillows and turning her haggard face, with its large frightened eyes, toward the girl. . "Yes, indeed, I will gladly," answered Meroe, but her head fell wearily on her bosom, baring her fat neck. Both were silent, Octavia's head shook as if the muscles of her neck had become

121

enfeebled by age. It was a piteous spectacle to see that proud, noble head tremble. After a longer pause she added,—"Perhaps we shall not be together long; how will you live in this world then?"

"Oh, no, no," sighed the attendant, wearily raising her head with its drooping eyelids.

"Yes, my end is drawing near," the Empress began again; "my position is daily growing more insecure; already my friends hardly dare to speak to me. All shun me, and various remarks which the Caesar has let fall concerning me forebode the worst. I shall soon see my brother, Meroe, soon embrace his beloved shade. Just think, dear one, Andromachus begged the Emperor to banish me; and Nero is said to have answered that I might as well die in Rome. Is it not sad, my child, to have death ever before the eyes, and yet be unable to die? I often feel as though I had long been dead. Tell me, will you sprinkle my funeral pyre with wine; when the flames consume my body, will you shed tears for me, Meroe?"

But, before Octavia had finished speaking, Meroe's regular breathing announced that she: had fallen asleep* Octavia smiled mournfully.

"Go to bed, poor girl," she said, shaking her gently by the shoulder.

"Here is the book," Meroe gasped, waking, rubbing her eyes, and looking around her in terror. "I am so tired," she whimpered.

"Go to bed," her mistress repeated, and turned from her.

Meroe stretched herself like a cat, yawned once more, and staggered sleepily away. Octavia, with a keen pang in her breast, pressed her face into the pillows and tried to drive away the misanthropic thoughts which strove to take possession of her heart.

The bust of Socrates stood opposite to her bed; and with a sort of despair she tried to concentrate her mind upon it, as if this bust could afford her a refuge. The snub-nosed face seemed to smile compassionately; its grotesque shadow on the floor, the illumination of the bald skull, the profound silence around, the night-breeze which floated through the room like a kind word,—all produced an impression upon her, and thus, absorbed in contemplation, she succeeded in ceasing to think. True, a warning often glided through her consciousness; but mental exhaustion robbed all these warnings or fears of their positiveness, their painful sharpness.

The royal lady, accustomed from childhood to suffering, had acquired a power of banishing from her imagination everything that might become dangerous to it. She was cruel to herself, and took pleasure in this cruelty; she was her own tyrant. In this way she had cherished Metellus's image in her mind, without really thinking of him. He was like a light which illumined her soul without her seeing it; she did not think of him, yet he was present, ever present to her. No matter what she might do, he formed the background of all her thoughts.

Gradually the bust of Socrates melted into a white mist, the lamp gave the ornaments on the ceiling uncertain outlines; at last its dim rays merged into the shadows of the furniture. Then Octavia, as if she could no longer endure her weariness, closed her eyes; she still felt the cool breath of the night wind on her cheek; then care-dispelling slumber floated down upon her. Her bosom rose and fell with deep, regular breathing; but this breathing, her smile of relief, had been watched for several minutes.

He whose image still lingered in the depths of her soul, Metellus, had been standing for some time by the gilded bed-posts in the shadow of the curtain. He had stolen in and now gazed with hard, dull eyes at the sleeping woman, whose oval face rested on the pillows amid the tresses of her loosened hair. The beautiful arm lying across her bosom rose and fell with it; a noble peace surrounded the whole form.

Metellus dared not rouse her, though he felt neither reverence nor yearning love in her presence. His soul was empty, lifeless, since his heart had experienced universal disappointment; existence seemed valueless, love worthless; all desire appeared to be dead within him, yet passion still glimmered under the ashes. This woman was no longer the incarnation of everything noble and beautiful; the yearning humility he had previously felt at the sight of her had yielded to disdain; the rapture which, a few days before, had thrilled him in her presence had given place to an almost scornful indifference. As he stood gazing down at the sleeper, trying to crush every stir of any deeper emotion, the deceptive flicker of the lamp conjured up a strange illusion in his mind. A mirror stood opposite to the bed, and in this mirror the youth saw Octavia' 3> face, but paler and bodiless. He instantly thought of a beheaded corpse. The face in the golden frame of the mirror had just that livid, lifeless aspect.

A sharp pang pierced his breast; compassion forced tears to his eyes, which now rested with a gentler expression on the sleeper. She had grown paler and thinner; there were dark rings around her closed eyes; the misery and suffering of her whole desolate life looked forth from the peace of her slumber. As he stood watching her, and felt his heart grow softer, he tried to struggle against the weakness, and the conflict became so impetuous that his lips voiced in a whisper the emotions contending in his mind. At last the word " folly " unconsciously escaped them in a louder tone, and this one word was enough to break Octavia's light slumber. She sighed, contracted her brows as if in pain, and called sadly,—

"Is it you, Meroe?" She called a second time, and, receiving no answer, raised herself on the pillows, murmuring sorrowfully: "Oh, I was sleeping so well!" She was about to lie down again, but perceiving a shadow moving near the curtain she turned toward it.

"It is I, my Mistress," said Metellus, quietly, standing motionless; and the Empress, who, with the instinct of unhappiness, instantly perceived by his calm expression that it was no light matter that had brought him here, scarcely started, but gazed at him with anxious, questioning eyes, and after, as it were, swallowing the anxious foreboding that oppressed her, said—

"Metellus, I was dreaming of you!"

The words fell on the sculptor's ear as if the voice belonged to a shade from the nether world, it was so dull, so colorless. A rapturous sorrow thrilled him as he closed his eyes and stood like one ensnared by an evil, yet blissful dream.

"I did not come to ask about your dreams," fell rudely from his almost motionless lips. Yet he felt a chill agitation stealing over him, and was forced to confess to himself, with shame, that this woman loved him far more purely and tenderly than he loved her, that he was unworthy of so unselfish a feeling. "How wicked I am! '•* cried a voice in his soul; "she loves me, who forgot her in Poppaea's embrace, me who even now do not love her as I ought!"

The Empress gazed at him absently with her large, mournful eyes, and said,—

"You are right to blame me; I ought to be thinking of the land where there are no more dreams." Then she rose, arranged her garments and her hair, and even looked into the mirror. She seemed unconscious of any other presence, as if she were a shade that had fled from Orcus to descend thither again after the allotted respite was over. The youth was so touched by this dreamy absence of mind that, although not a muscle of his face moved, burning tears rolled down his cheeks. Then Octavia at last sank wearily into a seat; she clasped her hands in her lap and looked at the youth with the strange, lifeless, yet touching expression of love subdued.

"You are weeping," she said; "do you mourn Octavia's fate?"

Metellus now first perceived that he was weeping, he hastily shook his head and was about to speak.

"You have cause to weep for me," she whispered dreamily, bending toward him with half-parted lips; "I know why you came; I have deserved that you should weep for me."

Metellus shook off the overwhelming sense of anguish, and, trying to appear harsh, said:

"Danger is at hand; your life is threatened."

Then, with the utmost composure, he revealed the plan which Nero had devised for her destruction; and not until he was forced to intimate that he himself had been used as the tool of her ruin, did his voice begin to tremble. At last he broke down. The unexpected disclosure made a stronger impression upon the hapless woman than Metellus had expected. She did not receive it with calmness and dignity. She had listened with compressed lips; now she trembled violently, her breathing grew labored, and her eyes glowed with the fever of mortal terror.

"I am weak and foolish, am I not?" she said apologetically. "I ought to be different, I know—" she pressed both hands on her temples as she spoke—" oh, in what power the gods placed me; what a terrible man!"

Metellus tried to find words of consolation, but uttered only inarticulate sounds.

"What a terrible man!" she repeated again, alluding to her husband, and then relapsed into silence. They heard Meroe snoring behind the curtain; it was the only sound that interrupted the stillness, and its animal comfort contrasted strangely with the mental anguish of the two watchers. A stronger gust of wind blew aside the curtain from the balcony; the disk of the moon looked sadly into the room; a withered leaf fluttered noiselessly in and, after drifting through the air, settled on the marble floor.

"Metellus," gasped Octavia, after a long pause, "Metellus, oh, it is terrible—I shall die—"

"Die? Can the thought horrify you?" replied Metellus.

"I am a woman!" she wailed, exerting all her mental power to repress her weakness; "we have not your courage—die! Oh, where shall I find comfort—I have nothing to which I could cling!"

She clasped her hands and gazed despairingly at the youth, whose expression, half pitying, half wonderingly reproving, made her realize the littleness of this sudden outburst. She humbly bowed her head, and fixed her eyes upon the floor in shame.

"Forgive my weakness," she said at last; "I will be strong; I will strive to be strong. One who has read Plato should not fear death. A plot to destroy me; oh, it is disgraceful! What wrong have I done, that they plan to remove me from the world? Oh, it is shameful!"

Metellus told her the details of the plot, and the surprise which was to take place in her sleeping-room that very night.

"I have come," he concluded, "to inform you of this, and then, before your foes can surprise us, to fly, perhaps to Baise, or wherever my feet can carry me."

The Empress could say nothing except: "Oh, it is shameful!" which she repeated mechanically, pressing her trembling arms upon her bosom. Her grief was the more touching because the struggle between it and the greatness of soul which she had acquired by study was plainly visible; the culture that she had gained bent its head, as it were, under the breath of death. When Metellus saw her in this condition, he felt as if he were being torn asunder by wild horses, the floor swayed under his feet, and his parched tongue stuck to his palate as he faltered,—

"Farewell, it is time for me to go; I must not be found longer in Rome to- night. If it is possible, I will try to save you; perhaps the populace will make an attempt to rescue you from the clutches of your destroyer."

As he muttered the words, half unintelligibly, he turned to go as quickly as possible, to end the scene with manly strength. But as the Empress saw him hurrying away, she roused herself by a violent effort from the paralyzing spell with which mental bewilderment bound her limbs. He had drawn the curtain back; the moon-lit park lay at his feet in the sultry night; the blue, sultry night, in which the leafage glistened with a golden haze, was mirrored in the polished marble walls; far away on the horizon a mass of dark clouds was rising, which sometimes emitted a low rumble of thunder as if fierce wrath was seething in their depths. But, before he reached the balcony that led to the grounds, Octavia rose and tottered several steps toward him* She seemed to be recovering her consciousness, and gradually understanding what he intended to do, for she looked at him questioningly, and he, with his hand on the metal railing of the balcony, gazed in bewilderment at hen

The slender figure of the Empress, around whose delicate limbs floated the folds of her light robe, stood steeped in the bluish moonlight. Trembling in every limb, as if a tremendous weight rested on his shoulders, the artist gazed reluctantly at her with an expression of yearning sorrow. Octavia flung her white arms above her head, her bosom heaving under the robe, and her lips moved, but no words issued from them. A stronger breeze, the harbinger of the approaching thunderstorm, swept through the room; all the hangings, garments, and scrolls rustled; the dark wall of clouds rolled swiftly nearer, like a legion hurrying to battle; often it flashed brightly as if glowing with secret fury, then rolled on black and threatening as before.

The two figures still stood irresolute; Metellus waited for her approach, she for his. A fold of the curtain was softly pushed aside at the end of the room; neither noticed it. The opening widened; a spying eye appeared; but only the bust of Socrates saw the spiteful face, heard the malicious whispering, the clank of weapons.

Octavia moved nearer to Metellus; at last she stood directly before him, agitated, it is is true, but calmer. She was endeavoring to show herself the Empress, to bear her sorrow with dignity. Both remained motionless. At last she murmured,—

"Tell me only one thing before death comes, Metellus—did you love me?"

With drooping head, he whispered almost under his breath: "Yes, my Mistress!"

"I thank you," she replied; "I shall die easier now."

Another gust of wind fluttered the garments of both; a peal of thunder, loud and menacing, shook the air, dying away in long reverberations.

"And you—you, oh, my Mistress," asked Metellus, in eager, breathless haste, "oh, speak, did you, too—" he hesitated.

"Hush, my friend," she interrupted gravely, "I am the Empress; it does not beseem me to love. Take the assurance that you have rendered the last day of my life beautiful. What can the love of a hapless woman avail you—but now! Farewell! It is time for you to go.

"Oh, not yet," he whispered, suddenly overpowered by the might of his passion.

"Consider my safety," she answered.

Not now," he repeated, "I cannot go yet—forgive me, my august Mistress—you are so beautiful—"

"How selfish it is to tell me this now!" she murmured. "You do not love me, or you would speak differently."

"Oh, let me touch your lips," he pleaded; "oh, how beautiful you are!"

She smiled and shook her head.

"Your hand, at least," he implored.

"You would kiss the hand of a dead woman," Octavia answered.

"Oh, I know, it is base in me!" he muttered.

"Not base," she said, pushing the hair back from his forehead; "poor boy," she added, "how gladly I would do everything for you, everything! And so you really love me? Poor boy—"

"Kiss me, and I shall be rich," he whispered.

Octavia gazed at him as if intoxicated, clasped his head between her hands, and pressed a long, ardent kiss upon his brow.

He was about to embrace her rapturously, but, as he looked up, his eyes rested upon the end of the room. He had delayed too long! They were there! A convulsive cry escaped his lips, he seized the railing of the balcony with both hands, and flung himself down, almost senseless, into the shrubbery of the park.

The Empress had turned; behind the curtained doorway of the adjoining room glittered the helmets of soldiers, curious faces were peering from the other two rooms; Petronius whispered a few words in the ear of the Emperor, who advanced several paces in front of his train, and, frowning gloomily, stood, with a gesture of surprise, in the centre of the chamber.

"He has fled," said Petronius, pointing to Octavia, while the Emperor, wrapping his night-robe closer around him, called for a pair of sandals for his bare feet, still fixing his eyes upon his wife.

"I rushed from my bed, unwilling to believe it," said Nero, with studied dignity, turning to his attendants; "but I am forced to do so—look, the Lord of the World does not even possess what every honest citizen has,—a faithful wife! I am dishonored! Say what the woman deserves who has done this!"

The attendants stood motionless; every eye was fixed upon Octavia. The Empress flushed then paled, as she recognized her husband. A frantic, maniacal fury gradually distorted her beautiful features almost beyond recognition, as she continued to gaze into Nero's brutal, hypocritical face.

"Is this a fitting hour to be modelled? Can you deny that the sculptor visited you?" the Emperor continued. "I have long suspected you; this time I have gained my object,—the proofs of your infidelity are in my hands. The judges of Rome will pronounce your doom; the people of Rome will see whom they have honored in you. Until that time, I will place you under military guard, that you may not be able, by night, to translate into prose Ovid's 'Art of Love.'"

Octavia had been searching his face with eyes that he shunned.

"You?" she gasped, clinging to the railing of the balcony, "you?—dishonored—faithless to you—you?" she was struggling vainly to find words in her overwhelming excitement.

"There is no name for your corruption," she shrieked, and, as Nero approached her, she could no longer control herself, but spit into his face. With the act, the strength she had maintained with so much difficulty failed, she sank moaning to the floor of the balcony, wrapping herself, with half unconscious modesty, in the folds of the curtains. Nero left the room with a look of foolish rage on his embarrassed face, while Octavia lay a long time before her terrified servants ventured to raise the senseless figure.

CHAPTER XI

POPPAEA SABINA was still sleeping, when, early in the morning, the Caesar hastened to her couch. The light of the lamp which streamed from the ceiling upon the pillows mingled with the first rosy hues of dawn, as Nero cautiously drew back the curtain, and 'pressed a kiss upon the fair curls of his love. Poppaea yawned, and asked very peevishly who had the insolence to rob her of the delicious morning nap; and even the face of her august patron, peeping forth mischievously from the folds of drapery behind which he had hidden himself, did not immediately smooth her frowning brow.

"What folly," she cried, "to wake me! Don't you know that the lover should never surprise the object of his affection at her toilet?"

"At her toilet?" asked Nero, in amazement.

"Yes, look here!" cried Poppaea angrily, pushing the curtain entirely aside; at which the Caesar, startled, drew back several paces from the couch. Poppaea's whole face was covered with a thick crust composed of bread dough moistened with milk. This was intended to give the complexion smoothness; and Poppaea, who, like all beautiful women, did not wish to have the secrets of her toilet exposed, was inconsolable because her lover had seen her in this condition. In fact, very little of her beauty was visible: her hair was wound up in rolls; her face looked like the raw hide of an animal; her bosom and hands were covered with oiled cloths; her whole person resembled a newly embalmed mummy. Nero had soiled his face and hands with the dough, besides scratching his finger with a hairpin, and seemed to be somewhat disenchanted by the spectacle of this disfigured beauty. At last Poppaea called her maid, who instantly appeared with a bowl of warm milk and a towel, and, by her mistress's orders, washed off the dough. The fair face soon appeared from under the black crust; and, without troubling herself about her illustrious visitor, Poppaea rose from her couch, ordered the cloths to be removed, and finally said she must be left alone with her servant,—she would never permit the Emperor to know still more about the arts of her toilet.

"I Know still more?" laughed Nero, who was again in the best possible humor. "What greater surprise could be in store for me? Will it appear that the charms I have embraced did not belong to you at all? You had your bosom sent from Greece; your hair from Germany; your arms from Syria,—where did you get your teeth? And what salve do I kiss instead of your lips?"

Leave me at once," she answered angrily; "you see I am ugly to-day, and shall constantly become uglier. If you don't go, I'll arm my slave women with hairpins, and prick you out of the door."

128

"Suppose I should tell you that our wedding will take place in a few days," answered Nero,—" what will you do to me then?"

"What!" cried Poppaea,—" our wedding? Are you telling the truth?"

"Octavia is already accused of a crime whose doom is death; the sentence will be executed in a few days."

Nero related the incidents of the previous night, whereupon Poppaea's mood instantly brightened.

"I! Empress of Rome! My rival dishonored, overthrown?" cried the reckless woman, exultingly. "Oh, you are my god! Come, let me embrace you, my Jupiter!"

"Not Jupiter!" said Nero, as she impetuously showered kisses upon him. "Let me be your Hercules! I intend to strangle a lion—a trained one, of course—in the Circus before the people very soon,—so let me be your Hercules."

Poppaea now cautiously inquired about Metellus, and, when she learned that he had fled, she concealed her dismay, which, however, increased when Nero declared that the fugitive would be pursued and rendered harmless, as he might be dangerous. Poppaea became remarkably quiet, fixed her eyes on the floor, and only nodded occasionally when the Emperor elaborately explained his intention of calling Rome Neropolis, in order to render his name immortal.

At last she ventured to interrupt him to ask, in a tone of forced indifference, whether it was absolutely necessary that Metellus should die. The Caesar looked at her in surprise, carelessly answered, "Of course," and went on with his former conversation. When he was about to leave her, she again tried to return to Metellus by remarking, with a laugh, that it was a pity for the handsome fellow to die. They ought to let him live. Nero became thoughtful, and, sighing, began to say a few words about the transitoriness of life, the perishableness of beauty, till Poppaea hoped that, in this philosophical mood, he would pardon the fugitive; but he suddenly broke off, asking her whether the name " Neropolis " would not sound very musical, after which, when she had assented, he left her.

Poppaea allowed her maids to dress her with all the care which her toilet required, during which time, to the surprise of all, no words of reproof, usually so often uttered, escaped her lips. For the first time, she showed a certain indifference to the salves, mirrors, and ornaments. Even the arrangement of her "amber locks" won very little attention.

Toward noon she had herself carried in a litter to Rufus, whom the Caesar's favor had already made a legate. His very richly furnished mansion was near the Forum, and when Poppaea entered the splendid, but showy, inartistic rooms, she did not wait long for their master. Rufus seemed to have become more timid, more gloomy. The smile with which he invited his visitor to sit down was meaningless and cold. Poppaea did not treat him like an upstart, but as if he was a member of the old nobility, praised the furniture of the rooms, which displayed very little taste, but a great deal of money, spoke of the Emperor, and inquired for Esther, his mother, which question Rufus evaded. She was ill and could not be seen, he said, and then awkwardly turned the conversation to a statue of Apollo which stood near.

"It cost me ten thousand denarii," he said, "when I sent to Greece for it. Would you suppose, from looking at the marble, that it was so expensive?"

The soldier continued to talk about the costly uselessness of such work, remarking that one of his well-drilled recruits, if soundly drubbed, would produce such a statue gratis. Poppaea waited impatiently till he had finished, and then alluded so abruptly, and with such evident decision, to the event to which Rufus owed all his wealth and honors, that the warrior, suspecting some evil, started.

Who can it have been," she whispered, that wanted to murder the Emperor? People say it was Octavia? Do you believe it?"

She watched Rufus's startled face, listened to his faltered words, and soon convinced herself that she had touched the right spot to make him useful to her. She instantly dropped the subject, and, before her antagonist had recovered himself, spoke, without any intervening comment, of the fugitive Metellus, so that the suspicion could not fail to enter the soldier's mind that he could render her an important service—which she would repay by another—by keeping silence concerning some vague occurrence. A pleasant smile instantly rested upon Rufus's face. "She suspects everything," he said to himself, but he answered aloud,—

"Mistress, you know that you can command me—we are alone! Speak."

Poppaea's face flushed.

"We must aid one another in life," she replied, equivocally; "the greatest services which we can render often consist in keeping silence."

Then she rose to take leave. Rufus followed her slowly, doubtfully, with the expression of a man who is listening intently for some disclosure; but Poppaea did not turn toward him again until they entered the last room, from which the outer door opened.

"It occurs to me," she said, "this Metellus, or whatever his name is—" she paused.

"Yes, this Metellus," replied Rufus, averting his face to make it easier for her to continue.

"Yes, lest I should forget," she went on, blushing, "he is pursued."

"Pursued?" repeated the soldier.

"They want to kill him."

"Kill him?"

"Is it not cruel? He is still so young. Could he not be saved?"

Rufus looked into Poppaea's face, which had grown a shade paler. Then he reflected.

"If there should be a pretext of keeping him a prisoner," he answered, " he might be saved."

"Very well, I will arrange through the Emperor that you shall be sent in pursuit of him," replied Poppaea. Rufus smiled.

"I understand, my Mistress. One service deserves another," he said, "you know that the Emperor has given me a villa on the Gulf of Baiae."

"Certainly."

"Well, I will make this villa the prison of a certain man. You understand."

With these words in her ears, the noble lady departed.

"Oh, that she still lives!" muttered Rufus, after Poppaea had gone, pressing his clenched hands to his brow; "she is old but strong, and I love her, yet, yet she ought not to live longer."

To whom did he allude in these words?

CHAPTER XII

SEVERAL days after the catastrophe previously related, the Emperor had himself carried to his gardens, where, in the presence of his applauders, he was trying to reach the "high note." This note, which was to interrupt the singing rhythmically, almost like the accompanying melody, was especially pleasing to the ear of the royal singer on account of its exquisite time, and the difficulty of its execution. So to-day he stood on a chair, while about a thousand young lads, with beautifully curled locks, encircled him, their eyes fixed upon him, their hands raised to applaud. Surrounded by the floating folds of his toga, with the laurel wreath on his reddish locks, he swept his hands over the strings of the lyre, glittering* in the sunlight, whose notes accompanied the affected distortions of the face which the exertion of singing extorted. His voice sounded hollow; the veins on his forehead swelled prominently as soon as he was obliged to force higher tones from his throat.

The applause was intended to occur exactly in the pauses of the song, which, however, was difficult to manage, as usually the hands, moving too soon, spoiled the close of the delivery, so that there was danger that, in the execution of the music, a large part of the Emperor's divine tones would be lost to the people. Menecrates stood beside the chair, marking the time. A trill had just completed " the death of Clytemnestra," when a slave glided up to Menecrates to whisper a message. This was the day which had been—appointed for Octavia's execution; her sentence (to obtain which false witnesses had been summoned) had been pronounced; at this hour, which the Emperor was devoting to singing exercises, the Empress was to see the light of the sun for the last time. Nero asked the slave what news he brought, and learned that Andromachus had refused to open the Empress's veins, indignantly exclaiming that he was a leech to preserve life, not to destroy it.

"This woman torments me even in her death," replied the Caesar. "Then call a barber or some other leech," he added angrily; "but /do not interrupt me now. If you had even the slightest appreciation of Art, you would not disturb my leisure hours with such unpleasant subjects."

Yet it cost the royal singer some efFort to continue his song, though his most intimate friends scarcely noticed it. But he often struck a false note, and once he even gazed thoughtfully into vacancy, as if secret thoughts disturbed him.

"I slept very badly last night," he whispered to Menecrates; "I dreamed that Octavia was dragging me through a dark passage to an abyss. I see that I am in no mood to sing to-day. I will practise racing." • The applauders were dismissed, and Nero, whose brow was still clouded, called upon his court fool, Vatinius, to cheer him. As Vatinius vainly sought for jests, his master ordered him to tell him some funny stories quickly, or he should feel the lash.

"You pretend to be a fool, so prove yourself one whenever I want you to amuse me," said Nero.

"I will give you the funniest jests I can invent. Lord," said the frightened fool; "but laughing depends upon yourself; I am not master of the muscles which produce it."

Then he strove most eagerly to invent comical quips, phrases with double meaning. But no one laughed at the dirty witticisms of the misshapen dwarf; and the Caesar was just entering the chariot that stood waiting, when another messenger arrived.

"Octavia requests that no one except Andromachus shall open her veins," he announced.

"Let that message be taken to Andromachus," Nero commanded. Then he turned to Petronius.

"How does she meet death?" he asked in a low tone. Petronius shrugged his shoulders. She scarcely speaks," he answered gloomily. Does she make any remark about the Caesar?" Nero went on. "Condemning? Cursing?"

"None at all," replied Petronius.

"I do not like that," Nero burst forth; "she ought to hate me. If she had only cursed me! Why does she not curse me?"

"She was reading Plato until the guards entered to announce the death- sentence."

"Plato? Well? And then?" Nero went on, examining the reins of the horses to hide his suspense.

"Then she laid down the book and nodded, as if assenting to the words of the sage," answered Petronius. •" And did not utter one word of hate?"

"No."

"Nor show the slightest fear of death?"

"No," replied the courtier again, shrugging his shoulders.

"She defies me to the end," murmured Nero,

"Her cheeks began to flush," Petronius added; "her breathing grew more labored, and the veins in her temples throbbed."

Here the Emperor whispered something; his face wore a spiteful, satisfied smile, then instantly assumed a look of mournful approval.

"Afterwards she stepped out upon the balcony and gazed up at the sun a long time, until her eyes ached. She seemed to be taking leave of the world, for she raised her hand as if greeting the sky. Then she ordered water to be brought, and watered her favorite plants, looked out into the park again, and silently drew the curtain before the balcony."

"Poison would have been quicker," muttered Nero, grasping the whip; " what do the people say?"

"They remain quiet," replied Petronius. "See that Metellus is captured," he whispered as he entered the chariot; "his death is necessary, as you can easily perceive."

Petronius withdrew, and the Emperor drove slowly to the Circus to practise racing, of which he was passionately fond. When, toward noon, wearied and dusty, he reached the palace, news of his wife's death was brought to him, which he received in silence. Later he said to his confidant, Spiculus,— "Let her go and toy with her brother."

Toward evening Burrus and Andromachus met in a hall of the palace. Andromachus had attended Poppaea, who was suffering from a slight indisposition; Burrus, who was in command of the night-guard, waited for him. Both shook hands silently, and went to the gardens, where they lost themselves in the winding paths. It was a stormy night; the trees rustled; leaves whirled by; trunks groaned; and the moon often disappeared behind clouds. For a long time not a word was exchanged between them; each knew what secretly engrossed the other's thoughts, each respected the other's sorrow, until at last Burrus broke the silence.

"Will you not tell me how the Empress died?" he asked.

I!" replied the leech, in a harsh tone. Why should I?"

They say that you opened her veins," replied the commander of the Praetorians.

"So you know it?" said the physician, painfully affected; "that is another one; I thought you would not know—oh, Burrus—it was a terrible hour—she entreated me to do it."

Both were silent.

"Now the doors are thrown wide open to corruption," muttered Burrus, grinding his teeth; "now that she is gone, the tyrant will permit himself everything. Madness sits upon the throne, and stupidity worships it. Oh, an admirable world!"

The physician passed his hand over his brow, while Burrus laughed hoarsely.

"When I entered her room," Andromachus began, "I saw her, surrounded by her weeping women, sitting on a chair beside the bed, which she had just left. Her dress showed special attention; her hair was carefully arranged and adorned with the imperial diadem. She held in her lap a jewel-casket, from which she was giving her maids pearls, rings, and pins.

"'Faithful service is ill repaid with gold, it is true,' she said quietly; 'but you know that it is intended only for a memento of your mistress. Take it, and take with it the highest reward that I can give.' As she spoke, she told the maids to kneel down in a row, and kissed each one on her forehead, while she checked the convulsive weeping of several, saying: 'She herself was glad to be permitted to leave this world, but sorry that she could no longer see her good attendants.'

"'Poor girls,' she added, 'I wished to give you your freedom; but this was refused me. So you must patiently endure the yoke until the hour comes which is now approaching me, and which will break your chains. Have patience with me, if I say no more; and do not, as is customary, strive to rouse the compassion of your tyrant and mine. It is hard for me to speak.' You can imagine, Burrus, how these words pierced my heart; I did not venture to advance, but remained standing at the back of the chamber. Then she gazed with dull eyes into the distance as if seeking some vague, joy-giving vision.

"'The kind Mistress will die,' said Meroe, wonderingly, looking inquisitively into the quiet face whose large dark eyes were almost ghostly in their expression. Of what was she thinking, Burrus? It was as still as a sick chamber. The maids moved noiselessly, and repressed their tears. In the distance the fountain in the ante-room plashed musically. The coolness of the dusky room invited sleep, and death seemed only like sleep's quieter brother. As I went nearer, she saw me, and a grateful, contented smile flitted over her worn features.

"'I thank you for coming,' she said; 'I wish to die by your hand only.' I sighed deeply. 'You are right. Friends should render one another this service of love too,' I replied. 'Since it must be done, no bungler shall mutilate the body of my royal friend.'

"She again sank into a dreamy reverie; and when I asked the subject of her thoughts, she murmured: 'Oh, do not disturb me! I see so many beautiful things. I hear loving words too. Oh, Andromachus, it is not hard to die, when we love!'

"I ordered the waiting-women in the next room to prepare a warm bath, drew my box of instruments from my toga, opened it, and selected a very sharp one. Several of the maids shrieked at the sight of the glittering knife. Octavia looked around her with an expression of great annoyance; and I motioned to the soldier on guard, who took the girls away.

"'Meroe shall stay,' said Octavia; 'give me your hand, my good girl.'

"'Oh, let me go too!' Meroe entreated, sighing, 'I cannot see it, Mistress, I cannot see blood—'

"'Do you wish to forsake your mistress in this hour?' answered Octavia, reproachfully; and the slave-girl sat down again, groaning and averting her face, beside her mistress.

"'Is the bath ready?' I asked to divert my wandering thoughts. The soldier on duty answered that it was, and I said to Octavia: 'Shall I begin?'

"'Only one word more,' she whispered, shaken by a sudden chill that affected my nerves also, 'have you any news of him?'

"'Of Metellus?' I asked.

"'Yes,' she replied.

"I shook my head.

"'If you love me, Andromachus,' she whispered, pressing my hand to her lips, 'if you wish to sweeten the tortures of my last hour, promise to find the boy, to provide for his future. Oh, Andromachus! I loved him deeply!' She gave free course to her tears a moment, but forced them back again as quickly as they had come. I promised to fulfil her wishes, and she pressed my hand gently.

"'That is kind,' she gasped, uttering the words with difficulty; 'I—am—ready—'

"Then she again asked for Plato, read the speech which Socrates addressed to his judges after his sentence, laid the book aside, and again said: 'I am ready!'

"She held out her beautiful arms to me as she spoke; I clasped her right hand, taking the instrument from the table; and now there was such a roaring in my ears, and I trembled so violently, that I was obliged to make a vehement effort to calm myself. I think I stammered something about painlessness, or gave some other consolation which I did not believe. We physicians must always have comfort at hand, like sea-captains in a storm. Meroe rose, clutching her mistress's robe.

"'No, no,' she groaned, half averting her face.

"'Is this the only consolation you have for me, Meroe?' asked the Empress, in a hollow tone which sent a thrill of horror through me. Her face was colorless.

"'Oh, don't scream. Mistress,' wailed the fool of a slave, 'I can't bear it; oh, don't scream—' Whereupon her mistress made a gesture of the hand which probably meant: leave me! I was forced to touch the skin thrice with the knife before I could bring myself to cut the beautiful blue veins; the third time Octavia shook her head disapprovingly, exclaiming: 'It will not hurt, Paetus!' Then, bursting into tears, I cut despairingly; but the blood would not flow, it had probably gone back toward the centre of the body; for fear contracts the blood-vessels. Her heart was beating as if she was in the most terrible fever. Scarcely had the incision been made, when foolish Meroe shrieked and ran away. My knees trembled; I saw nothing more; but the Empress tried to speak, smiling pleasantly, as if she wished to say: 'You are innocent of it.' I cut again, deeper. At last, with much difficulty, she uttered the words: 'Bath—the warm bath.'

"I called her women, not one of whom had the courage to come; though they screamed as if they, not she, were to die; so I was obliged to carry the half unconscious woman into the adjoining room. I tried to induce her to undress; but she refused, her pale cheeks flushing crimson for a moment. The warm water, as soon as she was placed in it, grew scarlet—but I—let me stop—this is enough. I held her hands, shaking them under the water that the blood might flow faster; and she smiled, and nodded gratefully as long as she had strength to do so; the smile on her features grew more expressionless, her eyes became glassy, her head drooped over the edge of the tub till her beautiful hair touched the floor, and her chaste bosom no longer moved. I was obliged to release my hand by force from her cold, clinging fingers."

Burrus had covered his face with his mantle before Andromachus finished speaking. Andromachus would not disturb his friend's grief, and withdrew, regretting in his troubled soul that he had allowed himself to describe Octavia's death-agony so minutely to a man who cherished her image so tenderly in his heart. He glanced back once, and saw the Praetorian commander still standing motionless; the leaves were whirling around him through the darkness, and the moon cast a fleeting ray upon the muffled face, clearly revealing the folds of the mantle.

Later, when Burrus, after pacing to and fro in the gardens a long time, approached the palace, a lank, long-haired figure stepped from the shadow of a pine, and he recognized the poet whom Seneca patronized. The figure wiped its eyes with its ragged toga, apparently scarcely able to endure its burden of sorrow.

"Oh, the noble-hearted Empress!" wailed the long-haired author, "that she must die so young! What a lofty nature she possessed, and what a generous patroness of Art she was! Alas! You know how attentively she listened to my drama, and then ordered wine to be set before me."

Burrus, walking on, made a contemptuous gesture of the hand; but the fellow followed like his shadow, constantly pouring forth fulsome praises.

"Art will go to ruin, now that she is no more," he lamented; "bread and wine will no longer be given to the poets; they will suffer cold and hunger, and be tossed in soldiers' blankets in the streets. Oh, how they will suffer from hunger!"

Burrus, who had reached the palace, was about to enter, when the dramatist made a last effort to attain his purpose.

"I have composed a paean to the noble Octavia," he said, seizing the soldier's cloak. "See," he unrolled the papyrus, "I wrote two hundred and twenty-three iambics by the dim oil lamp in my attic room, with no food except an onion. The people say she was unfaithful to her husband; I have sung her chastity in my verses."

Burrus was tempted to deal the intrusive fellow a blow on his starving mouth, but controlled his anger.

"The dead need poets less than the living," he said; "take this and begone!" He. gave him a denarius as he spoke, which the poet hastily pocketed, retiring with many bows.

"But my paean," he called, holding up the roll.

"It can be arranged to suit some other death," answered the soldier. " You can put it on the funeral pyre of the famous poisoner, Locusta."

As Burrus entered the palace, the wailing of the women guided him to the room where Octavia's body had lain. When, hurrying through the ante-room, he reached the chamber, he found Meroe prostrate beside an empty bier. He turned inquiringly to another maid: "The corpse has been removed," was her reply. The articles scattered about,— mirrors, wreaths, garments,—lighted by a dim oil lamp, gave the impression that the occupant of the apartment had just gone away on a journey; the bier alone indicated its goal. The lamp sent circling wreaths of smoke toward the ceiling, and its feeble rays were reflected from the blood-stained water of a tub. The floor was soiled, and showed the wet prints of bare feet.

Burrus went out and met in the adjoining room one of Octavia's women. A young palace servant was patting her chin.

"You never took any notice of me before," whispered the girl.

"What? She gave you this bracelet," said the fellow, tenderly; "give it to me, and you will find no lover more faithful than your Fabius."

"Go! She is scarcely dead, and you are talking in this way," pouted the maid.

"What of that! Dead is dead," cried the lad, laughing, and snatched the bracelet, kissing and embracing her, while she, after a short struggle, submitted.

CHAPTER XIII

NEAR Baiae, on the highway from Rome, a villa whose white walls afforded a view across the moonlit surface of the water to the swelling hills on the opposite shore, lay close to the edge of the gulf. The night was already far advanced; no boats filled with gay parties floated on the waves, on whose crests, scarcely rippled by the night-breezes the moon shone radiantly. A broad golden pathway streamed from the bright disk of Selene across the surface of the water to the vine-clad terrace of the villa on which Rufus and Lucretia were sitting. But Rufus, on whom Nero had bestowed it, looked gloomy, and paid little or no attention to his wife's timid tokens of affection. To her question concerning the subject of his thoughts, he made no reply. Was he perhaps thinking of her to whom he owed his grandeur and happiness! Did the thought that the woman who had glided to the Emperor's wine-cup with the vial of poison in her hand, still lived, disturb him? Had he perceived the worthlessness of the worldly greatness for which he had so long labored? Was he recalling the words of the street-astrologer whom he had once consulted concerning his future and who had said: "Beware of woman!" Who could tell? Only it was evident that the wealth which surrounded him, the high position he occupied, had made him neither more cheerful nor more affable. He had no appreciation of the witchery of the moonlit night, but gazed into the blue dusk as if it were a prison; every gust of wind startled him like the clanking of chains, every dash of the waves like the voices of traitors.

Lucretia, with her head resting on his breast, gave herself up to her doubtful happiness, the happiness of being the object of this stern, gloomy man's love. She was thinking of her parents, who lived in Rome, by whose command she had given her hand to her preserver. Gratitude bound her to this heart, but even this gratitude had gradually yielded to a sense of fear. She had no will in his presence; she was a tremulous breath which his lips could shape according to his will. So she flattered him, served him, was subject to him more from a timid sense of duty than under the lion's claws, her firmness of character had been crushed, the horror of that time still weighed upon her heart. When Rufus visited her in her illness, he made a favorable impression upon her, his resolute nature awed her, and she dared not oppose her parents' wishes. But, since the Jew had become one of the Emperor's favorites, she no longer understood him.

Gazing out into the blue radiance of the moonlight, she ventured to sing a song under her breath. Rufus asked harshly what it meant, and she stopped,—

"I will light a lamp," she said timidly.

"Why? The moon shines brightly enough," he answered. Lucretia suppressed a yawn; and he asked whether she always felt sleepy in his society, and when her eyes filled with tears, he looked at her so sternly that she forced them back in alarm. Her fear seemed to touch his heart. Kissing her, he said: "Do not be angry with me, Lucretia! You know I do not mean what I say." The words had their effect upon her timid nature, and she embraced him with her white arms, while, for a time, he condescended to treat her tenderly.

"Oh, how beautiful the night is at your side!" she whispered, almost believing that she loved the gloomy man. And for a moment he really felt sincere devotion.

Suddenly the distant rattle of arms interrupted the stillness; the red glare of torches crimsoned the foliage in the garden; and Rufus started up in dread.

"What is the matter? Why do you turn pale?" cried Lucretia, anxiously. " Are you ill?"

"Hush," he answered, "some one is coming."

A slave came out on the terrace and said: "Armed men have entered the garden, and wish to see the owner of the villa."

Rufus's knees trembled, but he controlled himself and said: "Bring them to me."

"You are seriously ill, dearest," cried Lucretia, embracing his shaking knees, as he sank down exhausted.

"Nonsense," he muttered, pushing her caressing hand rudely away. The soldiers entered, casting the red glare of their torches on the floor.

"What do you want of me?" asked Rufus, controlling himself by a powerful effort.

"You have a young man named Metellus in your villa?" said the leader of the band. "Am I right?"

"I have," replied Rufus, with a sigh of relief.

"Well, this fellow is—you could not know it—a traitor to the state; we are sent, by the Emperor's orders, to kill him."

"Far be it from me to shield a traitor," exclaimed Rufus; "consider this villa your own; do your duty."

"I know that you are a friend of the Caesar. Where is the man who has fallen under the ban of the law?"

138

"Order one of the slaves to show you to the room; it overlooks the sea, at the right of this terrace."

"Very well."

The soldiers withdrew, pressing their weapons to their breasts to prevent their clanking.

Rufus gazed into vacancy, pondering.

"Poppaea Sabina would thank me if I saved him," he murmured; "shall I send old Cato up quickly? If he should anticipate the lictors, the youth might escape yet."

"What work have they in hand?" asked Lucretia, in alarm. "Does it concern the young man whom you received into the villa when he begged for protection?"

Rufus, as if urged by some noble impulse, went to the entrance of the villa, stood there irresolute, stepped forward, and then came slowly back as his eyes chanced to fall upon the white marble bust of Nero, which stood beside the entrance.

"I am a friend of the Emperor," he muttered in a hollow tone, listening to hear whether the Praetorians had commenced their work or even completed it.

While this scene was taking place in the lower part of the house, Metellus was sitting on the flat vine-covered roof at a table, busily engaged in reading. Stephanus lay asleep beside his chair; the reed-flute on which he had been playing still rested between his half-parted lips.

"How refreshing is this stillness, this peace," murmured the youth, "after the days of excitement!" He let his head droop dreamily and closed his eyes. The cool breeze, blowing from the moonlit water, played with his hair, and bore with the perfume of the flowers blooming on the distant hills visions of half-forgotten days. His passion had been partially crowded out of his heart during the terror of the flight; the love of life, so powerful at his age, had awakened in him; and though he confessed with shame that the love of the noble woman had far surpassed his in strength and endurance, he felt calmer and more content. Charming, rapturous as his love might seem to a woman, on his part it was rather a sweet natural impulse to kiss. He easily succeeded in throwing off the fetters as soon as they chafed his flesh, and yet one could not be angry with him for this carelessness. Perhaps his affection for Stephanus had always been much more tender than his love.

"Oh, you must learn whether she still lives," a voice in his dream whispered, "and whether you can save her. Surely you can! What sweetness lies in the consciousness of being loved, even though the object of that love is far away, and can never become your own! Yet it would have been better, had you contented yourself with friendship, and never learned to know the glowing, life consuming goddess. Oh, how sweet it is to rest in the arms of friendship; how treacherous, how mysterious is the power of love!"

So the dream swayed his thoughts; and suddenly it seemed as if the light of the lamp which stood before him grew dimmer and bluer, a mist rose from it, the air above the blue flame expanded and formed into a glittering frame, and in this frame—was it illusion or reality—he started up, sighing, and gazed sleepily around, suddenly overpowered by a vague sense of fear.

"Stephanus," he cried, panting for breath, "Stephanus—"

"Master—" stammered the boy, rubbing his eyes.

"Did you see nothing?" asked Metellus, trembling, his eyes rolling feverishly.

"I saw in my dreams a white horse with wings," replied the boy; "it was flying toward the sky—it sounded sweet—oh, dear, now it is gone!"

"No! I mean—did not you see—a woman—"

"A woman—"

"Here above the flame; her eyes were so dull, so glassy—her veins were cut at the wrists—blood was flowing over her whole body—"

"Oh, master, you are dreaming, you are raving—"

"Alas, Stephanus! She is dead! I know it—"he stammered mournfully, and, bursting into tears, clasped the boy to his heart.

"Oh, do not weep!" said the lad, compassionately; "I will play for you, master, then you will be happy again."

"She is dead and I live," fell sighing from the lips pressed upon Stephanus's curls.

"Do not weep; show me the star that shines upon Greece," urged the slave, patting his master's cheek; "why do you make yourself unhappy? You promised to take me to Greece. Come let us start i At once!"

Metellus made no answer, but wept long and bitterly before he at last wiped his eyes and, with his lower lip still quivering convulsively, stroked the boy's curls.

"Hark, some one is coming," said the little fellow. "I hear footsteps and voices on the stairs."

"You are my only comfort now, Stephanus," said Metellus, in a broken voice; "be good and love me, will you?"

Stephanus was about to answer, when the clash of arms interrupted him. Directly after a helmet appeared beneath the curtain at the doorway, below the glittering metal frowned a stern, pale face.

"Is it you, Rufus?" cried Metellus, seizing the lamp, whose dim light would not permit him to recognize the soldier.

The curtain parted; a centurion stepped out upon the roof, saluted respectfully, and said to the astonished youth,—"I come from Rome," then moving nearer, and covering his mouth with his hand, he whispered: "Octavia sends me to you!"

"Octavia?" cried Metellus, in joyful surprise, "then she is still alive?"

"She is still alive," replied the soldier, bowing his head.

"So the vision in my dream deceived me! But speak! What have you to tell me from her, quick!" said the excited artist.

"It is he," muttered the Praetorian under his breath, and then continued,—"She is not only living, but near you!" Near me! Oh, ye gods!" I was commanded to conduct you to her secretly."

"Then she is making her escape?"

"As you say, making her escape!"

The soldier, declining to answer any further questions, invited the unsuspicious sculptor to accompany him, the rest would be explained as soon as they reached the other shore of the Gulf; he had strict orders to keep silence.

"Don't go without me, master," pleaded

Stephanus; but Metellus did not hear, he was rushing, as if in a delirious frenzy, down the steps into the garden. She is still alive, was his sole thought, which floated like a radiant divinity before his soul.

"You must know, lord," said the soldier, when both stepped out into the moonlit night, "you must know that Octavia is on the opposite shore of the Gulf. A little boat lies hidden among the bushes yonder on the beach; I will row you across as fast as possible. You cannot stay after sunrise."

"Very well," replied Metellus, wholly absorbed in his own thoughts, walking on at the centurion's side. He scarcely noticed how they went to the shore, that the soldier unfastened the boat, or that another armed man, emerging from the bushes, sprang into the skiff as it pushed off; he might have been wounded at this moment without perceiving it; his mind seemed dazed by the anticipation of the meeting.

"Everything is going well, Julius," said the second soldier, laughing spitefully as he gave the centurion a poke in the ribs.

"The Caesar can rely upon me," said the other; "whatever I undertake succeeds; but this cursed oar is broken. Push the boat off against yonder rock, that we may get afloat."

The man obeyed the command, replying: "Only let us not be overhasty. He who is going to the nether world can be allowed plenty of time!"

"Don't chatter, but row," retorted the centurion.

"Chatter is the spice of all work," answered his companion, grasping the oars. A silvery mist veiled the moon; a cool breeze swept over the waves; the little boat, impelled by the strokes, danced lightly over the glittering surface; not a breath, not a sound in nature gave a premonition of the future; the world lay like an innocent, sleeping child. Metellus gazed, shivering, at the moonlit water without hearing the talk of the two men. Beyond the silver wavelets, where the low hills rose, glimmered the walls of a little villa. Was that the. goal of the voyage?

"Cannot you tell me in what way Octavia escaped her foes?" asked Metellus.

Unfortunately, no, lord," replied the rower; I was not present. But I think Andromachus skilfully assisted her; and, you know, when such a leech is in attendance, people are soon released from all suffering."

"Then you belong to the Empress's, attendants?"

"Yes, lord."

"I suppose she is spending the night in yonder villa," continued the sculptor, who could no longer control his emotion.

"She is spending the night there," laughed the rower; "she is well cared for; by Zeus! spending the night is good."

"Hush, Marcus," ordered the centurion.

"You will soon be with her, lord," the bold fellow added. Metellus was again absorbed in his own thoughts; his heart was throbbing; a sigh of happiness escaped his yearning breast.

"I love her still," cried a voice in his heart. "I feel it by the flush upon my cheeks! She will be like a loving sister! At her side I shall lead a pure and noble life; nothing dark or base will venture to approach me.

"Where does she intend to fly?" he asked after another pause.

"Where?" grinned Marcus, "just where you will go yourself!"

"Perhaps to Egypt?"

"Somewhat farther."

"To Ethiopia?"

"Have patience, you will be there sooner than you desire."

Metellus was already imagining the pleasure of a journey together, when he noticed that the rower called to the centurion in a low tone: "Here?" The other muttered: "Not yet! Farther!" and the man rowed on.

They were now about a hundred feet from the shore; the villa seemed close at hand. Metellus could no longer remain seated in the boat; he rose and eagerly inhaled the cool sea-breeze that fanned his brow. Just at that moment a pang pierced his soul at the thought that, in the bewilderment of the moment, he had entirely forgotten Stephanus. Poor, forsaken boy! If he left Italy with Octavia, where would the lad, who had already become dearer than a brother, find protection?" Oh, Stephanus, come!" he murmured, and was turning to tell the centurion that they must row back to the shore again; but to his surprise the centurion was standing directly behind him.

"Row—" the betrayed youth could say no more; a blow in the back robbed him of speech and destroyed his balance so that he only saved himself from falling overboard by hastily grasping the edge of the boat.

"What clumsiness!" he gasped; "take care."

"Take care? He thinks it was an accident," cried the rower, laughing. "Zeus help me! He is hard of hearing."

"What do you mean? What do you want of me?" stammered the deceived youth, and now, as they tried by force to wrench his fingers from the boat, a light dawned upon his brain.

"So that is your plan; you want to kill me?" he cried, through his set teeth, struggling desperately with the centurion, who was vainly trying to force him out of the boat.

"I am betrayed," rang far over the calm surface of the water; "help, help!"

"Stop his mouth," panted the centurion; "help me throw him overboard."

The other soldier seized the victim's feet. Metellus struck wildly around him; he saw, as if through a blood-red veil, the surface of the water glimmering so calmly, so deceitfully before him; the tension of his nerves

142

was so great that the shore seemed whirling before him, the moon danced before his eyes; he felt the approach of the cold lonely death in the still water. And the love of life awoke with terrible, passionate power! Mere breathing now appeared to him so sweet, all the sorrows of life grew insignificant in comparison to the mysterious, uncertain void of death. The soldier's rude hand thrust his struggling head nearer and nearer to the water. The anguish of death oppressed his mind. It rested on him as a falling rock crushes a butterfly. Nay, he became weak, contemptible— clasping his hands as well as his position would permit, he begged piteously for his life,—the life which he had so often despised. Nay, more! The fear of death made him base, rendered him a shameless liar.

"I did not love Octavia," he wailed; "I hate her; I never wish to see her again." He hesitated, the falsehood of his words pierced his heart, but as if hunted by an invisible power, he went on without reflection; "put me on shore, I will fly to a distant country, and the Emperor shall never hear of me again; you can tell him confidently that you have accomplished your work of executioners."

The men released him, and whispered softly together, while their victim, with wild eyes, cowered in the bottom of the boat.

"He is a handsome fellow," said the centurion; "we will let him live."

But the other opposed him.

"What, do you want to let him live because he is good-looking? So are other people, yet they must die too."

"Well then," replied the centurion, "I will take it upon myself." Turning to the kneeling figure, panting for breath, he said,—

"Jump into the water and try to reach the shore. Can you swim?"

"Yes," murmured the exhausted youth.

"Then go!" cried the soldier, spurning him with his foot.

"What do you say?" asked the bewildered artist.

"You are to try to escape," replied the centurion; then, turning to Marcus, he added laughing,—

"If he reaches the shore, he will escape us; if he does not, so much the better."

Metellus uttered a sigh of relief.

"Ye gods, I thank ye," he gasped, then swung himself over the edge of the boat into the water, which dashed upward around him, and, trembling, divided the cold waves, while the two men watched him. They gazed long at the white spot shimmering amid the black waters,—the white neck of a half mad man who was exerting all his strength to gain the shore.

"He will not reach it," said Marcus.

"He is strong," replied the other; "he will."

The wind had risen. The waves dashed higher; they rowed on behind the swimmer, and suddenly saw him turn. "Help me!" came faintly from his lips.

"Only keep on," shouted the centurion, "a few more strokes, and you will reach the shore."

Metellus's strength had failed; he felt a relaxation of the nerves,

143

against which it was impossible to struggle. The terror of death had affected his muscles too powerfully. The chill of the water was robbing him of breath. To divert his thoughts, he counted from one to one hundred, and often murmured: "Stephanus, help me!" or, "Octavia, where are you?" With his eyes fixed intently upon a dark clump of bushes on the shore, he strained his arms to the utmost; but the outer world was already vanishing. He began to swallow the water. Then it seemed as though a voice was droning incessantly in his ear: "I will not die!" but another voice, with an icy laugh, responded: "You must."

Slower and slower grew the swimmer's movements, more and more languid, again a half-stifled: "Help me!" floated over the waves, then the white form sank. The neck shone with a greenish glimmer through the flood; there was a gurgling sound, a few bubbles of air, and the surface of the water rippled as peacefully as before in the bright, shining moonlight.

THE END